INTO THE NEBULA

Look for STAR TREK Fiction from Pocket Books

Star Trek: The Original Series

Star Trek: The Next Generation

Star Trek: Deep Space Nine

Star Trek: Voyager

STAR TREK
THE NEXT GENERATION®

INTO THE NEBULA

GENE DeWEESE

POCKET BOOKS

New York   London   Toronto   Sydney   Tokyo   Singapore

An *Original* Publication of POCKET BOOKS

POCKET BOOKS, a division of Simon & Schuster Inc.
1230 Avenue of the Americas, New York, NY 10020

STAR TREK is a Registered Trademark of
Paramount Pictures.

A VIACOM COMPANY

This book is published by Pocket Books, a division of
Simon & Schuster Inc., under exclusive license from
Paramount Pictures.

ISBN: 0-671-89453-6

First Pocket Books printing July 1995

10 9 8 7 6 5 4 3 2 1

POCKET and colophon are registered trademarks of
Simon & Schuster Inc.

Printed in the U.S.A.

In memory of Don Thompson.

And for those interested in such things, a historical note: The Ensign Thompson herein is a direct descendant of the police reporter and record reviewer of the same name in *Now You See It/Him/Them.* . . .

INTO THE NEBULA

Chapter One

THE MAPPING NEVER STOPS.

As long as a starship computer system has the power to function and sensor inputs to process, some part of that system is analyzing those inputs, comparing the results with its own internal image of the external universe and correcting that image when differences are detected. Even under battle conditions—*especially* under battle conditions, when even the smallest of discrepancies between image and reality could conceivably spell disaster—this nanosecond-by-nanosecond updating is going on.

The only time the updating stops is when the sensors encounter an anomaly, something that is simply outside the parameters of what the computer, acting on both its programming and its experience, defines as "normal." Of course, the incoming data continues to be stored, so that, when and if the anomalous data is proven to be correct, it is still available.

The first thing the computer does when it encounters such an anomaly is run a complete diagnostic of the sensors involved, then of itself. If no malfunctions, no miscalibrations are found, it alerts the crew and awaits instructions.

"Come in."

Lieutenant Commander Data did not look up from the tricorder as the door to his living quarters hissed open and Commander Geordi La Forge stepped inside. His cat, Spot, on the other hand, darted under the bed.

"Data, does that cat hate everyone? Or is it just me?" Geordi shook his head. "Never mind. Just tell me, why did you want to see me? And *what* is so fascinating about your tricorder?"

"I do not believe she hates anyone," Data said, still not looking up. "Most of the material I have been able to access indicates that, except when directly threatened, cats are essentially indifferent to humans."

"I wouldn't call that a display of indifference," Geordi said, glancing toward the space beneath the bed, where Spot's high feline body temperature still produced a distinctive infrared signature in his VISOR even though the cat had retreated to the far side, completely out of sight.

"Perhaps not," Data said, finally looking up from his tricorder, "but neither is it open hostility."

"I'll take your word for it," Geordi sighed, wondering if beating around the bush was part of Data's continuing effort to be more human, "but you still haven't told me why you wanted to see me."

"As you know, I have been observing Spot's behavior for some time now, and I often find it most intriguing. For example, I have noticed that Spot will often dart suddenly from one place to another. I have been unable to detect any visual, auditory, or olfactory stimulus to which she might be responding, so I have been attempting—"

"You're using a tricorder to find out what sets her off? Data, she's just being a cat! I'm no expert on feline behavior, but even I know that much. Something in her tiny little cat mind makes her decide she has to be somewhere else—immediately. And she goes."

"If you are suggesting that her actions are the result of random synaptic discharges or similar phenomena, I do not believe that to be the case."

Geordi chuckled as he shook his head. Data no longer took every remark as literally as he once had, but he still had his moments. "That's not what I meant, Data. I just meant—actually, I don't know what I meant. But nobody knows what a cat thinks about, if anything. Maybe she just suddenly remembers that she liked it a lot better someplace else, so she decides to check it out. You should probably get Counselor Troi down here. If you could get Spot to perform for her, maybe she could at least tell if Spot is frightened or happy or whatever it is cats feel."

Data seemed to consider the advice for a moment. "That is an excellent suggestion, Geordi," he said. "I will ask the counselor."

"Then you won't be needing me." Geordi started to turn toward the door.

"I still would like your assistance, Geordi."

Geordi sighed again and turned back to Data. "All right. But you still haven't told me just what it is you want me to do."

"I would like you to watch Spot."

Geordi shook his head. "No, thanks, Data. I did

that once, remember? We just didn't get along. Maybe Worf—"

"I did not mean I wished you to care for her, only to watch her. A possibility exists that your VISOR might enable you to detect something that would not be detectable either by myself or by the tricorder."

"When she does her 'I-gotta-be-someplace-else' act?"

"That is correct, Geordi. I realize it might take some time before such an event occurs, but—"

"Hold on a minute. You want me to just sit around and stare at your cat? For hours? I don't think so. Look, Data, I don't want to dampen your scientific curiosity, but I really think you're wasting your time. Cats have been around since the pyramids and no one's been able to figure them out yet. And frankly— no offense intended, Spot—it's probably because there's nothing there to figure out."

"Perhaps you are right, Geordi, but there is a great deal of research indicating that cats and other animals are able to sense phenomena that humans can not. For example, there is strong statistical evidence that both cats and dogs sense impending earthquakes."

"Statistical?" Geordi frowned skeptically. "Sure, lots of people talk about how their cat or dog went bananas before an earthquake, but that's anecdotal, not statistical."

"I understand that, Geordi, and that is not the phenomenon I was referring to. There were a number of statistical studies made of the classified advertisements in newspapers in areas in which earthquakes occurred. In a significant percentage of instances, the number of advertisements for missing and runaway pets, both feline and canine, increased by fifty percent or more in the week immediately prior to a significant earthquake."

Geordi grinned. "Data, unless I missed a Starfleet bulletin recently, an earthquake is one of the few hazards a starship doesn't have to worry about, so I seriously doubt that that's what's making Spot twitchy."

"Of course not, Geordi. I merely cited that as an example of animal behavior that has never been adequately explained. However, there is much that has never been fully understood about the natural abilities of not only cats but of other animals. Migrating birds, for example—"

"Data, don't go mystical on me. Birds have a directional sense. I don't remember how it works, exactly, but I do know that scientific explanations were found all the way back in the twentieth century."

"That is precisely my point, Geordi. Among the explanations for certain migratory birds was a sensitivity both to earth's magnetic field and to polarized light. Even lower life-forms were found to have similar sensitivities. Certain worms, for example, determined 'up' and 'down' in response to the magnetic field."

Geordi laughed. "You're joking, right? Worms?"

"I am not joking, Geordi. A number of experiments were conducted with worms taken from Earth's southern hemisphere to the northern, where the direction of the vertical component of the magnetic field was essentially reversed. The worms consistently behaved in ways that indicated they thought up was down and vice versa."

"With a worm, how can you tell?"

"I do not know, Geordi. However, I can access the complete text of the reports if you wish. The rationale of the experiments—"

"No, thanks, Data. Thanks, but no thanks."

As if to add her own commentary, Spot chose that

moment to dart from under the bed, streak across the floor, and disappear behind Data's desk.

"I didn't see a thing," Geordi said hastily as he turned to the door, "and I'm probably needed in engineering."

A moment later, to his surprise, the voice of the computer confirmed that he actually was needed in engineering, on a matter involving anomalous sensor data. It added that Data's presence on the bridge would also be appreciated regarding the same matter.

Captain Jean-Luc Picard was in his quarters, grimly working on the seemingly never-ending crew fitness reports, when the computer, in effect, threw in the towel and asked for help. Picard, who welcomed any interruption of this particular duty, quickly abandoned the barely started reports and headed for the bridge even though he knew he could have just as easily handled the situation—whatever it turned out to be—from his quarters. Lieutenant Commander Data and Commander La Forge were far better qualified than he to deal with whatever the computer was worrying about—Mr. Data if the anomaly proved to be out there in the real world, Mr. La Forge if it proved to be the result of some momentary glitch within the *Enterprise* itself. Nonetheless, if rank had its obligations—such as having to struggle with the fitness reports—it also had its privileges, such as being able to delay that particular struggle on a relatively flimsy pretext.

Data was already seating himself at the ops console when Picard emerged onto the bridge. A red-haired ensign—Curtis, Picard noted automatically, among the top ten percent in her class last year at the Academy—sat at the conn. The unmoving starfield on the main viewscreen indicated that the *Enterprise* had dropped out of warp drive, standard procedure under the circumstances.

Picard gave Data a few seconds to pull the necessary information from his console, then asked, "What seems to be the problem, Mr. Data?"

"There are two anomalies, Captain, both related to a star approximately half a parsec distant, bearing forty-two-point-six-three, mark twenty-seven-point-one-four. Visual spectroscopic analysis indicates a middle-aged star similar to Earth's sun. It has at least four planets, but there is also a substantial ring of what appears to be nebular dust centered on the ecliptic. Such a ring would be typical of a young sun whose planets had not yet formed but decidedly atypical of a mature sun with an existing family of planets."

"You said it 'appears' to be nebular dust." There was no change in Picard's voice or demeanor, but an anticipatory tingle rippled up his spine, as it always did when the *Enterprise* encountered something new and unexpected in unexplored space. "What, precisely, is its makeup?"

"That is the second anomaly, Captain. The sensors cannot obtain a reliable analysis. There is interference of some sort, possibly a systemwide energy field."

Picard frowned. Red flags, born of other encounters and other times, sprang up in his mind, intensifying the tingle and partially changing its nature, from anticipatory to apprehensive. "A shield, you mean?"

"No, Captain, a different sort of interference. The sensors do not appear to be blocked in any way, but the information they return from the dust cloud varies widely from moment to moment and is therefore obviously unreliable."

"And the source of this interfering energy field, if that's what it is?"

"Unknown, Captain. I cannot be certain that it is even an energy field. It is possible that the interference is the result of a property of space itself in that region. Were we to approach more closely, however, the sensors might be able to—"

"Not yet, Mr. Data. What you describe indicates the possible existence of a highly advanced technology. It also suggests that the possessors of that technology feel they have something to hide. It is not a situation to charge into blindly." He turned to Lieutenant Worf at the tactical station. "Is there any indication of communication traffic, Mr. Worf, either subspace or old-style?"

"None in the system, sir," the Klingon rumbled, then paused, his massive fingers moving deftly across the console before him. "There is a faint EM signal originating at least a quarter parsec outside the system."

"Source, Mr. Data? Or is it subject to interference as well?"

"The interference appears to be limited to the star system itself, Captain. I will redirect the long-range sensors."

"Mr. Worf, the nature of the signal? Information content?"

"It appears to employ a form of frequency modulation, sir. The limited bandwidth indicates that whatever information is present is almost certainly limited to audio. The signal is being fed into the computer for analysis."

"Put it on the speakers as soon as you get anything, intelligible or not."

"Yes, sir."

As Picard turned back to Data and the viewscreen, Commander Will Riker, looking a bit flushed but otherwise presentable, strode onto the bridge. "Holodeck exercise," he said hastily as he joined Picard in the command area behind Data and Ensign Curtis. "Counselor Troi convinced me I should try the new table-tennis program. That game is *not* as easy as it looks. Now, what have we run into that stumped the computer?"

Tersely, Picard explained. As he finished, the image on the main viewscreen went from the slow-moving starfield in front of the *Enterprise* to a seemingly stationary one. In the center of the screen was a faint, metallic dot. A ship of some kind?

"Maximum magnification," Picard ordered, the tingle spreading out from his spine to brush at his entire body. "Is that the source of the EM signal?"

"It would appear to be, Captain," Data said.

On the screen, the dot further confirmed Picard's suspicion by expanding into a slowly rotating ship. Without realizing he was doing it, he leaned forward a fraction of an inch in his chair, as if by that minuscule motion he could bring the ship closer, force it to reveal its secrets more quickly. The forward section, he saw, was an almost featureless cylinder. At the rear of the cylinder, protruding dozens of meters in all directions like a massive Elizabethan collar, was a disk-shaped shield. Beyond the shield, only partly visible from this angle, was a second, smaller segment, presumably containing the ship's drive.

"And there is only the one ship?" Picard prompted.

"The only one in that immediate vicinity, Captain," Data replied. "We would have to conduct a comprehensive sensor scan of the entire volume of space surrounding the star to determine if other ships exist but are not generating detectable subspace or EM signals."

"Life-forms, Mr. Data?" Picard had voiced the question in one form or another more times than he could remember, in more parts of the galaxy than once he could have dreamed of seeing, but each time it was as fresh as the first, an unneeded reminder of one of the central reasons for the existence of the *Enterprise* and of Starfleet itself.

"Approximately ten thousand humanoid life-forms in the forward cylinder, Captain, and abundant plant and animal life."

"A generation ship?"

"It would appear to be, Captain. It is rotating at a rate that would provide approximately one gravity at the outermost point of the cylindrical habitat. And the drive is pre-impulse, powered by a primitive form of nuclear fission," Data said, but even as he spoke, the stubby rear section of the ship came into view, not a cylinder but a squat oval with numerous protrusions that—

Abruptly, a sinking sensation in Picard's stomach muted the tingle that still played along his spine. Protruding haphazardly from the rear of the ship was a series of what must once have been massive jets. But now they were barely recognizable, looking as if they had partially melted and then rehardened into Dali-like caricatures of themselves.

The ship was, Picard realized, a derelict, but a derelict with roughly ten thousand living, intelligent beings aboard.

Chapter Two

EACH NIGHT when finally sleep approached, Koralus vowed that when he awakened he would make the announcement. He would share with the Ten Thousand the secret—the burden—that had dominated his life for more than ten years.

Each morning, faced with the reality of the ship and the Ten Thousand whose lives he was planning to disrupt, he would hesitate. Most mornings he got no farther than the entrance to the dozen flights of metal steps that led to the long-vacant bridge. Perhaps one time in ten, he would reach the top and speak the code that unlocked the door, only to enter and stare at the now-useless controls and the slowly turning but otherwise unchanging starfield that still filled the forward port. A dozen times in the last year, he had gone so far as to activate the seldom-used shipwide system of screens and speakers, but each time, when the acknowledgments from the sector leaders had begun to come in and he had seen their expectant, trusting faces one by one, his resolve had failed and he had passed it off as simply another test of the system.

What was the point in shattering their lives for no reason other than to lessen his own burden, his own isolation?

In truth, there *was* no point. There was nothing any of them could do. There was nothing *he* could do, either for himself or for them. Except keep them safe, for a time, from a truth they had no need to know, a truth that would make their very existence pointless.

As it had already made his.

The original Ten Thousand had known from the moment the *Hope of Krantin* had been launched that they would die in space without ever again setting foot on the surface of a planet—any planet. A dying Krantin was being left irrevocably behind, and the hypothetical worlds that circled the star that was their destination were centuries distant, if they existed at all. If they did not, it would be even more centuries and more generations to the next likely star.

But the Ten Thousand had been filled with optimism and hope, if not for themselves, then for their descendants, a dozen generations down the line, and for the Krantinese civilization that would be rebuilt on one of those worlds. If they had not, they would never have volunteered. If they had not believed in Koralus and the handful of others who had stood against all odds to get the ships built, they would have thrown all their efforts into the sealing of the cities and lived their lives out on Krantin among their friends and families rather than isolated in mammoth metal canisters drifting through space.

And Koralus, though he dared not share it with any of the Ten Thousand, not even the one who might otherwise have been his wife, had even entertained some hope for himself personally, for himself and the rest of the One Hundred. If the statistical models proved true, at least one in four of their group would survive the series of hibernations and awakenings. Beyond that, theory said, it was up to them. If during their waking periods they were able to teach and train each new generation, if they were able to maintain the *Hope*—including their own hibernation chambers— through the centuries, they would survive. If they were able to maintain the reality of Krantin—and of their destination worlds—in the minds of the Ten Thousand through generation after generation of knowing only the world of the ship, then Krantin itself would have a chance, not of surviving but of being reborn through their descendants. Even Koralus himself, fifty years old when the *Hope* departed, could conceivably live to see the beginnings of that rebirth.

Or so he had hoped.

But then, less than ninety years into their journey, barely a month into what had been scheduled to be his first five-year watch, those hopes had been shattered. All of the hopes, not just those for himself personally.

The drive had failed, not in any of the thousands of failure modes its designers and builders had predicted but in one that none had anticipated. He had awakened nearly a quarter of the One Hundred to try to right the situation, but all to no avail. He had been able only to watch as they lost their lives, slowly and painfully, journeying down the central core past the shield to the drive pod again and again, with nothing gained for their sacrifice except the certainty of failure. The last of the awakened technicians had restored and diverted the power that still maintained life-support and other necessities in the sections forward of the shield, but the drive remained dead, unrepairable without the facilities that were ninety years behind them and probably no longer existed in any case.

He had donned a suit himself at the last, but he had been met by the final returning party in the core passageway before he reached the shield. The telltales on their suits had already told them they would be dead within days if not hours, but collectively they had had the strength to turn him back and the compassion to convince him that his own death would serve no purpose, could only make matters worse for the Ten Thousand for however many years or decades the *Hope* had left.

Repeatedly, then, he transmitted a message to Krantin, tersely informing them of the *Hope*'s fate, but he had no expectation of a reply. Krantin had been silent for decades; he had no reason to think that word of his failure—if there was anyone still alive on Krantin to hear it—would spur any survivors to new activity. Messages to the other ships were still being sent, though expectations of a reply from that quarter were equally low. Since the first decade after launch, there had been no intership communication. The other ships might have suffered even more disastrous failures than the *Hope*.

And even if they were still functioning, even if one of them did reply, even offer to help, Koralus could not accept that help. The others had their own destinations. Diverting them to rendezvous with the *Hope* would only add more generations and more dangers to their journeys, and that was the last thing he wanted. He could only warn them of what had happened to the *Hope* and remind them that their own survival was therefore all the more important.

This particular morning had so far proved little different from the thousands that had gone before. If anything, his decision to yet again delay the announcement had come more easily, more quickly than usual; his memory of the previous night's resolve was more tenuous, as if he were finally beginning to acknowledge that it was only a ritual, that its only meaning, its only importance was in its contribution to his own psychological survival.

Tired in spite of his decreasing weight, he climbed—almost floated—the last dozen steps to the entrance to the bridge, his eyes avoiding the other door, the one that led to the total weightlessness of the core and the frost-rimed hibernation chambers where the remnants of the One Hundred waited. Waited accusingly, he imagined for the thousandth time. As accusingly as the Ten Thousand would look at him if they knew the truth, that the *Hope* was doomed and that he was one of the handful most responsible for their presence on it, for its very existence.

For a long moment he hovered at the top of the stairs, not so much debating whether or not to continue but simply existing, like a particle caught between two energy states. Finally, as if nudged by an errant breeze from the air-circulation system, he drifted toward the door. He heard his own voice speaking the code that released the door, though he hadn't been conscious of making the decision to speak.

The door slid open, as soundlessly as it had the day they had launched from orbit. It, at least, was still in perfect working order.

He stepped—glided—in.

And froze, his stomach knotting, his heart suddenly racing.

On a panel far to the left of the ponderously rotating starfield, a light glowed—a light that had not come alive even once in the years since he had been awakened. A light he had never expected—nor, truth be known, wanted—to see.

A twin to the light that had been glowing intermittently since his own messages had begun to be transmitted.

A reply.

Or at least a signal. From somewhere. The first in more than ninety years.

Surprised at the intensity of his reaction, Koralus gripped the waist-high handrail and pulled his virtually weightless body to the panel and strapped himself into the seat in front of the glowing light.

How long, he wondered, had it shone unnoticed? Not that it mattered, he told himself grimly as he fought to keep his hands from shaking as he reached out to the controls. When the nearest possible source—one of the *Hope*'s sister ships—was half a light-year distant, there was little urgency for an immediate reply.

And it was far too late for warnings like the ones the *Hope* continued to send out to be of any use to the *Hope* itself.

His stomach twisted painfully as he worked the controls that would play back the message. If there was a message, if the light and the recorders had not simply been triggered by a random burst of static. If it had not been the result of yet another malfunction—

A voice emerged from the console, a voice that could have been a twin to his own.

Koralus frowned puzzledly as the brief message began to repeat itself. The words were familiar, but his mind refused to make sense of them. *Federation?* What Federation? Far back in Krantin's history, there had been alliances that might have called themselves Federations, but those had been gone for centuries.

Starship? The *Hope* and its five sister ships were the only starships. There was no way Krantin could have built more, even if the Plague had reversed itself the very day the *Hope* had been launched.

The message was repeating itself for perhaps the tenth time when Koralus finally realized that, despite the fact that the words were in the one surviving Krantinese language and that the voice was almost indistinguishable from his own, the speaker was not from Krantin or any of the *Hope*'s sister ships.

It was an alien, from another star system.

And it was offering assistance.

A mixture of hope and fear twisted at him as he darted a look at the still-rotating, still-empty starfield and reached again for the controls.

Picard turned back to the main viewscreen and the slowly rotating alien ship that now half-filled it. The situation was not as bad as he had feared when he had first seen the distorted, almost unrecognizable drive jets. Early on, the *Enterprise* sensors had shown that, though the jets themselves were useless, the fission reactor, buried deep within the bulbous drive unit, still functioned and supplied power to the habitat cylinder.

Then the Universal Translator program had mastered the almost melodic language of the alien ship's automated message, and the evidence of the sensors had been confirmed by the words of one who called himself Koralus.

But still there was no response to a continuous hail on all EM frequencies within hundreds of megahertz of the frequency that carried the message.

"Is their receiving equipment functional, Mr. Data?" Picard asked finally.

"It appears to be, Captain. It is possible they are

simply not monitoring it, however, and are not aware of our hail."

"How many years have they been traveling?" Riker wondered, seeming to echo Picard's own thought. "If it's been as long as their present velocity indicates, it's no wonder they aren't listening every minute."

"That is true, Commander," Data volunteered. "In fact, if their life spans are equivalent to those of humans, it is doubtful that any presently aboard were alive when the journey began."

"Then it's certain—they originated in the star system that stumped the computer?"

"Not certain, Commander, but highly likely. Assuming that their present speed and direction have remained essentially constant, the ship either originated in or passed through that system approximately one hundred years ago."

"A generation ship," Riker said, a touch of admiration in his voice. "Earth was lucky Cochrane came up with the warp drive when he did. Without it, I doubt that we'd ever have gotten outside the Sol system."

"If our system were in the same shape theirs is, Number One, I suspect we would not have," Picard said.

"Whatever shape that is," Riker countered. He looked again at the ship on the screen. "I suggest an away team, Captain. From the condition of their drive, they obviously need help, even if they aren't answering our hail."

"Not yet, Number One, not before we gather more information." The red flags raised by the unexplained sensor interference in the nearby star system still dictated caution to Picard. "Ensign, take us in to a thousand kilometers, quarter impulse."

"Aye, Captain."

"Mr. Data, is there still no evidence of weaponry?"

"None that I can detect, Captain. The ship itself is completely unarmed, and there are no energy signatures indicating personal energy weapons. Based on the technology level of the ship, however, it is unlikely they would have developed phasers or disruptors. They might still be dependent upon projectile weapons, which our sensors could not detect."

Riker shook his head. "Projectile weapons on a spacecraft? Not likely."

"Not likely," Picard agreed, "but far from impossible." Supposedly intelligent beings had done far more foolish things, he thought as the misshapen drive jets grew clearer on the viewscreen. One, he saw, had folded in on itself and appeared completely sealed, and he couldn't help but wonder if Koralus's message had told the complete truth when it spoke of the damage being solely the result of equipment malfunction.

"How long can they survive on their own, Mr. Data?" he asked grimly.

"That is impossible to estimate accurately, Captain. The reactor has been repaired in makeshift ways, but it could continue to function for decades, though with increasing radiation leakage. Ultimately, however, the repairs will fail and the reactor will destroy itself and the ship."

Picard grimaced mentally, the only outward sign a slight tightening of his lips. He had listened to the endlessly repeating message at least a half-dozen times, and each time the feeling of kinship with the speaker, the one who called himself Koralus, had grown more pronounced. The message was straightforward and to the point, a simple account of the essentially hopeless situation his ship, the *Hope of Krantin*, found itself in, followed by a succinct description of the warning signs that had preceded the failure of the drive—warning signs that, if reacted to differently and more quickly on other ships, might save them from the same fate.

Picard hoped that the message was true, but even more he hoped that the man who had recorded it and started it on its snail-like way across the light-years was still alive to see it answered, and not just because of the kinship he felt. If Koralus was dead or no longer in control, if no one responded to their hail and an away team was forced to beam onto the ship with no idea of the current lay of the land—

"Mr. Data," Picard said abruptly, "are there unpopulated areas of the ship to which an away team could beam unnoticed?"

"Many, Captain. The entire central section—the core—is essentially unoccupied except for one large area that might be employed for recreation."

"A zero-g rec room?" Riker murmured. "Interesting." A momentary smile pulled at his neatly bearded face as his words brought a sidelong glance from Picard.

"There is something else, Captain," Data went on. "The sensors are beginning to indicate that another part of the core is a hibernation facility."

Picard frowned. "In a generation ship?"

"That is correct, Captain," Data said, continuing to study the ops console readouts. "Though there are approximately ten thousand fully active humanoid life-forms, there are also approximately seventy similar life-forms whose metabolic rates indicate that they have undergone some type of cryonic preservation. Their life signs were too faint for our sensors to detect at greater distances."

"That area would appear to be the place to start, Number One. You can get a look at them without—"

"Captain," Worf broke in, "they are responding to our hail."

A moment later, the same voice they had heard on the recorded message emerged from the bridge speakers.

"This is Koralus of the *Hope of Krantin.* Who are you?"

So he *was* still alive! Picard thought with relief. Quickly, he began to identify himself and the *Enterprise,* but before he could finish, the voice broke in. "That is the same as the message I have already heard, and it means nothing to me. *What* are you? Where are you from? What is this Federation you speak of?"

Patiently, fully understanding Koralus's impatient desire for information, Picard tried to explain, weaving his way around the other's rapid-fire and often incisive questions. When he finished, the alien was silent for several seconds.

"This offer of assistance—" Koralus began finally. "You have heard my message, so you understand our situation. What type of assistance can you offer? Can you repair our drive, for example?"

"Based on our preliminary observations, that would be difficult," Picard admitted. "It would be easier to return your people to your own world or take you to another habitable one."

"Your ship is that large?" The Universal Translator did little to disguise the mixture of skepticism and suspicion in Koralus's voice.

"We could handle your ten thousand for as long as it would take to move you, yes."

There was a long silence before Koralus's voice returned. "'As long as it would take . . .' How long would that be? We are almost a light-year from our own world and farther than that from any other."

"A few hours at most," Picard said. "Transferring your people from your ship to the *Enterprise* would likely take longer than the trip itself."

"You are speaking of subjective time, surely," Koralus said after a moment, his voice still skeptical. "Even if you approached the speed of light—"

"We have a way around that particular limitation." Picard glanced briefly toward Riker. "Perhaps it would be best if some of our people came aboard the *Hope* to evaluate your situation firsthand."

"Came aboard? No, I would prefer no one come aboard at this time."

Picard frowned at the hastily spoken protest. Had his feeling of kinship for this alien captain been misplaced? "Why not, Koralus?"

There was a long silence before the voice returned. "Our nuclear power generator is no longer safe. Our section of the ship is protected from its radiation by a shield, but surrounding space is not. It would be unsafe for you to approach."

"We are aware of the radiation levels surrounding your drive unit," Picard said, certain that the alien had not yet revealed his real reasons. "They do not pose a threat to us."

Another uneasy silence, and then Koralus said, "I will be honest. I do not wish to offend, but I must know more before I allow your presence to be known to the others."

The real reason this time, but far from a complete explanation. "There is no need for anyone other than yourself to know of our presence on your ship until you wish to disclose it."

"That is not possible. The *Hope* has only one airlock, and anyone entering through it could not avoid being seen by—"

"We have a way around that problem, too," Picard

interrupted. "Our people can transport directly to any point within your ship that you specify."

"Transport? I do not understand."

"It is how we often come and go from our own ship. It is a form of matter transmission. Perhaps a demonstration would—"

"You can simply disappear from your ship and reappear here, on the *Hope?*"

"Precisely."

"How would you get back to your ship, then?"

"We can transport both ways."

For several seconds, there was only silence. Then: "You can simply move things—people—from one point to another, regardless of any barriers between the points?"

"Within certain limits, yes."

"You can go 'through' the hulls of both our ships?"

"Easily."

Another silent pause. "Does that mean you could bring *me* aboard *your* ship in the same manner? Without our two ships ever coming in physical contact?"

"It could be done, yes. We are already within transporter range."

"Then that is what I would like, if it is permissible."

Picard considered. He still felt that his initial impression of this alien was correct, even though the always-present analytical—skeptical—part of his mind knew that this feeling could be nothing more than wishful thinking. However, if Koralus could *not* be trusted, it would be safer to bring him aboard the *Enterprise* than to send an away team to the *Hope*.

"Very well, Koralus," Picard said. "If that is your wish, it is acceptable to us. However, you will have to tell us precisely where you are within your ship. And you must separate yourself from everyone else."

"I imagine I am already at least a hundred meters away from anyone else. I am in the bridge. That is essentially at the center of the forward end of the ship, within a few meters of the rotational axis."

"Is that sufficient, Mr. Data?"

"I believe it is, Captain. I have identified a single humanoid life-form at approximately the location described."

"Transfer the coordinates to the transporters." Picard stood up and headed for the turbolift. "Number One, with me. And ask Counselor Troi to join us in transporter room number two."

He wanted to trust Koralus, but there was no point in taking unnecessary chances.

Koralus stood waiting, his heart pounding. What was he letting himself in for? Matter transmission? It was an absurd idea on the face of it, but so was their claim of being able to "get around" the limit of the speed of light.

But if it was all true . . .

He shivered, wondering suddenly if there was hope not only for himself and the Ten Thousand but for Krantin as well. With the kind of technology these people obviously had—or claimed to have—almost anything was possible. They might even be able to find what Krantin's scientists had failed to find—the source of the Plague, a reason for its existence, even a way of turning it back.

On the other hand, everything they said could be a lie, a trick. These beings, if they indeed had the powers they claimed, particularly the ability to "transport" objects unseen through space, might even be the ones responsible for the Plague in the first place.

Or others like them. The one who called himself

Picard had spoken of a "Federation," which meant there must indeed *be* others out there in the galaxy with equal or greater powers. Who was to say they had not visited Krantin in the past? Who could say what they might have done?

He shivered again, waiting, his mind whirling, his stomach queasy with a sudden feeling of utter helplessness. If they had the powers they claimed, if they were capable of creating—or stopping—the Plague, there was nothing he could do that would keep them from doing whatever they wished, nothing he could do to make them do anything they didn't wish to do. He only hoped that when—

A sudden tingling sensation gripped him and spread instantaneously throughout his entire body. Involuntarily, he started to pull back, but before he had more than tensed his muscles, he was frozen, unmoving. The bridge shimmered around him and faded out of existence, replaced by a surreal, silvery light that refused to hold still.

Then he was in another room, several times the size of the bridge of the *Hope*, standing on a raised platform. A woman stood at a console of some kind at the far end of the room. To one side, two men and a woman, all wearing odd, one-piece garments, their exposed skin several shades darker than his own sunless white, stood watching him.

The shorter man, almost totally hairless, stepped forward. "Welcome to the *Enterprise*, Mr. Koralus."

So, he thought, *they were telling the truth. About their "transporter," at least.*

Chapter Three

THE BRIEF TOUR of the *Enterprise* completed, Koralus and six of the starship's officers adjourned to what they called a "conference room." Koralus lowered himself uneasily into a seat at one end of a table long enough to accommodate a dozen or more. The captain, the hairless one named Picard, sat at the opposite end, hunched slightly forward, his hands clasped on the table in front of him. His second-in-command, Commander Riker, sat easily on Picard's left. Next was Commander La Forge, an extremely dark-skinned man with a strange silvery device hiding his eyes. He was the one who, if any repairs to the *Hope* were found to be possible, would do the work or watch over those who did. Troi, the woman who had been in the transporter room to greet him, was on Picard's right. Her function—"counselor"—was unclear except that she seemed to be the one the others looked to when they wanted to know if he was telling the truth. Crusher, another woman, a doctor who could learn the most remarkable things about a person simply by running a small device over that person's body, was on Koralus's left. On his right was the one called Data, the only one whose skin tone matched his own. They described him as an android, an artificial human, but he was also considered an officer like the others.

The final participant was the frightening-looking creature they called Worf. A "Klingon," whatever that was. Koralus watched him uneasily. Despite their assurances, he could not completely overcome the terror that had gripped him when he had emerged onto the bridge and almost run into the creature.

Visible through a series of windows—or viewscreens?—in one wall of the conference room were the stars, motionless. There was no need for the constant rotation the *Hope* required, they had said. Their gravity was another of their technological miracles, generated at will. On their bridge, they had shown him an image of the *Hope* on a huge screen, and for the first time he had been able to see what it was that had killed two dozen of his friends. And why it was beyond repair. It was only luck—and the skill and courage of those who had died—that had kept the habitat section of the *Hope* intact and the nuclear power generator even marginally functional.

Uneasily, still not certain of their motives, Koralus nonetheless answered their questions, truthfully in the main, about the *Hope,* about its sister ships, but mostly about the Plague, never letting his suspicions show through his words.

"Nebular dust," they called it at first, until he told them that it fouled Krantin's atmosphere even more than it did the surrounding space, and their seeming puzzlement at that information both encouraged and frightened him. Encouraged because their seeming ignorance indicated that they were not the ones responsible for the Plague. Frightened because their puzzlement cast doubt on their ability to help.

Five hundred years ago there had been no Plague, he assured them when they expressed not only puzzlement but doubt. The stars had shone as brightly on Krantin as they did here in interstellar space. Five hundred years ago, when Krantin's technology had just begun to develop and the world was emerging from a long agricultural stage, the atmosphere had been clean and breathable, and more than a billion had lived on the planet's surface.

No one was sure precisely when the Plague began. Krantin's fledgling industrialization began to pollute the air, and for nearly a century, most assumed that was the sole source of the pollution. But then, as efforts to eliminate it evolved from determined to desperate, scientists gradually came to see that there had to be another source. Finally, Krantin's technology reached a point at which its machines produced virtually no pollution of any kind, and still the atmosphere continued to grow worse. It was as if the very air was being converted into toxic materials of all kinds. Even radioactive contaminants began to appear, though no one realized at the time what they were. It was another fifty years before Krantin developed nuclear power and scientists recognized the radioactive parts of the pollution for what they were: elements found in the waste products of nuclear-fission power plants.

Meanwhile, the Plague had apparently spread to space. The "nebular dust" had begun to appear in their asteroid belt and slowly thickened and expanded until the cloud—the Plague—enveloped Krantin itself. The stars faded year by year until finally they were invisible altogether from Krantin. Even their sun began to dim and redden in the sky.

The atmospheric Plague was the critical factor, however. Long before the dust in space had enveloped Krantin, the atmosphere had become a disaster. Entire species of plants and animals were dying off, and breathing masks were becoming a necessity. Finally, when all else failed and they seemed faced with extinction, they began a campaign to enclose their largest cities and to convert all their food production to hydroponics. Soon after the first of the enclosures was begun, Koralus and several others managed to divert some of the money and resources to building the *Hope* and its sister ships. Even the enclosures could not protect the Krantinese forever, Koralus had argued. Small amounts of pollution were already appearing within supposedly airtight individual structures, indicating that, in the long run, the Plague could not be kept out, no matter how tightly sealed the cities became.

There were only two chances for long-term survival of the race, Koralus and his allies said. Either the scientists must find the source of the Plague and stop it, or ships must be built to allow at least a few tens of thousands to attempt to reach other star systems. Enough people agreed for enough time to construct and launch the *Hope* and five other ships. It all ended when a seventh ship nearing completion was destroyed by a group of workers who became furious when they found they would not be among the one in ten who would be given space on the ships they were building.

"That was the end of the program," Koralus said. "The seventh ship and three others under construction were also destroyed, along with most of the orbital facilities needed for the construction. Tens of thousands of stranded workers died as well, including the ones who caused the destruction. After that . . ."

He paused, lowering his eyes to the glistening surface of the conference table. "After that, I don't know what happened. We were a year on our way, and the few messages we received after the disaster indicated that there were no plans to even try to build any more ships. All their efforts were going to be concentrated on enclosing the cities. Most wanted to simply forget that any ships had ever been built. Some, I think, would have killed us all if they had been able to reach us. Because the ships had been built, they said, fewer cities would be enclosed and more people would have to die." He shook his head. "Perhaps they were right. Perhaps Krantin would have been served better had we all concentrated on enclosing the cities and searching for the source of the Plague. There have been no messages from the other ships. None of them may have survived. At this point, I don't even know if anyone is still alive on Krantin."

Once again on the bridge, Picard watched the irregular torus that Koralus called the Plague grow ever larger on the viewscreen. Koralus, his face a stoic mask, sat in Riker's chair while the commander stood to one side. The alien had rejected the suggestion that he return to the *Hope* and explain the situation to his ten thousand charges.

"Until I know there is a world they can return to," he had said, "I would prefer not to have to tell them the *Hope* is doomed. Nor do I wish to raise false hopes. That is the reason I did not want you come aboard the *Hope* and reveal your existence to them."

A billion kilometers from the outer edge of the Plague cloud, the *Enterprise* slowed to quarter impulse.

"Is it safe to enter, Mr. Data?" Picard asked.

"I believe it is, Captain. Though the associated energy field is highly variable both from one moment to the next and from one location to another, the intensity is too low, even at its peak levels, to have a significant effect on either physical structures or life-forms."

"What effect would higher levels have?"

"I could not say, Captain. The energy itself bears a superficial resemblance to some of the energies involved in molecular-level transporter operation, but its only observable effect is to interfere with the sensor beams."

"But you say it varies wildly in intensity. Is there a pattern to the variability?"

"None that the computer can discern. It appears totally random from moment to moment and location to location. It is also impossible to rule out sudden, massive upswings at any moment, in any location."

"And the dust itself?"

"At our present distance, interference from the energy field prevents reliable sensor readings."

"Can the interference be compensated for?"

"I have been attempting to do so, but the random variations make it impossible."

"Mr. La Forge, is there anything Engineering can do?"

"I've been trying, too, Captain," Geordi's voice came from the Engineering deck, "but I think getting closer is the only solution. I tried boosting the power to the sensors and narrowing their focus, which helped a little, but not enough to give us anything reliable. It's like trying to look into a lake that's constantly being stirred up by millions of little storms. Up close, I think the extra power and tight

31

focus will give us relatively reliable readings, at least for small areas."

"Very well. Keep me informed, Mr. La Forge, Mr. Data. Ensign, take us in, minimum impulse."

Once again, though he still didn't realize he was doing it, Picard leaned forward a fraction in his chair. This was something he never tired of, was never completely comfortable with and probably never would be—never should be. If the time came when approaching an unknown star system became routine, that would be the time to retire to a desk somewhere in the depths of Starfleet—before such an attitude had a chance to kill him or his crew.

At a million kilometers, Data reported the first stable readings, but only of the outer fringes of the cloud, where the energy field was as attenuated as the cloud.

"This is quite remarkable, Captain," he reported after a moment's silence. "Sensors indicate the presence of hundreds of elements and compounds but nothing larger than individual atoms and molecules. More appear to be coming into existence every moment."

"'Coming into existence,' Mr. Data?" Picard's pulse quickened. "Are you positive this isn't still a result of the energy field's interference?"

"I cannot be one hundred percent positive at this distance, Captain."

At a hundred thousand kilometers, Data and Geordi agreed—they were positive. The sensors still wouldn't penetrate more than a few thousand kilometers into the cloud, but the readings at the very fringes, where the energy field was weakest, were now rock solid.

"Matter is being *created* right before our eyes—our sensors?" Picard stood abruptly and moved to look over Data's shoulders at the ops readouts. "Are you saying we've stumbled across a pocket of steady-state matter creation?"

"That is unlikely, Captain. There have been no confirmed instances of such a phenomenon in Starfleet history."

"But there's always a first time."

"That is correct, Captain. However, the theory regarding such hypothetical phenomena states that the matter thus created would be of a more elemental nature, primarily individual particles. Helium atoms are the most complex that could be produced within the framework of current theory."

Koralus had come to stand next to Picard. "Captain, you have said that an energy field of some kind blankets virtually the entire Krantin system, and that this energy is similar in some ways to the energy you use for your so-called transporters. Have I understood the situation correctly?"

"Essentially, yes," Picard admitted.

"Then is it possible that someone is *doing* this? Transporting this material here, from another part of space?"

Frowning, Picard turned to Data. The thought had crossed his mind, but he had not verbalized it yet, perhaps hoping it would be proven wrong before speaking it aloud made it real. "Possible, Mr. Data?"

"I would never say anything is totally impossible, Captain, but it is highly unlikely. There is no obvious source for the material within sensor range. To transport anything over the necessary distance would require a subspace transporter, which itself would leave a distinctive signature."

"Is it any more unlikely than that—that 'steady state' idea?" Koralus asked.

"With no more information than we have," Data

said, "both suggestions can be said to be equally unlikely."

"But you don't have anything to offer that's any *more* likely!" Koralus persisted testily.

"I suggest, gentlemen," Picard broke in, "that we move on to Krantin itself. Perhaps the scientists there have found something that will be helpful."

"If there are any still alive," Koralus said bleakly.

Picard's eyes were on Koralus as often as they were on the viewscreen as the *Enterprise* skirted the upper surface of the cloud, more than ten million kilometers above the orbital plane of the planets. It was obvious from the alien's expression and occasional muttered words that the situation he was being confronted with after his hundred years' absence was even worse than he had feared.

The alien shuddered as, at the orbit of Krantin, the ship nosed down into the Plague at minimum impulse. Before they had descended half the distance to where Krantin lay hidden, the stars had faded to invisibility. By the time they reached Krantin and went into orbit around it, the sun was the only other object visible, and even it was reduced to an indistinct red ball.

The planet itself was almost as indistinct. Its entire surface, land and water alike, was obscured by a reddish orange haze, translucent in some places, opaque in others.

And the energy field in the vicinity of the planet, Data reported, was several times as powerful as anywhere else.

"It would be inadvisable to use the transporters to reach the surface from a standard orbit, Captain," the android went on. "A strong possibility exists that the

matter stream could be interfered with, if not interrupted entirely."

"We can take a shuttle—if there is a reason for us to
descend to the surface," Picard said. "Are there any
life-form readings?"

"Yes, Captain, but they convey only the most
rudimentary information. Many areas of the surface
appear totally lifeless. Others show minimal signs of
lower life-forms, both plant and animal. Even the
upper layers of the oceans appear sparsely popu-
lated."

"And humanoid life-forms?"

"Unknown, Captain. There is only one area in
which higher life-forms are present in great enough
concentration to register despite the interference. The
sensors cannot determine if they are specifically
humanoid."

"Only one?" Koralus broke in. "They were working on enclosures for ten cities when communication ceased. They were hoping to build a hundred
more." He shuddered. "How many? How many are
left alive?"

Data glanced questioningly at Picard, who nodded
assent. "It is impossible to determine the number to
any degree of accuracy under the present conditions,"
Data explained. "However, there are certainly no
more than a few million."

Koralus slumped. "A few million . . ." he murmured, and after a moment he turned his back to the
bleak image on the viewscreen. "There were more
than a billion. . . ."

"Power sources, Mr. Data?" Picard prompted,
though his eyes remained on Koralus. "Energy
usage?"

"There is what appears to be a functioning nuclear

fusion power source approximately one hundred kilometers from the concentration of life-forms. It appears to be delivering its output in the form of electrical energy to the area of the life-form concentration itself, where there are indications of extensive electrical activity."

"But no communications of any kind?"

"None that the sensors can detect, Captain."

Picard turned to the alien. "Your assessment?" he asked quietly.

Koralus shook his head. "I don't know. Obviously, enclosing the cities was not as successful as they hoped."

"Obviously. However, the immediate question is, how do we contact anyone if they aren't listening to any frequency?"

"Sir," Lieutenant Worf broke in, "a localized surge in the energy field, bearing approximately one-sixty mark forty."

Picard turned sharply toward the tactical station. "Distance?"

"Unknown, sir. The sensors are not reliable beyond fifty thousand kilometers, and—" The Klingon broke off, scowling at the tactical station readouts. "It is gone, sir."

"How powerful was the surge?"

"Also unknown, sir, but at a minimum it was a hundredfold increase."

"Any residual effects?"

"None detectable, sir."

"Mr. Data? Anything else?"

"I cannot be positive, Captain, but there appears to have been a qualitative as well as a quantitative difference in the localized surge."

"It was a different *kind* of energy, Mr. Data?"

"Not entirely, Captain. It still bears a strong resemblance to the energy fields associated with transporter operation. However, while the low-level energy resembles that associated with molecular-resolution transport, the pattern and frequency of the surge energy indicated a finer resolution."

"Quantum level, Mr. Data? Suitable for transmission of living matter?"

"Again, Captain, not entirely. The readings themselves are unreliable, so a precise comparison is impossible. However, even taking that unreliability into account, the indicated resolution was very probably not at a quantum level. At best, the resolution would be at some intermediate level of precision."

Picard glanced at Koralus, then back at the shrouded planet that still filled the viewscreen. Whatever the resolution level, this sudden burst lent weight to Koralus's suggestion—and his own suspicion—that the Plague was not entirely a natural phenomenon.

More importantly, it provided a new avenue of investigation. "Ensign, take us out of orbit, quarter impulse, heading one-sixty mark forty. Full stop the moment any artificial construct—or another energy surge—is detected."

Chapter Four

ALONG WITH EVERYONE BUT DATA, Captain Jean-Luc Picard could not completely suppress another wince as the fiery display on the viewscreen once again flared even brighter, as if the *Enterprise* were swooping through a star's corona. All the flare really meant, though, was that they had just passed through a slightly denser area of the Plague. The constant and coruscating bow shock that preceded and half surrounded the *Enterprise* simply marked the location of the forward shields as they plowed through the molecular soup of the Plague. Without them, even at quarter impulse, the unprotected duranium hull would start to show damage within minutes. At full impulse, even the shields could not protect the ship for long, any more than they could protect it forever against a sustained barrage of phaser fire. The raw energies involved would not be dissimilar.

They had gone nearly two hundred million kilometers and passed within range of more than a hundred asteroids when Worf barked out a command for full stop. Instantly the flare of the bow shock vanished from the viewscreen, replaced by the featureless haze of the Plague. "Object directly ahead," Worf announced, "range less than one hundred thousand kilometers."

"A ship, Mr. Worf?"

"Unknown, sir. Sensors indicate that the object is artificial, but beyond that, all readings are inconclusive at this range."

"Very well. Ensign, take us closer, minimum impulse."

The shields flared again, this time at a lower, almost undetectable level, as the *Enterprise* crept forward.

"The object directly ahead appears to be another asteroid, Captain," Data announced minutes later, "diameter more than fifty kilometers."

"An artificial asteroid?"

"No, Captain. The sensors are beginning to detect a second object approximately five hundred kilometers from the asteroid. This second object is almost certainly responsible for the earlier readings. Because of the interference, the sensors could not previously determine that there were two objects rather than one."

"Ensign, alter course to close with the new object. Full stop as soon as sensor readings are reliable."

"Aye, Captain."

"Sir," Worf rumbled a minute later, "we have just crossed the trail of an impulse drive. The signature is unmistakable and is less than a day old. There is no trace of the ship that produced it."

A jolt of adrenaline nudged Picard's level of concentration even higher at this further indication of the unnatural "nature" of the so-called Plague.

Koralus had sworn that Krantin had never developed an impulse engine, and yet an impulse-drive ship had passed through this very spot only hours ago.

Picard turned toward the alien as, slowly, the *Enterprise* continued forward. "Could your world have developed impulse technology in the time since you left?" he asked, though he knew what the answer must be.

Koralus shook his head. "I can't imagine how. From the few communications we received after the ships under construction were destroyed, it was obvious that space travel was dead and no one was interested in reviving it. And you saw Krantin just now. Your machines say there are only a few million left alive, huddled in a single city."

Picard nodded imperceptibly as he turned back to the viewscreen. "Nonetheless," he said softly, *"someone* with impulse-drive technology has been here within the last twenty-four hours."

On the viewscreen, the shields flared more brightly as Data announced they were again passing through a denser-than-average pocket of the cloud. Almost as soon as the incandescence returned to its "normal" level, Worf brought the ship again to a full stop.

"The object is definitely a ship, sir," he said a moment later. "Mass is in the thousand-ton range."

"Impulse drive?"

Worf was silent a moment, adding to his everyday scowl as he studied the tactical station readouts. "Yes, sir, but of extremely low power for a vessel of that size. It is little more powerful than those that drive our shuttlecraft."

"It appears to be a cargo ship of some kind, Captain," Data supplied. "There is a single humanoid life-form aboard, and most of the mass appears to consist of several hundred tons of ore, containing iron, nickel, and traces of uranium."

"Hail it, Mr. Worf, all EM channels. Ensign, take us in to visual range, directly in its path."

As if emerging from a fog, a bulbous ship took shape on the viewscreen. There were no rockets or other drives visible, only sets of comparatively tiny attitude-control jets. At the front, a tiny bubble protruded from the otherwise featureless surface. It was coasting directly across the path of the *Enterprise*. Slowly, the *Enterprise* moved ahead of it, and then kept pace with it at a distance of little more than a kilometer.

"No response to our hail, sir," Worf reported, but even as he spoke, the ship on the screen fired a series of attitude jets, which set it slowly to turning. After a quarter turn, the ship began to lumber away, apparently under impulse power.

"Stay in front of it, Ensign, and maintain our present distance. Mr. Worf, keep trying to contact them."

"Yes, sir."

"Mr. Data—"

"It is emitting a signal," Worf rumbled, "but it does not appear to be directed at us. It is totally unmodulated, with no discernible information content."

"Captain," Data broke in, "the energy field surrounding the ship is increasing precipitately—"

The viewscreen flared blindingly bright.

When it cleared, the screen was empty except for the featureless cloud that was the Plague.

"Was it destroyed?" Picard asked sharply.

"I do not believe so, Captain," Data said. "There is no residue of any kind. Even destruction by maximum-strength phaser fire or photon torpedo leaves a residue."

"Then where is it? Could it have escaped while we were blinded by the flash?"

"Only if it accelerated to full impulse speed virtually instantaneously, which would be impossible for a ship of that mass with that size impulse engine, even without the Plague to contend with. And even if it were possible, the impulse drive would have left an easily identifiable energy trail, which it did not. The existing energy trail ends at precisely the point at which the ship vanished. Neither are there any indications of either the existence or the activation of a warp drive."

Picard scowled at the starless screen, forced to give voice to the thought that had been in his mind, unwelcomed, since moments after the flash. "It was transported away, then, is that what you're saying?"

"Not precisely, Captain, but it is a reasonable supposition. The energy burst was essentially identical to the earlier burst, although there was no indication of either a matter stream or a containment field, both of which are essential to transporters as we know them."

"Play the entire sequence back, Mr. Data. Go to slow motion for the final seconds."

The viewscreen flickered and went blank for an instant as Data's fingers darted across the controls. A moment later, the missing ship was once again emerging from the haze, coasting across the bow of the *Enterprise.*

"The pilot was in the pod at the front of the ship," Data said as the replay continued. "The pod also contained the impulse drive and appeared to be detachable, just as the saucer unit of the *Enterprise* is detachable. The remainder is essentially nothing but a large cargo hold."

Picard frowned. "It has no drive of its own?"

"Only the attitude jets, Captain."

"What kind of range would this combination have?"

"Extremely limited, Captain. Also, it would dare not venture close to any asteroid substantially larger than the ones we have so far encountered. Were it to approach one even a hundred kilometers in diameter, it could be trapped in the gravity well."

Once again the massive ship made its turn and began to lumber away, essentially being towed by the tiny control and drive pod. It was, Picard couldn't help but think, as if the *Enterprise* were to be towed by one of the shuttlecraft. But what was the point? Why drag a thousand tons of mass through space at a snail's pace when you have the ability to instantaneously transport objects to—to somewhere else? Perhaps they could only transport objects from certain points in space? Or perhaps it was *easier* to do it from certain points, but it was possible, in an emergency—such as being confronted by an unknown and potentially dangerous alien craft like the *Enterprise*—to do it from anywhere? And perhaps the signal it had emitted was a distress call, a demand to be rescued then and there, regardless of the difficulty, regardless of the power required?

Picard shook his head. As was so often the case, all he had was questions, not answers.

On the screen, the alien ship was once more seen head-on. The *Enterprise* had maneuvered in front of it after the ninety-degree turn.

"This is when the signal was emitted," Data continued. "The computer is still unable to detect any form of modulation."

Abruptly, the image seemed to freeze. The only

43

perceptible motion was the exhaust from the attitude jets as they continued to fire to slow the ship's rotation.

"This is the point at which the energy buildup began," Data supplied a few seconds later. The image of the ship remained unchanged, except that the attitude jets had stopped firing. "It is almost certainly a form of transporter energy, but it is equally certainly not consistent with the quantum-level resolution required for transporting life-forms safely. At best, it operates at the level of individual atoms."

"Then whoever was aboard the ship was killed?"

"Not necessarily, Captain. There might be damage at the cellular level and below, but there is no way of knowing how serious that damage is, or how reversible."

On the screen, a brilliant pinpoint of light appeared near the center of the ship. An instant later, the pinpoint had become a blinding sheet of light enveloping half the ship. Another instant, and the ship was swallowed up entirely.

"Can it be slowed down any more?" Picard asked as the entire screen was flooded with the light. There was a maddening familiarity to the images, but its source eluded him.

"Not in the sense that I believe you mean, Captain. What you have seen was the individual images that the computer, operating at its maximum speed, captured from the sensors. The actual time that elapsed between the first appearance of the light and the full envelopment of the ship was less than a millisecond."

On the screen, the light vanished almost as quickly as it had appeared, taking five images instead of three to shrink from the ship-enveloping size to a pinpoint.

Then it was gone.

And so was the ship.

"The light, and presumably the ship, were gone within less than two milliseconds," Data went on. "The energy field accompanying the light took approximately two seconds to build up and another two seconds to decay."

Picard turned to Koralus, who had been watching the screen in scowling puzzlement. "Could that have been a Krantinese ship?"

"I cannot imagine how it could be—unless the situation on Krantin is radically different from what it seems."

Precisely Picard's own assessment. "Perhaps it's time we found out," he said, turning back to the viewscreen. "Ensign, take us out of this—this 'plague' and back to Krantin."

"Sir," Worf rumbled from the tactical station before the order could be carried out, "something is approaching, bearing one-ten mark eighty-five."

"Onscreen," Picard snapped.

"It is not within visual range," Data volunteered, "under current conditions."

"Focus the sensors on it as tightly as possible, Mr. Data. Get whatever you can before it gets here."

"I am working on it, Captain. It appears to be moving at a speed consistent with an impulse drive, but the sensor readings are becoming even more erratic."

"There is a concentration of the energy field, sir," Worf reported, "that appears to be moving with the object. That could be causing the added interference with the sensors."

"Or it could *be* the object," Riker said, "a moving energy field. Captain, whatever it is, I suggest we raise the shields until we know more about it."

"Agreed, Number One. Make it so."

They waited.

Finally, what looked like a tiny fireball emerged from the haze of the dust cloud. It was small, little larger than a two-person shuttlepod, apparently powered by an impulse engine similar in size to the one in the previous, much larger ship.

Beyond the signature of an impulse drive, however, even the most tightly focused sensor beams revealed little—except that the pyrotechnic display surrounding it was associated with a concentrated form of the energy field that permeated this system. Apparently the ship—if there was indeed a ship inside the fireball—was using it for the same purpose the *Enterprise* used its shields when traveling through the cloud at impulse speeds: to protect it from the cloud of matter it was racing through.

Abruptly, the newcomer stopped less than ten kilometers distant. The energy field collapsed instantly, the attendant flare vanishing with it.

"One humanoid life-form aboard, Captain," Data reported a moment later. "No indication of energy weapons. Power is provided by hydrogen fusion."

"Lower shields," Picard ordered. "Mr. Worf, hail it on all EM frequencies."

But it didn't respond. Almost as quickly as the tiny ship had stopped, it turned about and raced away, its image on the viewscreen turning instantly from ship to fireball.

"Tractor beam," Picard snapped, and a moment later the fireball lurched to a halt and once again became a ship. "Maintain position, Ensign. Number One, assemble an away team in the shuttlebay. I want—"

"Sir," Worf broke in, "the alien has transmitted the same signal as the first ship."

Almost before the Klingon had finished speaking,

the viewscreen was once again swamped by a blinding flash of light, immeasurably brighter than the fireball had been. The *Enterprise* lurched very slightly as the tractor beam found itself focusing on nothing.

When the viewscreen cleared, it was once again empty.

Another moment, and Worf reported a second surge in the energy field, this one almost directly astern.

Then another, this one in the general direction of Krantin.

And another, now from high above the ecliptic.

And another.

And another.

There were seventeen in all when finally they stopped.

Picard grimaced mentally as he sat down in the command chair and tugged automatically at his uniform. In the back of his mind, he wondered if each of the surges marked the departure—or arrival?—of another of the alien ships. At the same time, the elusive reason for the feeling of familiarity triggered by the images of the first disappearance continued to hover just beyond reach.

"Take us back to Krantin, Ensign," he said. "Let's hope *it* doesn't vanish as well."

Koralus watched the viewscreen with apprehension as the giant ship once again approached Krantin. On the trip back from the asteroid belt, the *Enterprise* sensors had detected, he was told, over a hundred more "energy bursts." They had come in groups of ten to twenty, with no discernible pattern except that all the bursts in a single group seemed to come from the same general volume of space, and all groups originated, as best their hampered instruments could determine, within the Plague cloud, possibly within the asteroid belt.

Whatever was going on, it was beyond him. He didn't know whether to be encouraged or frightened that it seemed to be beyond these people as well. Either way, there wasn't a lot he could do about it, which wasn't that much of a change from his position the last ten years on the *Hope*.

But at least now there was a chance—if these people and the "Federation" they said they represented could be taken at their word. And if whatever had been happening in the Krantin system for the last five hundred years wasn't as far beyond their abilities as theirs were beyond Krantin's.

Again, as they slid into orbit smoothly and effortlessly, they did whatever it was they did to try to find a way to communicate with someone on the surface of Krantin. But there apparently was nothing to be found. Their calls, like his own messages of a decade ago, went unanswered, if they were even received.

Finally, the captain ordered the second-in-command, the Klingon, and the android to descend to the surface in one of their auxiliary ships, a so-called shuttlecraft. It was not ordered but strongly suggested that Koralus accompany them and lend them his "native perspective."

"Survey the situation from the air before you commit yourself to landing," the captain instructed. "And relay all sensor data directly to the *Enterprise*. Unless the energy field within the atmosphere is more powerful than it appears, the shuttle sensors should provide us with considerably more information than we can obtain from up here."

Then the four of them were in the shuttlecraft and swooping down through the hazy upper atmosphere and into a layer of clouds that blanketed more than half of the main continent.

Antrovar, Koralus thought, and wondered if the name was still used. Were any of the names still used, now that virtually everyone apparently lived in a single, enclosed city?

Koralus suppressed a gasp as they emerged from the low-hanging clouds and the ground was suddenly visible.

He had been prepared for desolation, but not this. When he had left a hundred years ago, there had been plant life. Not the lush and abundant forests and fields and meadows that pre-Plague paintings and even some early photographs showed, but *something.* More land had been covered than was bare. Hundreds of species had survived seemingly unchanged—certain hardy breeds of grass, a scattering of long-lived trees, enough food plants to let the dwindling population survive until the conversion to hydroponics was completed.

But now . . .

The only trees were leafless, lifeless skeletons.

Here and there were grotesque patches of green and purple and gray groundcover, surrounded by bare ground or rock or mud.

The little ship's sensors apparently had things to say about the vegetation and the few animals still living. Koralus understood little of it, but he understood enough. "Mutated" he understood—and the android's emotionlessly delivered verdict: "Even using the most optimistic assumptions, there will be nothing alive in twenty years."

So this is what it comes to.

49

Then the city—Jalkor? once the greatest metropolis on Krantin?—became visible through the haze, and Koralus's heart sank even further. It was not one of the graceful domes the original planners had envisioned, nor even one of the low, smooth hexagonal shapes that had been the plan when the *Hope* had departed. Instead, it was a squat, misshapen box, each corroded, irregular side at least fifty kilometers long and fifty meters high. The "roof" was an endless collection of flat, slightly sloped terraced segments, as if the height of the roof at any given point had been determined by the height of the buildings beneath it. Some areas near the center were at least five hundred meters high. All around the outside of the enclosure were skeletal remnants of tens of thousands of what might have once been houses, apparently abandoned and cannibalized for what they could contribute to the enclosure and what was inside.

Inside, if he was to believe what he heard as the android and the Klingon read the craft's instruments, was a haphazard mixture, again as if a sprawling city of twenty or forty million or more had simply been roofed over and modified. Streets and individual houses still existed in many areas, while in others they had been torn down and replaced by kilometer after kilometer of boxlike hydroponic enclosures. In still others they had been replaced by hivelike buildings, each capable of housing tens of thousands. In the center were warrens of cramped passageways and corridors, as if offices and apartments and industrial structures had been fused into a single block, half of which had been converted to living quarters, the rest to house more hydroponics and food-processing plants. There were even remnants of half a dozen of what must have been parks, but the vegetation was long since dead.

And beneath it all, just barely within reach of those same instruments, the android described what Koralus recognized as the remnants of a vast underground complex of tunnels and storerooms and sewers. Now there was one section with tens of thousands of sterile hydroponics tanks, although less than a quarter of them seemed to be in use. The rest was filled with pipes and machinery of every description, constantly taking in the waste of the millions and processing and reprocessing it and sending it back for yet another cycle. As in the hydroponics sections, less than half of what was there was functioning.

Better to die aboard the Hope *than here,* he thought despairingly.

There were dozens of tiny entrances—airlocks—scattered about the bases of the outer walls, but none appeared operational. Four massive airlocks, one on each side, led into what must once have been storage and repair areas for the machines used outside during the construction of the enclosure, but only one of those showed any signs of use or repair. The remnants of a road led out into the haze and desolation, through the long-dead and cannibalized "suburbs."

The one called Riker was scowling at the image when the Klingon looked up from the panel he had been hovering over since their entry into the atmosphere.

"Commander, I am detecting a signal."

A moment later, a crackling sound erupted from the panel. There were no voices, no sounds other than the static.

"Data, can you locate the source?"

"Not precisely, Commander. It is coming from the

direction of the fusion-power-generating facility that was detected from the *Enterprise*. The facility itself is approximately one hundred kilometers distant."

Riker was silent a moment, listening to the static. Then he straightened, his fingers darting to the control panel. "Let's take a closer look," he said, the image on the screen shifting as the shuttlecraft wheeled about.

Chapter Five

AHL DENBAHR COUGHED as she sealed the inner door of the driver's compartment of the converted hauler and pulled the clogged breathing mask from her sweat- and grime-streaked face. Like everything else that really mattered on Krantin, it was obviously not in the best working order. It was also desperately in need of recharging. It had not, after all, been designed for the kind of continuous use she had been putting it to. It had been designed to get her from her vehicle to the "safe" areas inside the sprawling plant, a journey of no more than a few minutes.

But there were no more safe areas, not the control cubicles, not the supply rooms, not the emergency access and inspection corridors and crawlspaces. For whatever reason, the filtering and recycling system had not started up at her remote command, and the air inside the plant had been almost as bad as the air

53

outside when she arrived. It was certainly not good enough to breathe unfiltered for hours on end.

But that was the least of her problems, she conceded to herself as she nursed the engine into noisy life and set the vehicle to lumbering down the last remnants of the hundred-kilometer road back to Jalkor. Theoretically, the plant had been designed to repair itself and continue functioning near maximum efficiency indefinitely, but for design theory to be translated into fact, an inventory of reliable spare parts had to be maintained, particularly the laser confinement units that were the heart of the fusion assemblies. The plant could replace its own decaying units once they were delivered to it, but it couldn't manufacture or repair them.

And neither, it was becoming increasingly apparent, could she or anyone else. The last dozen, brought to the plant barely a year ago, had already been used and ten of the twenty she had brought today had been scooped out of their "storage" compartments the moment she had deposited them. Worse, three of the modules that were being replaced were part of the twelve from the year before. They had lasted less than a year.

And, based on the final tests she had done on the new units, they would likely fail just as quickly. The high-level vacuums required for them to function safely, let alone efficiently, were becoming ever harder to produce and literally impossible to maintain.

Most of the last year, she had spent with the other technicians, testing and retesting, building and rebuilding the machines used in fabricating the units, and yet each day the vacuums degraded more rapidly and the life expectancy of the units decreased. Even Zalkan had spent several days with them, suggesting new techniques, new experiments, but his efforts had been as fruitless as hers. If the trend continued, the life expectancy of new laser confinement units would someday be too short for them to be transported to the plant and installed.

And then?

Then they would either shut the plant down, one fusion unit at a time, or they would miscalculate and wait too long, and the plant would shut itself down, permanently and probably catastrophically.

Either way, once the power plant failed, Jalkor would go the way of all the other cities.

It would be over.

The Plague would have won its final victory. Five hundred years of struggle would be over. Only the dying would be left, and death would be quick in coming.

And the Deserters would have been proven right.

For a moment, anger pulsed through her, not against the Deserters but against herself for continuing this futile struggle. And against Zalkan for having "rescued" her from the electronic womb she had retreated into a dozen years before. Like millions of other "survivors," she had one day looked at the world around her and realized she was no longer able to deny what her future—what Krantin's future—was. Like millions of others, she had cursed her parents for having brought her into a world so obviously dying.

And she had surrendered.

Unlike millions of others, however, she had "recovered." After two years—she still had trouble believing it had been only two years, so endless had it finally begun to seem—after two years of emerging from the computer-generated fantasies only long enough to eat and sleep, she had awakened one day to find the fantasies temporarily replaced by the frail figure of a man she had never seen before, awake or dreaming. His name was Zalkan, he said, and he was the latest to take up the increasingly impossible task of maintaining the machinery that kept the city alive. He was searching out all who had worked for his predecessors, trying to coax and bully them back into the real world, where they and thousands of others were desperately needed. Unlike most, Ahl Denbahr had been ready to return.

For all the good it had done.

The power plant—the single most critical piece of machinery; if it went, everything went—was barely limping along, as was everything else. If demand had not decreased—the hundred million who had filled Jalkor when it had been sealed had dwindled to five million or less—the systems would have long ago broken down completely.

But if the population had not decreased, if more and more of those who remained had not simply given up and retreated from reality, then there would have been more than enough skilled and willing workers to keep the systems going, even improve and replace them. Or such was Zalkan's constant litany against the sin of surrender.

Sometimes Ahl agreed with him, sometimes she didn't. Today she had serious doubts. No matter how skilled or how willing a workforce existed, there was still only so much that could be done in the face of the Plague. The inability to produce new units for the power plant was only one example, though by far the most critical. More and more often, surrender to the inevitable was once again striking her as the rational alternative, while constant struggle seemed both futile and foolish. It certainly wasn't pleasant, and more than once she had found herself envying those who were able to simply retreat into the fantasies and, unlike herself, resist the temptation to be drawn back to reality.

Coughing again, she wondered if, this time, the mask had let something truly deadly into her lungs. Shoving the useless thought away, she switched on the radio and tried to raise Zalkan.

But there was no response.

Sighing, she set the call on automatic and settled back to drive and wait. She couldn't blame Zalkan for not responding instantly. Though he never complained, his health was obviously bad. He had never been strong, even ten years ago when he had dragged her back to reality, and in the last few months he had seemed increasingly frail, as if he had finally reached a point at which even his iron will and determination were not enough to keep him going much longer.

Also, he was doubtless anticipating what her report would be, and he could be no more eager to hear it than she was to deliver it.

The Plague was winning even faster than they had feared, and there was nothing that could be done about it.

Zalkan insisted—had always insisted—that the only solution that held any real hope was, first, to build new construction and storage facilities deep underground, and then to build a new power plant at the same depth. The Plague, he believed, grew progressively weaker the deeper underground they went. Go far enough down, and it would be weak enough to overcome, or at least work around.

But a massive project such as that—far more massive than the sealing of Jalkor had been—would require, first and foremost, massive numbers of workers, tens of thousands if not hundreds of thousands, even millions. And Zalkan knew all too well that such numbers were impossible. After more than a decade of coaxing and cajoling and threatening, he had begun to lose ground, with more workers surrendering than he was able to recruit. "We'll all be dead in another five years or maybe a year, maybe even a month," he was told again and again, when he received an answer at all, "and I'm not going to spend what little time is left working myself to death even faster."

Even the Council, the only governing body left, such as it was, refused to use what little power it still retained to back Zalkan. "You might as well ask us to build a new fleet of Deserter ships!" was a typical response whenever Zalkan or anyone else brought the subject up.

Only Council President Khozak had ever had even limited enthusiasm for the project, and he had long ago realized it was hopeless. There simply weren't enough willing workers to even scratch the surface of such a project. There weren't even enough to properly hold the city together, let alone start something new. Most of the people had retreated into their computer-generated fantasies, while more and more of those who stayed in the real world had abandoned all discipline, taking and doing and destroying whatever they wanted. Some had even attempted to breach the city's walls, and more and more of Khozak's dwindling security forces had to be given over to fighting that and other lesser kinds of pointless destruction.

No, Denbahr thought, the Plague was winning, and there was nothing Zalkan or Khozak or anyone could do about it at this late date. A hundred years ago, if her ancestors had known what she knew now, if they had thrown all their efforts into building more and better ships instead of fighting among themselves and, in the end, abandoning space altogether, things would be better. Not specifically for her or for the few million still existing in the patchwork monstrosity

Jalkor had become, but for Krantin. She and most of the others, without the covered cities, would never have been born. Their ancestors, their parents and grandparents, would have been long dead. Nothing could change that. But at least a few more tens of thousands, possibly as many as a million, could have been—not saved, necessarily, but at least put on the road to finding a new home for their many-times-removed great-grandchildren.

But the kind of selflessness required for such a project was rare. Few were willing to work for years, even decades, under the harshest of conditions, not to save themselves but to save, at best, the distant descendants of one in a hundred of their fellow workers, particularly when there were those who, despite the disquieting evidence that was beginning to appear even then, insisted that sealing the cities was a better, safer way. Sealing the cities would not save a paltry million but virtually everyone.

Domes, they had said at first, but that had been when they thought they would have fifty years before the Plague drove them from the open air. When the Plague had accelerated, leaving them twenty, then ten years, the planners and engineers had thrown up their hands. They abandoned the domes, they abandoned excavations for the barely begun subterranean complexes planned to hold all the hydroponics, all the food production, all the recycling machinery—in short, everything needed to keep the city alive. Instead, to beat the Plague's accelerating deadline, they had improvised, done what they could with what materials they could get their hands on. Great tracts of "wasteful" individual homes were wiped out, replaced by square kilometer after square kilometer of hydroponics enclosures and everything else that they had hoped to seal neatly underground. Other tracts were replaced by hastily constructed "hives," each capable of housing tens of thousands. Instead of a complex series of massive domes, simple walls and roofs and support columns were all that could be managed. Even the "glow panels" planned to cover the inner surface of the domes, then the roofs, could not be perfected in time and were replaced by rings of harsher light that circled the upper reaches of the support columns.

It had been the same everywhere, every city for itself. Cooperation had vanished as each city raced to complete its own enclosure, of whatever size or shape it could manage.

And for another eighty years they had continued to struggle to survive even as they continued to die out. Most of the enclosures were never finished. Lack of raw materials, lack of energy, lack of time, lack of will, a lack of the same kind of selflessness that would have been needed to complete another hundred Deserter ships—all contributed to the failures and the wars and the deaths.

And it had all been for nothing. Jalkor had been the largest, and now it was the last. Originally holding more than a hundred million within its five thousand square kilometers, it had been reduced to less than five million by four generations of desperation. And less than one in a hundred of that five million spent more than an hour or two a day in the real world. And half of those, she thought with a new flare of anger, were not trying to save themselves or the city but, one way or another, trying to destroy it even more quickly than the Plague. Barring a miracle, Jalkor would soon be as dead as all the others, as dead as the barren landscape outside the—

A rasping buzz filled the tiny driver's compartment.

"Zalkan?" she said, almost shouting over the rumble of the engine as she slowed it to a somewhat less deafening idle. "It's even worse than you thought. Unless we find a way to produce and maintain a hard vacuum—"

"My name is Koralus," an oddly accented voice broke in. "I must speak with you."

"What?" Ahl frowned at the unfamiliar voice and name. "Where's Zalkan?"

"I know nothing of anyone named Zalkan," the voice said. "Please, I must—"

"Who are you? Whoever you are, get off the air! I don't have time for any—"

Another, deeper voice with the same odd accent broke in. "Look up, in front of your vehicle."

"What? Are you insane?" Despite her protest, she looked up. "Now, just who—"

She broke off, her jaw dropping. Hanging motionless in the hazy air not twenty meters away, half that high off the ground, was—*something*.

At least twice the size of her own lumbering vehicle, it looked like a rectangular box with a streamlined front end and a pair of eerily glowing tubes running the length of the sides.

Fighting down a growing feeling of panic, she turned back to the radio. "*What* are you? What do you want?"

And the voices explained.

If not for the apparition floating in plain sight in front of her, she would have assumed that, like countless others in recent years, the owners of the voices had been pushed over the edge into insanity by the strain that living on Krantin had become. With that *thing* staring her in the face, however, she realized that she was more likely the one who had been pushed over the edge. She was simply having an elaborate, pointless hallucination of her own, without even the help of the computer.

Unless this whole thing—her whole life the last ten years—had been a computer-generated fantasy. Unless, rather than being pulled back into reality by Zalkan, his appearance had simply marked the beginning of a grimmer fantasy—

She shook her head sharply. Hallucination or not, it was not in her nature to ignore it, and she forced herself to listen and to absorb what they were saying about federations and generation ships and someone named Koralus who—

Abruptly, the name clicked into place in her mind. Someone named Koralus, according to the histories, had been a leader of the Deserters! He had departed on one of half a dozen ships that had left orbit around Krantin a hundred years ago! They had not been heard of for at least ninety years. For a few years after the departures, the surviving supporters of the program struggled to keep in touch, and for another few years, isolated individuals continued to listen for transmissions from the ships even though they had no means of replying. Within a decade, the so-called Desertions had begun to recede from public awareness until they became just another unpleasant incident on the downslope of Krantinese history, one small but bitter skirmish in the long, losing battle with the Plague.

And now one of these voices was saying *he* was Koralus, one of the leaders of this almost forgotten exodus?

It was of course impossible, she told herself, just another symptom of her insanity, or a new twist in the fantasy she was still trapped in. Only minutes before, she had been thinking about the Deserters and the ships they had left in, and now, conveniently, here was a disembodied voice coming from a glowing, floating apparition saying he *was* Koralus, that he had been rescued by the other voices and brought back to Krantin in a magical ship that blithely defied the laws of physics!

At least, she thought, it was an interesting hallucination. And a persistent one.

Finally, one of the voices—the one that called itself Commander Riker—asked if she would like to come on board his ship. He called it a "shuttlecraft," which, the Koralus voice explained, was an auxiliary ship of some kind, carried by the main ship and used to take small numbers of people places the main ship couldn't go—like to the surface of a planet.

Sighing, she acquiesced. If this was all happening in her own mind or in the semiconductor synapses of a computer, what did she have to lose?

And if, by any chance, it was real . . .

Only a few minutes earlier, she had been thinking that only a miracle could save Krantin. And she couldn't help thinking now, despite all common sense, that maybe, just maybe, this was it.

In her stained coverall, Ahl Denbahr reminded Riker of an attractive Starfleet engineering cadet who had just emerged from one of the belowdecks training exercises the Academy liked to throw you into without warning. As Riker had hoped, bringing her aboard the shuttlecraft seemed to dispel her suspicion that she was hallucinating. "There's no way I could imagine *that!*" she said, recovering from a momentary Worf-induced paralysis.

After that, she was willing, even eager, to answer their questions, as long as they would answer hers in return.

Unfortunately, her answers did nothing to clear up the mystery of the disappearing ships. Not only had Krantin not developed impulse drive in the century since the *Hope* had departed from orbit, they had not sent a single ship of any kind into space since the destruction of the half-constructed generation ships—"Deserter ships," she called them, a hint of apology in her voice—and most of the orbital construction facilities.

Nor had they made any progress in understanding or stopping the Plague. "There may be people still working on it besides Zalkan," she said, grimacing, "but whoever they are, if they've made any progress, they haven't let me in on it. The few of us that haven't given up altogether are just trying to cope with the *effects*. And losing ground faster every day."

She looked around at the group and at the image of Picard and the *Enterprise* bridge on the tiny viewscreen. "Now you people think these mysterious ships may have something to do with the Plague? But you can't catch one to ask? Have I got that right?"

Riker suppressed a smile. He only hoped that whoever else they would have to deal with was equally sharp and as adaptable. "You have," he said.

"Meanwhile," she went on, looking toward Koralus, "you're hoping to have your ten thousand brought back to Krantin."

Koralus shook his head. "No more. Unless the Plague is overcome, they—we—will be better off on the *Hope*."

She leaned toward the viewscreen and the miniature image of Picard. "So, what are our chances against the Plague? Can you help us? Are you *willing* to help us?"

"If we are able," he replied. "We must first speak

64

with your leaders, of course, and with those who have studied the phenomenon. In the meantime, our chief engineer has been listening in, and he would like to inspect your fusion power generators."

"Can he do something for them?"

"He won't know until he looks the situation over personally, but it is likely that he would be able to produce the replacement laser units you say are needed. He would like to begin by bringing one of your units on board the *Enterprise* to analyze."

She was silent for several seconds before closing her eyes briefly and pulling in a deep breath. "Tell your chief engineer I will be glad to give him anything he wants or needs. Assuming I can get in touch with Zalkan, and also assuming I don't get overruled. And if I am," she added with a laugh, "let me know how I can help you steal one."

She didn't get overruled, at least not by Zalkan. When he finally responded and she told him what had happened, all he wanted to know, after several seconds of silence, was "Are *you* convinced they are genuine?"

"As convinced as I can be. Either they're genuine or this entire thing, including this conversation with you, is one giant hallucination."

He was silent again, uncharacteristically so, for several more seconds. "Tell me about the one who calls himself Koralus. I would like—" He broke off. "No, I am wasting time. The laser unit is more important than my own curiosity. I will meet you at the airlock. I will try to have one of the laser units there as well," he said, then signed off.

After a brief discussion, Ahl was returned to her machine long enough to drive it back to the power plant, where it was left. Minutes later, she was back in their vehicle, waiting at the city's one functioning airlock, a wastefully massive thing that opened into what had once been the maintenance area for the countless machines that had, a hundred years ago, ventured out to aid in the final sealing of the city and then to scavenge the surrounding area for anything useful. Now it was a junkyard for all but a half-dozen of those machines, the only ones that were still functioning.

Their chief engineer, as dark as the one called Worf but not at all frightening despite a strange silvery device that covered his eyes, had arrived a few minutes later in a second vehicle, where he sat waiting at the controls. He was to pick up the laser unit from Zalkan and return it to their orbiting ship for analysis while she and Zalkan notified President Khozak of the aliens' arrival and their offer of help. If Khozak had any sense at all, he would arrange to meet with them and discuss their offer.

When, finally, the outer airlock door creaked open a couple of meters, she began to suspect that Khozak, not surprisingly, didn't have the requisite amount of sense and that, somehow, he had managed to interfere. Instead of Zalkan, a nervous young man in a breathing mask and a Council coverall several shades lighter than her own stood in the lock. Despite her uneasiness at this development, she couldn't help but grin as the young man flinched backward a step when he saw Worf emerge from the vehicle a step behind her.

"Welcome," the young man said, his voice stiff and uneasy at the same time. "President Khozak is most anxious to meet with you. Please come with me."

"Where is Zalkan?" Ahl demanded. "He said he

would meet us here. *With* one of the replacement laser units."

"You will have to discuss that with President Khozak," he said.

"Look, whoever you are, you're wasting time!" Ahl snapped. "Khozak has nothing to do with maintaining that plant. That's Zalkan's responsibility. And mine. Now, where is he? Why isn't he here?"

"I told you," the young man said, glancing nervously at Worf, "you will have to discuss that with President Khozak. In any event, please step inside. You of all people should know it is not safe to breathe this air any longer than absolutely necessary."

Ahl started to protest again, to tell the irritating young man that the tiny unit attached to her coverall was something called a "field-effect suit," but the one called Riker intervened before she had gotten out more than a half-dozen words.

"Yes, whatever disagreements we have," he said smoothly, "I suggest we discuss them where the air is less toxic. Geordi," he added, tapping the metallic emblem on the chest of his uniform, "you can return to the *Enterprise* until we get the situation sorted out." He turned to the Klingon as the second vehicle lifted off and vanished into the haze. "Lieutenant Worf, stay with the shuttlecraft. If our direct link with the *Enterprise* is interrupted for any reason, you can relay our messages."

The Klingon hesitated a moment; a new expression, equally as unreadable as the previous one, altered his features slightly. "As you wish, Commander," he said, then turned and marched back into the shuttlecraft.

As the vehicle's door closed behind him, the others, Ahl still frowning, stepped into the airlock. Slowly, the massive door slid down, almost as noisily as it had risen. When it reached bottom, the usual whirring noise started up, and the air gradually cleared.

Finally, the inner door inched up. When it reached approximately head height, several men in dark, loose-fitting jackets with the chevronlike insignia of Khozak's security forces on their sleeves stepped abruptly into view.

They all carried something she had rarely seen outside the computer fantasies she had once been trapped in, something she had never wished to see again: guns.

And every one was leveled at Ahl and the group in the airlock.

Chapter Six

PRESIDENT KHOZAK WORRIEDLY PACED the length of the empty Council Chambers. Had Zalkan lost his mind? First, without even asking for authorization, the scientist and one of his technicians had taken one of the newly and laboriously produced laser units from storage. Khozak would never have known except for a sharp-eyed security officer.

And when the two of them had been stopped, Zalkan had first blustered something about its being none of the officer's business. Even when Khozak himself, on the officer's radio, had demanded an explanation, Zalkan had lied, saying it was for Denbahr, the technician he had sent to the power plant. She had not taken enough with her and needed this one to replace a unit that was about to fail. Denbahr, however, couldn't possibly be back for another five hours, and the idea of Zalkan, in his condition, trekking a hundred kilometers across that no-man's-land out there in one of the converted construction machines they used was ridiculous.

Finally, either from desperation or insanity, Zalkan had spun a fairy tale so ludicrous it defied imagination. Apparently with a straight face, he had spewed out a story of how one of the leaders of the Deserters had not only returned from the dead but been ferried back to Krantin from the depths of interstellar space by some magical star-traveling ship that just happened to be in the neighborhood. And the beings on this ship had offered to produce new laser units for the power plant, in order to do which they needed a sample unit. They were, Zalkan had said angrily, waiting outside the airlock while valuable time was being wasted by "interfering" guards.

Ordinarily—if anything about this could be thought of as ordinary—that piece of insanity would have been the end of it. Khozak had never completely trusted Zalkan, and Zalkan had from the very start seemed to take an instinctive dislike to the president. And the scientist was far too secretive and independent for Khozak's liking.

But Zalkan was also good. He had kept what was left of the city running, after his predecessor had simply surrendered and retreated into the fantasy world of the computer, and Khozak was forced to accept his eccentricities, no matter how annoying they might be. Even so, this outlandish story was pushing things too far, even for Zalkan, and Khozak had been on the verge of ordering the scientist and his accomplice locked away until Denbahr returned from the power plant and could help make some sense of the situation. But the security officer had, on his own initiative, checked the one monitor that still sporadically relayed indistinct images from outside the air-lock.

And there was, the guard said nervously, something there! Two somethings! A pair of strange, glowing objects, they were obviously not the cumbersome, rumbling vehicles the technicians used on their trips to the power plant. But what they *were,* neither the security officer nor Khozak had any idea.

So Khozak had pulled a dozen off-duty security officers together and sent them, grumbling, to the airlock. One of them, weaponless and out of uniform, had gone to the outer door. The others had remained inside.

And now six of the officers, along with Zalkan and the technician and the Koralus impostor and two of the "aliens," were on their way here. The weapons had not even been necessary, if the "aliens" were to be believed, which was something Khozak was far from ready to grant. They had been more than willing to accompany the officers, although one of them, according to Alkred, had decided at the last minute to stay with one of the "ships," and there had been nothing he could do about it. Nor had he been able to stop the second "ship" from leaving. Khozak was tempted to order the six who had remained at the airlock to go outside and take the remaining one over and find out what it really was, but that could wait until he learned more from its occupants. He would find the truth, one way or another—if not from them, then from Zalkan or his technician.

Abruptly the door to the corridor opened. An angry Zalkan, preceded by two of the security officers, stalked into the room, followed by his technician, three strangers, and the remainder of the guards. It was immediately obvious which of the three strangers were supposed to be the aliens, though physically they looked almost as human as the woman Denbahr. Both wore formfitting, one-piece uniforms that did not look at all utilitarian. In addition, one not only had a short growth of hair over much of the lower part of his face but had skin of a darker shade than had been seen on Krantin since the Plague had stolen the sun from the sky. The other, aside from oddly colored eyes, looked far less exotic, and Khozak wondered why, if they had gone to such trouble with the bearded one, they had not bothered to similarly darken the exposed features of the other.

"Welcome," Khozak said into the silence. "I am Khozak, president of the Council of Jalkor."

"Thank you," the bearded one said, or at least seemed to say. His lips moved, but the movements did not match the oddly accented Krantinese words. "I am Commander William Riker of the Federation *Starship Enterprise,* and this"—a glance at the less exotic alien—"is Lieutenant Commander Data."

"And you are Ahl Denbahr," Khozak said, turning to the woman, "the technician? You were the first to speak with these . . . beings?"

She nodded brusquely, taking no pains to hide either her impatience or her annoyance with his tone. "Their ship approached me as I was leaving the power plant."

"I see." His eyes settled on the third stranger, a conventional-appearing male, at least in his fifties. "And you, I am given to understand, are the Deserter Koralus."

The man grimaced at the obviously intentional slur, but when he spoke, his voice reflected no anger or injury, only a modicum of sarcasm. "I am given to understand I have been called that, yes."

"You look remarkably well for a man nearly a

hundred and fifty years old," Khozak said, smiling faintly.

"As would you, if you had spent more than eighty of them in cryogenic hibernation."

"President Khozak," Ahl Denbahr broke in, "I think we can all save some time if you'll allow a little demonstration."

"Demonstration?" Khozak looked more irritated than puzzled. "I don't understand."

"You obviously think this is a trick of some kind, am I right?"

"I did not say that. I merely—"

"You don't have to say it in so many words. And I can't say that I wouldn't feel the same, were I in your position. To be honest, I thought I was losing my mind when I first encountered these people, so I anticipated some level of skepticism on your part." She turned to the one called Data. "You don't mind? The little demonstration we discussed on the way in here?"

"Of course not, if it will facilitate our mission."

She smiled, turning toward the darker, bearded alien. "Too bad you left your Klingon outside, Commander. He would be all the demonstration we would need. Commander Riker?"

The one called Riker nodded and raised his hands to the back of the other alien's head—and carefully peeled up a wide strip of hair.

"What nonsense is this?" Khozak protested angrily.

"Just watch," Denbahr said, still smiling. "Lieutenant Commander Data, though he looks like a normal human on the outside, is actually an android, an artificially created life-form with a positronic brain."

Even as she spoke, a section of the alien's skull—or just scalp?—came loose under the bearded one's fingers and was raised up like a small door. Inside, where skull or brain should be, was a mass of tiny blinking lights and circuits.

Khozak's mouth gaped open. Zalkan looked startled but recovered quickly. Koralus smiled, his eyes meeting Denbahr's.

"Would you care to inspect it more closely, President Khozak?" Denbahr asked with exaggerated graciousness.

Steeling himself, Khozak stepped forward and looked closely.

And was convinced.

It was obvious to Riker as he resealed the access plate in Data's head that Khozak had been converted from skeptic to believer. Gone were the defiant posture and the patronizing tone that the Universal Translator had done nothing to disguise. In the first moments after Data's cranial circuitry had been exposed, the president's eyes had widened in confusion, perhaps even fear, but then, when he stood back from his inspection of the lights and circuits beneath the access plate, his expression had turned to something else, perhaps determination, though what the object of that determination was, Riker couldn't tell. It would be helpful if Deanna were here, he thought, but they would have to do without her, at least for the time being.

Dismissing all but one of the guards, Khozak motioned the group to seats around the long council table. Riker, after some necessarily imprecise answers to Khozak's frowning questions about the nature, size, and location of the Federation, explained briefly how they had discovered the *Hope* and had come to bring Koralus back to Krantin. Koralus remained silent except to lay out the fate of his own ship. "Do you know what happened to the other ships, President Khozak?" he asked when he had finished.

Khozak, looking as if he resented even being addressed by a Deserter, shook his head curtly. Denbahr, however, who Riker had noticed seemed to be forming a wordless alliance with Koralus, perhaps because of their shared and open dislike of Khozak, gave Koralus a brief, apologetic summary of what little she could remember.

"Your arrival," she finished, "is the first real news of any of the ships since the years immediately after their launch."

"And proof," Khozak said with a scowl, "if any were ever needed, that the Desertion was a criminal waste of valuable resources on a massive scale. If those same resources had been devoted to saving Krantin rather than attempting to escape from it—"

"I don't mean to sound impatient, President Khozak," Denbahr broke in with obvious impatience, "but who was right or wrong a hundred years ago doesn't matter now. What matters is that these people from the stars have offered to help us. And now that you're convinced they're genuine, I'd like to get on with it. In particular, I'd like to get that laser unit delivered to them, the laser unit that was supposed to be waiting for us at the airlock."

Khozak turned on her with a frown. "Let me understand this, Technician Denbahr. According to your reports to Zalkan, it will soon be impossible for us to produce certain units needed to keep the power plant running."

"The laser confinement units and a number of other items," Denbahr said, "but the laser units, with their hard vacuums, are the most pressing need."

"And these people," Khozak persisted, "have offered to produce a new and perhaps even better version of these items, but they will need one of ours to use as a model. Is that correct?"

"Essentially, yes."

He turned to Riker and Data. "Is this true? Can you indeed produce these units?"

"I believe we can," Riker said, "but I can't guarantee it."

"And how long will this take, once you've determined it's possible? Months? Years?"

Riker shook his head. "Hours, assuming it can be done at all."

Khozak's eyes widened. For a moment, he looked as if he were going to protest, or even scoff, but after a thoughtful glance at Data, he nodded. "Very well," he said, turning to Zalkan. "Have the unit brought up immediately. Technician Denbahr and I will accompany it."

"There's no need for you to—" Denbahr began to protest but was cut off by Khozak.

"As president, it is my responsibility. In addition," Khozak went on, turning to Riker, "it would be advisable for me to speak directly with your leader. Picard, I believe you said he was called. Is that acceptable to you?"

"Of course, Mr. President," Riker said in his best diplomatic voice. "I'm sure the captain will be more than pleased to speak with you." *With the conversation being monitored by Counselor Troi,* he added mentally.

Zalkan, despite a scowl that vanished as quickly as it appeared, did not protest. Instead, he joined Khozak in making the call that would get the confiscated laser unit once again on its way to the airlock. As he released the button on the wall-mounted communication unit, Denbahr heaved a sigh of obvious relief. Riker couldn't help but notice, however, that her eyes went to Koralus rather than to the scientist, and that a surreptitious smile softened her features as their eyes met.

Only a trace of the smile remained as she turned to Khozak. "Your suspicions are all wrong, by the way, Mr. President."

Riker was not surprised when Khozak's frown returned. "Suspicions? What are you talking about?"

She almost laughed. "Armed guards waiting for us at the airlock? I wouldn't call that being particularly trusting."

"There's little to inspire trust these days," Khozak said, "in anyone, let alone in beings who claim the things these do."

"You're right, of course," Denbahr admitted briskly. "But now that you realize they're real, you're thinking they might be the ones responsible for the Plague."

"Don't be ridiculous! That is—"

"That is one of the commonest of the fantasies the computer puts out," she interrupted, "the fantasy that we somehow discover who caused the Plague and then turn the tables on them. I should know. I lived in those fantasies for two years."

"I don't have time for such indulgences, Technician!"

"I didn't say you did, but you're obviously aware of them. But what I wanted to make clear was, these people are *not* the ones responsible for the Plague— but they may have stumbled across the ones who *are.*"

As both Khozak and Zalkan gaped at her, she hurried through an account of the disappearing ships and the rest. As he listened, Riker's estimate of her intelligence and adaptability escalated yet another notch. She had obviously understood his and Data's explanations, and now she produced an abbreviated and simplified account of the basics of the transporter system that would have done credit to an Academy instructor, followed by an account of how similar energies had been detected throughout what they called the Plague, particularly in the atmosphere of Krantin itself. Khozak, however, seemed to remain skeptical until Koralus recounted his own experience of being snatched literally from the middle of the *Hope* and deposited a moment later in the *Enterprise*.

When Denbahr and Koralus fell silent, Zalkan sat stony-faced, saying nothing. Khozak, too, was silent for several seconds before turning to Riker. "You're saying, then, that the Plague could be the result of these ships 'transporting' it here from somewhere else? From another star system?" He frowned suddenly. "From your Federation?"

Riker shook his head. "Not from the Federation, for a number of reasons. But, yes, it's possible that the matter that's been appearing in here in your solar system has been—and is still being—transported here from somewhere else. And if it is, then these ships are very probably involved in some way. It would be too much to think it was all just a coincidence."

"Then if you can destroy these ships—"

"Being 'involved' doesn't necessarily mean being 'responsible,'" Riker said quickly. "Before anyone starts shooting, it would be nice to find out where the ships and the rest of the matter are being transported from. And how it's being done."

Khozak's frown deepened. "Whoever is controlling these ships, then—you're saying their science is beyond even your understanding?"

"Not at all," Riker said. "The ships themselves were comparatively primitive. And our analysis of the transporter energy associated with them indicates that the technology that produced it is less advanced than our own. It's just that it's . . . different in some way we don't yet understand."

"It is only a matter of time, then, until you do understand it?" Khozak persisted.

"In all probability, yes, although we on the *Enterprise* may not be able to do it alone. We may need to bring in a team of specialists from the Federation."

"But when you do understand it, you will be able to devise a defense against it? To reverse it?"

"It's impossible to say at this point. All we can promise to do is gather as much information as we can and report back to the Federation."

"And what about the disappearing ships themselves?" Khozak asked. "If they are, as you say, primitive compared to your own ship, it should be easy enough for you to capture one and question the occupants."

"It hasn't been easy so far," Riker said ruefully. "We tried to restrain one with a tractor beam, and it vanished as quickly as the others."

"But what of your weapons? Surely you have weapons."

"We do."

"If you object to destroying these ships, could you not at least disable them? Prevent them from escaping and capture them?"

"Again, I don't know. It hasn't gotten to that point yet, and it won't until we know considerably more than we know now. In any event, as I understand it, the immediate priority is to save your reactor. Is the laser unit—"

Riker broke off as Worf's voice erupted from his comm unit. "Commander, there have been two more bursts of the transporter-like energy. They were—"

Riker suppressed a frown as he cut Worf off. Two more bursts were hardly news after the hundreds they had already detected. "Thank you, Lieutenant. We can discuss it when we return to—"

"This time the sources of the energy were not in space," Worf broke in. "Both were somewhere on or below the surface of this world."

Riker grimaced mentally at his own slip. He should have realized that Worf would not have contacted him if the information were not important.

"Can you be more specific, Lieutenant?" he asked, darting a glance at the Council president. He was relieved to see that Khozak looked genuinely startled, but he still wished Deanna were here. She would have to be given a chance at Khozak and the others before any final decisions were made.

"The first burst was in an easterly direction from our present location, sir," Worf was reporting. "It very probably originated well below ground. The distance is likely less than one hundred kilometers. The second, less than a minute later, was southerly and probably much more distant."

"Keep watch for any more," Riker said unnecessarily. *"Enterprise,* can you—"

"Commander!" Khozak broke in. "Does this mean these ships you found in space are now here on Krantin?"

"At this point, I don't know what it means."

"Can your ship—your 'shuttlecraft' go to where these energy bursts originated?"

"To the general areas, yes," Riker said impatiently, suppressing another frown as he wondered what Khozak was driving at.

"Then I suggest you send them there immediately. If there are more bursts, you would then be better able to pinpoint the location of the ships responsible for them. Am I not right?"

So that was it. "Possibly," Riker said, "if they were caused by ships. And *if* there are more bursts, and *if* they come from the same areas as the first. Do you have any reason to expect the bursts to continue?"

Khozak blinked, seemingly startled at the question. "Only what you have already told us—that each time you detected one in space, it was followed by several more. If the same is true here—"

"You are wasting time, Khozak," Zalkan broke in, his voice touched with anger despite its weakness. "If these ships and their 'energy bursts' do indeed have something to do with the Plague, they have most likely been here for hundreds of years and will just as likely continue to be for hundreds more. There is no need to rush out instantly to try to trap them or destroy them or whatever it is you want to do with them. On the other hand, our need for fully operational laser units could become critical at any moment. I insist that that be dealt with first, as quickly as possible. Do you understand?"

"Of course I understand!" Khozak snapped. "Do you think me a fool? In any case, the one need not interfere with the other. Am I right, Commander?" he asked, turning toward Riker. "A second of your ships is already on its way back down to pick up the laser unit, is it not?"

"It is. And I believe you and Technician Denbahr were planning to accompany it to the *Enterprise?*"

Khozak shook his head. "She was right when she protested. My presence would be purely ceremonial. She knows how the units operate and can answer any questions better than I. I will accompany you in your search for—"

"For the moment, President Khozak," Riker said firmly, "there will be no search. Before we do anything else, I suggest both you and Zalkan come with us to the *Enterprise*. You can speak directly with Captain Picard, and you can give us as much information on the Plague as you can. Then we can discuss the best course of action to take."

And Deanna can perhaps tell us who, if anyone, is telling the truth around here, he added to himself, remembering the weapons that had been leveled at him by Khozak's men little more than an hour earlier.

Chapter Seven

KHOZAK AND ZALKAN, once they recovered from their first sight of Worf, were silent as the shuttlecraft shot up through the hazy atmosphere and into only slightly less hazy space. As the approaching *Enterprise* loomed ever larger until its graceful lines and colorful lights were all they could see, Denbahr was the only one to speak.

"This thing actually *moves? Faster than light?*"

Riker only smiled and surreptitiously motioned Data to remain quiet. She had digested the rudiments of transporter technology with remarkable ease, but there was no reason, yet, to get into warp theory, which virtually no one truly understood.

As Riker had requested, Counselor Troi was waiting for them when they emerged from the shuttlecraft, her eyes meeting his in brief acknowledgment of their conspiracy before turning her full attention to the three Krantinese.

Except for Data, who had data to analyze, the entire group made their way to the bridge, where Picard was waiting. As they started from there to a conference room, Riker and Troi lagged behind, ostensibly waiting for a second turbolift.

Riker turned questioningly to Troi the moment the doors closed behind the others.

"The woman is by far the most open," Troi began without further prompting. "I can sense no desire to hold anything back, only a—a feeling of hope or optimism, something I gather she has not had before. There is also an overwhelming impatience to 'get on with it,' to waste no more time."

Riker nodded. "That's how she struck me as well, although she was very skeptical at first contact. But the moment she entered the shuttlecraft and saw Worf, it was as if every doubt she had vanished. From that point on, she's been focused almost entirely on getting help for her world. But what about the other two?"

"Both are very guarded. The one called Khozak is more suspicious than skeptical, I think. Each new sight, each new crew member he saw, he became more tense. He simply doesn't trust us or Koralus. He may not even believe we are who we say we are. He's very wary, very apprehensive. The other, the scientist, is more puzzling. With him, there is very little feeling of distrust, but a great sense of fear."

"Fear? Of what? Of us? Of the Plague?"

"It is difficult to tell. Perhaps I can learn more as you and the captain discuss things with him. But he is definitely holding things back to a much greater degree than President Khozak."

"Even though he trusts us?"

"Perhaps 'believes' is a better word. I don't think he

doubts that we are who we say we are, nor that we mean to help if we can. Khozak, on the other hand, reacts to all of us like someone who is afraid we might stab him in the back regardless of who we are or what we want. Zalkan's fear is different. It is not a fear of us but of something or someone else, and it is quite strong. At the same time, underneath it, there is a feeling of hope that is almost as strong as Denbahr's."

"I suppose I was being naive, hoping for a simple answer."

"Where feelings are concerned, Will," she said with a rueful smile, "answers are rarely simple."

Riker sighed. "Unfortunately true. There are times I envy Data."

"But not many, I sense."

A smile slipped briefly across his face. "No, I suppose not."

They were silent as the turbolift doors opened and deposited them a few meters from the conference room. "The scientist, Zalkan, is also quite ill, I believe," Troi said.

Riker nodded. "I suspected as much. Do you think he would allow Beverly to look him over?"

"It's hard to say, Will. He might. Khozak, never. He mistrusts us too much. Simply being on the *Enterprise* is as much as he can take."

"And Koralus?"

"He is much like the woman, except I don't feel that he shares her optimism. It's almost as if he were consciously trying to keep his hopes reined in."

"Understandable, considering what happened to him and the *Hope.* And possibly to the other generation ships as well."

Both fell silent as the door to the conference room hissed open and they stepped inside. Except for Data, everyone was there, Picard at the head of the table. Riker and Troi took two of the seats left vacant on Picard's right, facing the four aliens on the opposite side of the long table. Geordi, who had already delivered the laser unit to Engineering, was at the far end, next to Worf.

A moment later, the door hissed open again and Data came quickly through and seated himself next to Troi. Leaning close, in a voice barely audible to Riker, he said, "Counselor, if it is not entirely outside your purview, I would appreciate your spending a few moments observing Spot when you have the opportunity."

Troi's eyebrows rose slightly as she turned toward the android. "Your cat?"

"Yes, Counselor. I stopped in my quarters to assure myself she was all right, and she seemed unusually . . . nervous."

Troi smiled and Riker suppressed a laugh. "I assume you're familiar with the expression 'nervous as a cat,' Data," Troi said.

"Certainly, Counselor, but I do not believe it has ever been applicable to Spot. Even during her pregnancy and temporary devolution, she remained quite calm."

Before Troi could answer, Picard was speaking. "Mr. La Forge, a preliminary report?"

"The laser unit is being analyzed in Engineering. Based on its appearance and on Technician Denbahr's explanation of its function, we should be able to duplicate it with little difficulty."

Denbahr, directly across from Data, leaned back with a grin and an explosive sigh of relief. "I knew you could do it!"

Geordi smiled at her enthusiasm but shook his

head. "No guarantees, at least not until the analysis is complete. And even then, we won't be one hundred percent certain until a new unit is produced and is actually installed and operating."

"I understand," she said, but her grin remained broad despite Geordi's caveat and the disapproving frown directed at her by President Khozak.

Picard, after an almost imperceptible glance toward Troi, turned to the four Krantinese, and as he did, a hologram of the first of the two alien ships appeared in the air above the conference table.

All four looked startled, but only Khozak darted a frowning look toward Picard. The eyes of the other three seemed glued to the image, even those of Koralus, who had seen it all before on the main viewscreen.

Troi surveyed all four silently, with no show of emotion, but after a few seconds, her gaze settled on the scientist Zalkan.

"This is an image of the first ship we encountered in your system," Picard said. "It appears to be a cargo vessel with an impulse drive barely powerful enough to move it from one asteroid to the next. Is it familiar to any of you?"

Picard looked slowly and deliberately from one to the next, addressing each by name as his eyes met theirs. One by one, they denied it, Khozak belligerently, Denbahr with a puzzled shake of her head, Zalkan with an expressionless "No."

"Or this?" With Picard's words, the cargo vessel was replaced by the second, smaller ship. "It appeared to be a scout ship of some kind. It, too, was equipped with an impulse drive."

Khozak's frown became a scowl as he shook his head. "Your people were already told we know nothing of any ships—or anything else—that you may have found in the Plague! It has been a hundred years since we sent anything or anyone into space."

"I understand that, President Khozak," Picard said. "But I also understand that your world was in space for many years before you were forced to retreat to Krantin entirely."

"But we *did* retreat! We had no choice! I see no reason to show us these objects when it is perfectly obvious none of us could ever have seen anything like them!"

"Please accept my apologies for any offense you might feel," Picard said. "However, I felt it important to determine if these ships bore any resemblance to those that your people built and used in centuries past."

"I wouldn't know! The history of our efforts at space travel is not something that has ever occupied my thoughts! Except occasionally," he added with a glare at Koralus, "to curse the Deserters and the waste they were responsible for!"

"I can confirm that neither ship bears any resemblance to anything ever built or conceived of on Krantin," Koralus said softly, "at least prior to my departure. In my role as a leader of the so-called Deserters, I made it my business to be familiar with every type of spacecraft and propulsion system ever built or proposed, and I neither saw nor heard of anything like these two, certainly none powered by this 'impulse drive' you mention."

"Thank you," Picard said, returning his eyes to the image that still hung above the table. "This," he went on as the image started to move, "is what happened when it vanished."

Except for Khozak, who fidgeted irritably, the

Krantinese watched the image by image disappearance of both ships raptly.

"Those flashes," Denbahr said when the last image faded, "those are the 'transporter energies' you say you detected?"

"The flashes were only the visible signature of the energies involved," Data volunteered when Picard nodded in his direction. "In effect, what you saw was a waste product of the process."

Denbahr's eyes widened. "You're saying that was only a small part of the energy that made those ships disappear."

"That is correct. With our own transporters there is a similar but much smaller visible signature. The process used on these ships was much less efficient, almost crude by comparison."

"But even with this signature," Zalkan said, straightening in his chair with a visible effort, "you are unable to determine where these ships were transported to."

"So far, that is true," Picard said, and then continued, overriding any other questions, "What I would like now is for each of you to tell us as much as you can about the Plague. If we are to have any chance of understanding it, any chance of learning what, if any, connection it has with these ships, we will need all the information you can give us."

It was not surprising to Riker that Denbahr was the first to respond, nor that she responded enthusiastically and encyclopedically. Even so, except for outlining Zalkan's persistent suspicion that the effects of the Plague decreased as you went deeper underground, she provided little beyond the basics. No one knew precisely when the Plague had started. It had been fouling the atmosphere of Krantin for at least five hundred years, and it had been detected in nearby space, starting in the midst of the asteroid belt, not long after. No source had ever been found, certainly nothing as obvious as a fleet of ships like the ones the *Enterprise* had seen, and no barrier had ever proven perfect. Most but not all of the planetary pollution seemed to form in the upper reaches of the atmosphere and drift downward. Increasingly in the last few decades, however, it had been appearing lower down, including inside the enclosed cities, and only massive filtering and recirculation systems kept the interior air breathable. Worst of all, hard vacuums—the sort needed in the laser units—were becoming contaminated ever more rapidly.

When she was finished, there was little the others could add, nor did they try, except for Zalkan, who cautiously explained that it was the progression of the Plague downward through the atmosphere that was responsible for his theory and his subsequent efforts to move everything underground, starting with the power plant and the facilities used to build new laser units.

When nothing else was forthcoming except more of Khozak's questions about the Federation, Picard rose, cutting the discussion short and offering to arrange for a tour of the *Enterprise,* individually or together, before they were returned to Krantin. "I will be certain," he added to Khozak, "that whoever escorts you will be able to answer all of your questions."

The president accepted immediately, while Denbahr said she would very much like a tour as well, but could it wait until she and Commander La Forge checked on the progress with the laser unit. Only Zalkan was reluctant, wanting to return to Krantin as soon as possible, at which point Troi caught Picard's eye and almost imperceptibly shook her head.

"You can all wait here," Picard continued without missing a beat, "and I will send someone to escort whoever wishes to see the rest of the *Enterprise*. In the meantime, Commander La Forge, you can escort Technician Denbahr to Engineering to check on their progress with the laser unit."

A minute later, Picard and the other officers, except for Geordi, who was already on his way to Engineering with Denbahr, were in the corridor outside the conference room.

Hurriedly, Troi filled them in on what she had already told Riker and went on to tell them what she had learned in the conference room. "Zalkan recognized those ships," she said, "I'm sure of it. They are part of whatever it is that he's afraid of. The others recognized nothing. And the president, despite his lack of trust for us and his dislike of Koralus—which is completely mutual—did not appear to be lying in any way. Another odd thing is Zalkan's reaction to Koralus. He has said nothing, but I sense what I can only describe as a degree of admiration and affection in his feelings toward Koralus. And he was offended whenever Khozak made one of his remarks about the 'Deserters.'"

"Good work, Counselor," Picard said. "Do you have any suggestions for getting the truth out of Zalkan?"

"Other than questioning him directly, no," she said, "and I doubt that he would respond well to that. His fear of those ships or what they represent is too great, although this time I was able to detect an undercurrent of anger as well as fear."

"We could start," Riker volunteered, "by seeing if

he would be interested in our medical services. Deanna and I discussed this briefly before, and we feel that, in addition to possibly helping him, it could be informative."

Picard nodded thoughtfully. "Very well. Counselor, suggest it as tactfully as you can. See how he reacts."

The scientist's outward reaction was almost nonexistent, a slight tensing of the jaw but nothing more. Behind that mask, however, Troi sensed a flare of hope that for a moment overcame the fear that had been a constant, debilitating presence from the moment she had first encountered him in the shuttlebay. There was no anger at her presumption in making the suggestion, no hint of denial of his illness, just the sudden flare of hope, but an instant later, the fear flooded back, smothering the hope and turning it to despair.

Lowering his eyes, he shook his head in the gesture of negation that so many humanoid races seemed to adopt. "I appreciate the offer, but I must return to Krantin as soon as possible."

Troi smiled soothingly. "Our medical technology is such that Dr. Crusher could perform a reasonably comprehensive examination in a few minutes. It would be completed long before a shuttlecraft will be available to take you and the others down."

He was silent for several seconds, and Troi could sense the battle raging within him despite the continuing surface calm. Finally he nodded. "Very well," he said. "As long as my return is not delayed."

As he walked with her toward the turbolift, however, it was obvious to Troi that his inner battle was far from over. It was only slightly less obvious that Zalkan knew more than he was admitting about his own illness and that, at least in his mind, there was a connection between the illness and whatever it was about the disappearing ships that he feared.

The results of a complete scan with a medical tricorder were, at best, puzzling. No single reading or group of readings was radically different from those obtained from a similar scan given Koralus shortly after he first came on board. Every organ, every cell seemed to be functioning approximately the way it was intended to function—except at a drastically lowered level of efficiency.

Zalkan sighed when Dr. Crusher told him the results. "Old age," he murmured. "I take it that's one medical problem you haven't yet solved."

"Not entirely, no," she said. "However, your readings are not consistent with those resulting from normal aging."

"How can you be so certain? After all, your only reference points are the readings you obtained from Koralus."

"I can't be certain, of course. However, there is a progression that is common to most advanced lifeforms, almost universal to humanoids, and your readings do not conform to that progression."

"But there is nothing you can do to help me, am I right?"

"We have no magical cure for whatever this is, Zalkan, I'll admit that. However, if we were allowed to do a more detailed examination, comparing the inner workings of your cells with those of Koralus or others—"

"And this detailed comparison—I assume it would take more time than the few minutes it took to run your machine over my body."

"Longer, yes, hours perhaps."

"Or days?"

"That is also a possibility. It all depends on what we find and how deep we have to go."

He shook his head firmly. "No, I must return to Krantin with the others."

And that was his final word. He insisted on joining Denbahr, who was being shown around Engineering by Geordi now that she had been convinced there was nothing more she could do to help with the laser unit. Once there, Troi saw, the scientist became so involved with Geordi's running commentary that the cloud of fear and impatience that seemed to hover over him constantly almost dissipated. It returned with a vengeance, however, when they reached the towering matter-antimatter reactor and Geordi did his best to give them a simplified explanation of its inner workings, dilithium crystals and all. From then on, despite continued outer calm, Zalkan was so distracted it was doubtful that he heard one word in ten that Geordi spoke.

By the time the tour was completed and they rejoined Picard and Riker to make their way back to the shuttlebay, cracks in Zalkan's surface calm were beginning to show, and he flinched visibly when Picard revealed that a second pair of energy surges had been detected from roughly the same areas of Krantin that had produced the earlier surges.

"I hope, Captain Picard," Khozak said immediately, "that you and Commander Riker will now reconsider the decision to not conduct a search of the areas in which these energy surges originate."

"We will discuss the matter when we bring the new laser unit down," Riker said, glancing at Lieutenant Worf, who was standing in the door to the shuttlecraft. "As Zalkan suggested earlier, if these energy surges are associated with the Plague, they've been around for hundreds of years and are unlikely to stop overnight."

"Quite right," Zalkan added quickly. "In any event, I have difficulty believing that these particular surges have any relationship to the Plague. As I have pointed out for years, its direct effects are less drastic at the surface than they are higher in the atmosphere and are very likely even weaker the farther beneath the surface you go."

"Which is unproven nonsense!" Khozak snapped, glaring at the scientist.

"Unproven only because you have refused to give the necessary priority to the research necessary to prove it! If you were not so obsessed with controlling every aspect of—"

"Think of the search, then, Zalkan," Picard broke in, "as part of that research. Unless, of course," he added after an almost imperceptible sideward glance at Troi, "you know of some reasons that such a search would be inadvisable or even dangerous."

Zalkan opened his mouth as if to reply but halted himself abruptly. After a second, he shook his head. "No, I know of nothing. Waste your time if you wish."

With that, he turned and climbed past Worf into the waiting shuttlecraft, leaving Khozak to glare at his back while Denbahr hurried in after him.

"Conclusions?" Picard looked around at the group, gathered in the same conference room, joined this time by Guinan, whose latest peculiar garb didn't look quite as out of place as it seemed it should. "Guinan, you said you observed him for a time in Ten-Forward."

"I always observe my customers, Captain," she said

95

with a toothy smile, "particularly those who ask as many questions as your friend Khozak did."

"And you learned what from these observations?"

"Little more than the counselor has already told you, I'm sure. He was very curious and probably believed very little of what he was told."

"If he was questioning you, I wouldn't blame him," Riker said with a grin.

"Now, now, Commander. It's not my fault that the truth is usually more complex than you'd like."

"Your truth, at any rate. What sort of questions did he ask you?"

"Pretty much the same as he asked everyone else. What world was I from." She shrugged as she favored Riker with another smile. "Where was it. What did I know about the Federation. Had my world been forced to join. What was the *Enterprise* doing in this part of space. And he tried to avoid officers. He even asked me if there were any civilians he could talk to other than myself, although I can't imagine why he thought I might be a civilian."

Riker nodded. "Just what I would do if I were in a strange place and didn't know who to trust—avoid people in authority. They always have the most reason to be . . . less than completely truthful. Present company excepted, of course."

"Of course, Number One," Picard said dryly as he turned to Troi. "Counselor, you accompanied them to the shuttlebay. Was President Khozak any more trusting toward us than when he arrived?"

"Only slightly, Captain, and most of the gain was lost when Will refused to consider an immediate search for the source of the energy surges."

"And the scientist Zalkan?"

"He still believes we are who we say we are, but he's terrified of telling us whatever it is he's holding back."

"Were you able to learn anything about what that might be?"

"Nothing substantial, Captain. However, I'm certain it has something to do with the ships and, now, with the energy surges we detected on the planet."

Picard nodded. "I noticed his reaction when I told them of the second pair of surges. Does he fear them as well as the ships?"

"I don't know, Captain. I don't even know that he fears the ships themselves. All I know is that he is very fearful of *something,* and that fear was triggered or made worse whenever either the ships or the energy surges were mentioned. However, there was an anger sometimes associated with the ships but not with the planetary surges. Also, as I have noted before, I do not believe the fear is for himself personally."

"For what, then? All of Krantin?"

"Again, I do not know, but it is almost certainly not for himself. For one thing, based on his reaction to the results of Dr. Crusher's examination of him, I suspect he has resigned himself to dying."

"Is there anything you can do for him?" Picard asked, turning toward Dr. Crusher.

"Perhaps, but without further tests, I have no way of knowing, and I doubt that he will consent to that."

"And, Counselor, you said you suspect that he knows more about his own illness than he is saying?"

"I am almost positive, Captain. But he flatly denied knowing anything about it when Dr. Crusher questioned him."

"The same way," Riker said, a touch of sarcasm in his voice, "that he flatly denied knowing anything about the disappearing ships and those planetary energy surges. Could there be a connection between the lies?"

There was silence for a moment before Data spoke. "It is possible, Commander. If we assume that the disappearances are the result of the ships being transported somewhere, and if we additionally assume that he is not only familiar with the ships but has actually been aboard one when it was transported, then his 'illness' could be the result. All our sensor readings indicated that the associated transporter-like energies did not have full quantum-level resolution and therefore could damage living matter during the transport process."

Crusher's eyes widened, but then she nodded. "You're right, of course, Data. I don't know why I didn't think of it myself." She turned toward Picard. "Remember the rebels on Rutia Four, Jean-Luc—the device they used to kidnap us was a result of some form of transporter technology, and it caused irreversible damage to anyone using it often enough."

Picard grimaced as he suddenly realized why the images of the disappearing ships had seemed so elusively familiar to him. "I remember," he said, not elaborating. "But the problem there was not the resolution level, was it? Mr. Data?"

"It was not the primary problem, Captain, so far as we determined at the time. However, we did not analyze the resolution level once we discovered that the process was based on the Elway theorem. We assumed, as did the rebels, that the dimensional shifting involved in the process was the cause of the damage."

Dr. Crusher nodded. "And the damage to Zalkan, if that's what it is, is different. On Rutia Four, the damage was primarily to the DNA, and the pattern was identifiable. In Zalkan, the DNA may be damaged, but I haven't been able to detect it as yet. Instead, there appears to be simply a lowering of the efficiency of virtually every biological process at every level."

"As if," Riker said, "he had been transported and rematerialized, but not with full quantum-level resolution. As if he were alive but not quite *as* alive as he was before."

Crusher smiled faintly. "It's as good a way for a layman to look at it as any, Commander—as long as the layman doesn't try to develop a treatment based on the analogy." She sobered. "In any event, I've already fed the results of the blood and tissue analysis into the computer and initiated a search for possible remedies. Preliminary results, however, are not encouraging."

She glanced around the conference table. "I'm sure you're all familiar with CZ-fourteen."

Riker frowned. "That isn't still around, is it?"

"There are rumors that the Ferengi picked up the formula for either that or one of the other illicit descendants of cordrazine," Picard said, "but there is no proof as yet."

Crusher nodded. "No proof that the Ferengi were involved, but traces were positively identified in three would-be entrants in the Josarian games last year."

"I hope, Doctor," Picard said, "that you're not going to tell us that CZ-fourteen is what the computer sees as an antidote for Zalkan's condition."

"It *is* one of the strongest metabolic enhancers known, Captain, and the computer noted that it would be especially effective with the Krantinese metabolism."

"It is also often fatal in a matter of hours, Doctor."

"Exactly, Jean-Luc. As I said, it is not encouraging."

Picard nodded grimly. "As you said. Let me know if the computer comes up with anything more useful."

"Captain," Data spoke up, "your Rutian experience may have provided us with another clue. There could be a form of dimensional shifting involved here as well. However, instead of returning to this dimension, it is possible that the ships remain in that other dimension."

"An alternate universe, Mr. Data?" Picard frowned.

"The existence of such alternate realities has been proven many times, Captain."

"I fully realize that, Mr. Data. The *Enterprise* has been involved in such 'proof' more often than I like to remember. I was merely hoping that we were not involved once more."

"It would certainly explain why there were no indications of either a matter stream or a confinement field," Riker said. "And no traces of subspace energy."

"Captain," Ensign Thompson's voice emerged abruptly from Picard's comm unit, "Lieutenant Worf is reporting from the shuttlecraft."

"Patch him through, Ensign."

A moment later, Worf's voice replaced Ensign Thompson's. "Captain, there has been another pair of energy surges."

"Were you able to pinpoint the location of either?"

"To some extent, Captain. As instructed, I have been patrolling the area indicated by the surges nearer the city since delivering Khozak and the others. The second in this pair was, like the others, far to the south, but the first was almost directly beneath the shuttlecraft. It definitely originated deep underground, at least a kilometer, and in the same general area as the earlier surges."

"A cavern of some kind?"

"Possibly, sir. The shuttlecraft's sensors are not reliable at that depth, but they do indicate an extensive network of tunnels and shafts at levels closer to the surface."

"Are there any life-forms in the tunnels?"

"None in the levels accessible to the sensors, sir. At the level of the surge, it is impossible to tell."

"Very well. Good work, Lieutenant. Continue where you are for the time being. Keep watch for life-forms at any level."

When Picard signed off, Koralus spoke up. "Captain Picard, I may have knowledge of the tunnels that your lieutenant detected."

All eyes turned to Koralus. "Enlighten us, then," Riker said.

"They are abandoned mines. Over a hundred years ago—no, over two hundred years ago—that was the richest mining area in all of Krantin. Dozens of different minerals, from lead and iron to uranium, were found and extracted in great quantities. Those mines, in fact, were in part responsible for Jalkor becoming the largest and most powerful city on Krantin. The mining went on for at least fifty years, until the entire area, hundreds of square kilometers, was a honeycomb of tunnels more than a kilometer deep."

He paused, shaking his head. "Of course, I have no idea what has been done with them in the last hundred years, but Jalkor's records computer would certainly have the information. If anyone has bothered to keep it up to date."

Picard glanced at Troi, who nodded affirmatively. He was telling the truth.

"Very well," Picard said, standing, "we will contact President Khozak and see if he can—or will—fill in the blanks for us when you take the laser unit down tomorrow."

Chapter Eight

"Thank you for coming, Counselor," Data said as the door to his quarters hissed shut behind Troi. "I realize you are accustomed to dealing with more highly sentient beings than Spot, but—"

"That's perfectly all right, Data," she said with a smile. "I'm responsible for the emotional well-being of all the crew, and a pet, once it is adopted by a crew member, is one aspect of that well-being." She paused and looked around. "Where is she?"

"Under the bed. She was there when I returned and has refused to come out, even for food."

"Perhaps it is something physical, Data. When cats are ill, they tend to keep to themselves."

"I understand that, Counselor, but I do not believe that is the case with Spot. Dr. Crusher says she is in perfect health, except for a nascent furball. Also, I spoke with Ensign Thompson, who has Spot's brother, Fido, and he indicated that Fido has been similarly uneasy the last few hours."

Deanna smiled faintly. "I see. Well, perhaps I should examine the patient. Can you coax her out, or must I crawl under with her?"

Data seemed to consider for a moment. "I will get her out," he said, dropping to his knees next to the bed. "Your movements would be quite restricted, and that might not be entirely safe, considering Spot's present mood."

Dropping flat on his stomach, Data looked under the bed. "Counselor, if you could watch the other side of the bed while I approach her from this side . . ."

"Of course, Data." Dropping to her knees and leaning down, Deanna could see Spot near the head of the bed, watching Data apprehensively. As Data made what passed for soothing noises and reached under the bed, the cat pulled back for a moment, then streaked out under the foot of the bed, raced across the room, and disappeared over the back of the couch.

"I believe I have her now," Data said, standing effortlessly and crossing to the couch. Kneeling on the couch, he leaned over its back and darted his right hand down into the triangular area behind it. A moment later, he brought the squirming animal into view, placed it on the couch and, still restraining it gently, sat down next to it. It wasn't hissing, but its ears were laid back, its tail lashing.

"Spot, you are behaving quite badly," he said, scratching the top of the cat's head between its ears, which seemed to calm it slightly. "Counselor Troi is only here to help you."

Smiling at Data's so-human interaction with the cat, Deanna sat down on the other side of Spot. Cautiously, she extended her right hand, holding the fingers directly in front of the cat's muzzle. Just as cautiously, the cat stretched forward slightly and sniffed at the fingers.

After a minute, the tail slowed its lashing and the ears were at least partially raised. Finally, it rubbed the side of its mouth against the tips of Deanna's fingers.

"That is quite impressive, Counselor," Data said. "This is the calmest she has been for quite some time."

"It's nothing, Data, just a small amount of empathic feedback. I wasn't certain it would work with a non-Betazoid animal, least of all a cat."

"I see. But I am not surprised that it worked, Counselor. There is much anecdotal evidence regarding the ability of cats to sense emotions in humans, though I must admit there is considerable evidence as well that the ability is due to their keen sense of smell."

Deanna laughed. "Are you implying that I smell calm to Spot?"

"It is possible, Counselor. The fact that I do not possess the same scents as humans may in fact explain a part of Spot's uneasiness. While Ensign Thompson has noticed similar behavior in Fido, he has been able to calm him while I have been unable to do the same with Spot."

"Perhaps you're right, Data. You might want to test your hypothesis by having Ensign Thompson—"

Without warning, Spot tensed, and Troi was shaken by the sudden, sourceless fear that radiated from the animal. An instant later, the hair along the cat's spine bristled and her mouth opened in a teeth-baring hiss as she ducked her head and, half turning on her back, lashed out with her claws. Only Data's lightning-fast reaction kept the claws from raking Deanna's unprotected hand.

A moment later, the hiss turned to a yowl, and Data held the struggling animal only for the fraction of a second it took Deanna to pull away and stand up. The instant he released the cat, it streaked back under the bed.

"Something terrified her," Troi said, her eyes wide. "I could feel the fear."

"It would be interesting to learn if Fido or any of the other cats on board the *Enterprise*—"

"Commander Data, Counselor Troi," Picard's voice erupted from their comm units simultaneously, "to the bridge. There has been another surge of energy, the most powerful one yet."

"On our way, Captain," Data answered for them both. At the door, he paused. "Computer," he said, darting a look toward the bed that Spot still crouched under, "initiate constant visual and audio scan of these quarters. Retain all records until further notice."

Picard's eyes remained fixed on the viewscreen as Troi took her position on his left and Data slid smoothly into the ops station seat. Koralus was again in Riker's seat, while the commander stood to one side. Ensign Thompson, short and bearded and constantly on a diet, was at the tactical station in Worf's place. On the screen, Krantin had been replaced by the flare of the shields as the *Enterprise* moved at quarter impulse in the general direction of the source of the latest energy surge.

Barely a minute had gone by when Data reported an object almost dead ahead, moving toward the *Enterprise* at a similar velocity. "It would appear,"

Data said, "that the surge was not more powerful than the earlier ones, only closer. It may even have been in high orbit around the planet."

"Mr. Worf," Riker said, "was there another energy surge beneath the surface of the planet?"

"No, sir," Worf's voice came back a second later. "There has been no detectable activity since my last report."

"I knew that would be too easy," Riker said with a curt sigh, "for the ships to be coming from down there."

"Get us as close as possible to this new ship, Mr. Data," Picard said. "I want as reliable a set of readings as you can get before *it* disappears."

"Yes, Captain. Sensors at maximum."

Another minute, and a glowing dot appeared on the viewscreen.

"It appears to be similar to the object we encountered in the asteroid belt," Data said. "As with that one, the sensors cannot penetrate the shell of transporter-like energy that surrounds it. I can only assume that, like the first, it is using the energy field to clear a path through the dust."

"Another of the scout-type vessels?" Picard wondered aloud.

"It is probably of a similar size, Captain, but it is moving more rapidly, indicating that its impulse engines are more powerful than those of the previous ship. They might be the equal of one of our larger shuttlecraft."

For another minute, the glow grew larger and brighter on the viewscreen. Then, abruptly, it vanished and was replaced by the image of a ship, this one bearing a slight resemblance to Federation shuttlecraft of half a century earlier. It continued to move closer, but more slowly, the equivalent of minimum impulse.

"Captain," Data said an instant later, "there are two laser devices that can only be described as weapons, although they are not powerful enough to pose a threat to the *Enterprise*. They appear to be fully primed and ready to fire. There is one life-form on board, definitely humanoid, possibly Krantinese."

"Continue to monitor."

"Should I hail it, sir?" Ensign Thompson at the tactical station asked hesitantly.

Picard considered a moment. The previous ships had not responded to hails, only vanished. "Not yet, Ensign," he said, "not until it becomes obvious the pilot is aware of us."

On the screen, the image of the ship grew steadily larger and more detailed, finally revealing the snouts of what must have been the laser weapons.

"The pilot does appear to be indistinguishable from the Krantinese, Captain," Data announced finally.

"Koralus?" Riker looked down at the Krantinese. "Can you enlighten us in any way?"

Koralus shook his head vigorously. "This ship could not possibly be from Krantin!"

"Counselor?" Picard leaned toward Troi, who, taking her cue, whispered briefly in his ear, confirming the alien's truthfulness. Nodding, he turned his attention back to the viewscreen.

"It has stopped," Data announced. "I assume the pilot has become aware of us."

"Very well. Ensign, hail the ship, all EM channels."

"The laser devices are being redirected, Captain," Data said. "I suspect they are being aimed at the *Enterprise*. They could be fired at any moment."

"Ensign," Picard said, "on my command, transmit

my words on all EM channels." Pausing, he took the auxiliary earpiece from the panel in the arm of Riker's seat and handed it to Koralus. "If there is a response, Ensign, patch the raw sound through to Commander Riker's station. Koralus, listen and tell us if it is a language you recognize."

Obediently, the Krantinese inserted the tiny device in his right ear and waited as it adjusted itself to fit. By the time it had finished, Thompson had made the necessary adjustments to the comm panel controls. "Ready, sir."

"Now, Ensign," Picard said, beginning his message moments later when Thompson nodded acknowledgment.

"Unidentified ship, this is Captain Jean-Luc Picard of the Federation *Starship Enterprise.* Please identify yourself." Another pause, and then: "We are aware of the weapons you have trained on us."

For a full minute there was no response. Finally, it came. "Where are you from? Why are you here?"

"We represent the United Federation of Planets. We are currently negotiating with the natives of this world, Krantin, to assist them. Now we would like answers to the same questions from you."

There was another silence, not so long this time. "You have come here from another star?"

"That is correct. Now please, identify yourselves."

This time there was no verbal answer. Instead, as Picard began to again demand identification, the intruder's lasers fired. The *Enterprise* shields flared softly near the points of contact.

"Phasers on stun, fire," Picard snapped. "Lock on with tractor beam, full power."

"The humanoid is unconscious," Data announced an instant later.

"Energy surge beginning to build, sir," Thompson said, almost simultaneously.

A flare of light once again blinded the viewscreen. When the screen cleared, the tiny ship was gone.

Picard frowned, though he wasn't surprised. He had not really expected it to be that easy. "Deadman switch, Mr. Data?"

"I can only assume that is the case, Captain. The energy field began to build within three seconds of the humanoid's loss of consciousness."

"Koralus—the language?"

The Krantinese removed the earpiece. "It was like Krantinese, but different. Some of the words I recognized, others I did not."

"Counselor, could you pick up anything at all?"

"Not at this distance, Captain, not without a video link."

"Mr. Data, any other surges, anywhere?"

"None, Captain. However, if a second surge had occurred at a distance, simultaneous with the nearby one, the more distant one would have likely been masked by the nearer."

"Mr. Worf, did the shuttlecraft sensors pick up anything?"

"Only the surge in the vicinity of the *Enterprise,* sir."

Picard suppressed a sigh. "Very well. Mr. Data, take us through the incident again, image by image."

He didn't expect them to find anything new, and, to no one's surprise, they didn't.

The analysis of the latest incident completed, Data hurried back to his quarters to review the records the computer had been making of the area. He was not surprised to find that Spot had experienced another interlude of extreme agitation starting within seconds of the moment the latest ship had vanished.

Intrigued, he began a second-by-second review of the computer records for both of the most recent surges. When he was finished, he thought for a moment of informing the captain of the results, but he decided it would be premature. Instead, he contacted Ensign Thompson, who listened to Data's account and bemusedly agreed to allow Data to have the computer maintain a similar record of his own quarters and Fido's activity.

Chapter Nine

RIKER FIDGETED, earning an amused glance from Troi. Waiting was not something he did well or gracefully, particularly when he had nothing to do while others did all the work. It had been more than an hour since the party from the *Enterprise*—himself and Deanna, Data, and Geordi—had delivered the newly fabricated laser unit to Zalkan's cramped laboratory in the city's lower level. Technician Denbahr, with Zalkan and Geordi watching over her shoulder, was still performing her tests, which apparently included every one in the official checklist as well as several she had improvised based on what she had seen at the power station in recent months. If there had been room in the little lab, Riker would have been pacing, but there wasn't.

Finally, Denbahr looked up from the test console with a broad grin. "As far as I can tell," she announced, "this unit is identical to our own—except that it works at least as well as ours did fifty years ago." She looked questioningly toward Geordi, who had been monitoring the tests with his tricorder.

He shook his head. "It won't last as long—ten years at the most, assuming the Plague gets no worse than it is now. The vacuum started to degrade the moment it was formed. Your instruments can't detect it yet, and it's degrading less rapidly here than it was in the *Enterprise* or in the shuttlecraft on the way down, but it's still degrading."

Denbahr's smile faded for a moment but then returned, tinged with defiance. "So," she said, glancing at Zalkan, "we have ten years to find a permanent solution. Like beating the Plague."

"A worthy goal," the scientist said grimly, "but not one we're likely to accomplish."

"Not alone, maybe, but with a little help . . ."

"She's right," Riker said as Zalkan grimaced. It might be the contrast to Denbahr's infectious optimism, but Zalkan's seeming pessimism struck Riker as counterproductive at best. "I have the feeling that if we can just find out where those ships are coming from—and disappearing to—we'll have a good start."

"You're both more optimistic than I, Commander. Nonetheless, I applaud your efforts. At the moment, however, my greatest applause would be for another hundred laser units like this one."

"Of course," Riker said, glancing toward Geordi, who nodded assent. "As soon as this one is successfully installed and we see that it does indeed work as well as the tests indicate, we'll get things started." He turned to Denbahr. "I suggest we get under way. We can take you and Commander La Forge and the unit to the power plant whenever you're ready."

Before anyone could answer, the door opened and

President Khozak strode in. He had contacted Zalkan earlier, saying he would be at the lab shortly, but Riker had been hoping they would be gone before he arrived, as had Zalkan, if his scowl was any indication.

"Commander Riker," Khozak said without preamble, ignoring Zalkan's obvious annoyance, "after you informed me yesterday about the mines, I uncovered information that will, I think, cause you to reconsider your decision not to search at least the area of the mines for the source of the energy surges."

"Something in the records computer, you mean?" Riker asked, not volunteering that a search was already planned. "Just what did you find?"

Khozak smiled. "Nothing, literally nothing."

"If you found nothing," Zalkan snapped, "why are you wasting our time? The laser unit should be—"

"When I first discovered there was nothing about the mines in the computer," Khozak continued, his voice rolling over the frail scientist's words as if they didn't exist, "I assumed that your Deserter friend had been mistaken or was lying for reasons of his own. However, I quickly realized that a lack of information this complete was itself suspicious. And it *was* complete, totally complete. It was as if that entire area, several hundred square kilometers, hadn't existed for the last three hundred years. The last reference was at least that old, from about the time most records were being transferred to the computer, long before mining was begun. The area was referred to only as 'farmland.'

"So I located someone in what remains of the history department of the university, a Professor Gammelkar, and he confirmed what you had told me—that that area had indeed contained the richest mines on Krantin. And yet, when Professor

113

Gammelkar himself checked the records computer, he was no more successful than I in finding information about the area. It was as if those mines had never existed."

"Which tells you what?" Riker prompted when Khozak paused and looked around expectantly.

"Two things," Khozak said, and Riker didn't need Deanna's empathic talent to recognize the smugness in his tone. "First, that the surges your instruments detected in that area in all likelihood came from somewhere in those abandoned mines. And second, that someone has tampered with the records computer to try to keep the existence of those mines a secret."

"The people in the disappearing ships, you mean?" Zalkan said, his voice thick with sarcasm. "The people responsible for the Plague?"

Khozak nodded, seemingly oblivious to the sarcastic tone. "It seems to me a perfectly obvious conclusion. As it must to you as well; otherwise it would not have occurred to you so quickly."

"A perfectly insane conclusion, you mean!" Zalkan snapped.

Riker was about to suggest that the pointless wrangling was only delaying the installation of the laser unit when he recognized Deanna's restraining touch on his arm. Glancing down at her, he saw from the brief flicker of her eyes toward his that she had picked up something worth pursuing. Nodding almost imperceptibly, he said nothing, deferring to her.

"I wouldn't say the conclusion was obvious by any means," Troi said, "but it does seem at least possible, even plausible. Do you know of some reason it is not possible, Zalkan?"

"Just common sense!" Zalkan shot back. "You expect aliens from—from *somewhere* to not only get into a sealed city unnoticed but to be able to find the records computer *and* be allowed access to it?" The scientist snorted derisively. "And then to be able to operate the computer, to selectively remove information from it? That isn't easy even for the people who operate it every day. There are built-in safeguards against both intentional and accidental destruction of information." He shook his head. "It is impossible."

"Unfortunately, gaining access to the computer would present no problem," Khozak said. "Much as I deplore the situation, my security forces are stretched far too thin to cope with anything but open physical vandalism and violence. They have been for years. In any event, if these aliens can appear wherever they want, the way their ships apparently can, no amount of security forces could keep them out."

"And Lieutenant Commander Data," Troi added quietly, "given a little time, could almost certainly operate the computer well enough to remove whatever pieces of information he desired."

Zalkan scowled at the android. "Perhaps. But only because he is a computer himself!"

"So who's to say these aliens don't have similar creations?" Troi countered. "Do you know positively that they do not?"

Zalkan blinked. "Of course not! But from what you said about their ships, they're not nearly as technologically advanced as your Federation."

"But they are at least as advanced as Krantin," Troi persisted. "They must have computers at least as complex as yours. Given time, certainly their scientists could master your computer."

"Given time, perhaps. But they would have to have free access to it for weeks or months, and despite President Khozak's inadequate security forces, even despite their magical ability to pop out of nothing in a flash of light, I very much doubt that an alien working

115

at the records computer for the necessary length of time would not have attracted *someone's* attention!"

"Perhaps," Troi said, neither agreeing nor disagreeing. "However, considering that the Plague has been with you for at least five hundred years, you might assume the aliens have been here equally as long. They would have had more than adequate time to infiltrate Krantin." She smiled sympathetically. "For all you know, your computer may have been designed by one of them."

Khozak guffawed. "She has you there, Zalkan! For all I know, *you* could be an alien."

Zalkan spun on the president, obviously intending to reply angrily, but he seemed to catch himself. He turned back to Troi and Riker. "What did your doctor's machines say yesterday?" he asked stiffly. "Did they say I was an alien? Or a Krantinese?"

Troi smiled. "He has you there, President Khozak," she said, echoing the president's words of a moment before. "According to all the readings Dr. Crusher took, Zalkan is no more an alien than Koralus."

"Have we wasted enough time now?" Zalkan asked angrily. "I for one would like to see this new laser unit installed before the existing ones begin to fail!"

"And I," Khozak echoed, all traces of laughter gone from his voice. "And while Technician Denbahr and Commander La Forge are installing it, the rest of us can investigate the mysterious mines. Can we not, Commander Riker?"

Riker nodded. "We were planning to do just that. I take it you would like to accompany us rather than supervise the installation of the laser unit?"

"Of course."

"And you, Zalkan? Would you like to accompany us as well?"

Troi eyed the scientist as he remained nervously

silent for several seconds. Finally he said, "Khozak can waste his time as he wishes. I will assist with the installation."

With eight occupants and the laser unit as cargo, the shuttlecraft was full. As it lifted off, Worf at the controls, Troi pointed out the viewscreens to the three Krantinese and explained that they would give them a clear and constant view of the ground over which they were passing, regardless of the dim light and the haze.

Within a minute, a frowning Zalkan spoke up. "This is not the way to the power plant."

"We're taking a slight detour," Riker said, preparing to spin out the story he and Deanna and Data had improvised during the few private moments they had managed to have for themselves during the return to the shuttlecraft. He only hoped it would sound more convincing to Khozak and Zalkan than it had to him. "It will delay us only a few minutes at most. You see, the *Enterprise* computer detected a possible pattern in the timing of the energy surges in space. If the pattern is real and if a similar pattern applies to those on Krantin, the most likely time for another surge is in the next few minutes. And, as President Khozak pointed out yesterday, if such a surge occurs while we are nearby, we might be able to pinpoint the source more closely."

Khozak smiled while Zalkan's frown deepened. "You have been able to establish a pattern from only two surges?" Zalkan asked suspiciously. "Or have there been more that we were not told about?"

"There was another pair shortly after you left the *Enterprise* yesterday," Riker said, "but none since."

Zalkan looked like he wanted to ask more, but finally, with an angry shake of his head, he subsided into silence. His eyes, however, as well as those of the other two Krantinese, remained fixed on the viewscreen as the shrouded, barren landscape slid by. Patches of mosslike vegetation covered some of the hilltops, growing mostly on the rotting remains of long-dead trees and grasses. Occasional stands of live but stunted trees poked into the poisonous haze that was the air of Krantin.

At one point they passed low over a massive pit, an excavation several kilometers wide. To one side squatted the ruins of dozens of massive buildings. Within the pit were rusting hulks of almost equally massive strip-mining machines.

Khozak grimaced at the sight while Zalkan almost shuddered. Riker held himself expressionless, thinking that Earth of a few centuries back had been headed in this same direction, and they hadn't needed any help from alien intruders.

"This is what we had come to," Khozak said softly, "by the time the decision to seal the cities was finally made. There are thousands of these around the world. In those last decades there was no effort to operate 'cleanly,' only quickly, to get and process material to seal as many cities as possible. The Plague had won, and all we could do was retreat."

He fell silent as the pit disappeared into the haze, all of his earlier smugness seemingly gone. Zalkan was similarly subdued.

Minutes later, Worf slowed the shuttlecraft and began circling. "These are the coordinates, Commander," he announced.

On the viewscreens, the land below them was an irregular series of gently sloping hills, gigantic mounds hundreds of meters across except that the crowns of nearly half of them were sunken in like soft-edged volcanic craters.

Data did something to the sensor controls, and

circular outlines formed around the tops of each of the mounds, cratered and uncratered alike. "Those were the main entrances, Commander, the shafts leading down to all levels of the mines."

" 'Were,' Data?" Riker asked.

Khozak said, "According to Professor Gammelkar, they were all sealed when the mines were played out. All the surface buildings, the headframes, everything, were torn down. The land was returned to essentially the condition it was in before the mining began." He grimaced. "We were still being careful then, for all the good it did us."

"Many of them appear to have had a smaller entrance as well," Data said. Smaller circles appeared on the screen, located near the bottoms of several of the hills.

Khozak peered at the screen, then nodded. "As I said, we were being careful then. It wasn't always possible to fill in the entire shaft. Some of them were two kilometers deep. Instead, many were roofed over and covered with soil, even landscaped. As you can see, some of the roofs didn't hold up very well. The smaller entrances are associated with access tunnels that were dug after the mines were sealed. The intent was to allow workers to enter periodically to check and repair the roofs from the underside, to prevent just the sort of collapses that have obviously taken place in several instances." He gestured at the crater-like concavities that topped so many of the hills. "But that all ended more than a hundred years ago—like everything else. I suppose they must have sealed the access tunnels then, too. Or, more likely, abandoned them and let them collapse on their own."

Data nodded as he continued to study the sensor readouts. "They all appear to have collapsed naturally, Commander, except for one."

One of the smaller circles began pulsing more brightly than the others.

"What happened to that one?" Riker asked when Data didn't immediately continue. "Is it still open?"

"No, Commander, but it is the only one that was almost certainly closed intentionally. There are traces of explosives in the blocked portion."

Riker darted a look at the two Krantinese. Khozak looked almost triumphant, while Zalkan remained stiffly expressionless. "How recent?" Riker asked, turning back to Data. "Can you tell?"

"Not with any precision, Commander. I would say no more than twenty years, no less than five. A closer inspection with a tricorder will give a more precise time."

Khozak nodded. "This is undoubtedly the work of the aliens, Commander. No Krantinese has lived outside the cities for more than fifty years."

Zalkan said nothing, only shook his head in curt negation when Riker looked at him questioningly.

Riker turned back to Data. "Are there any signs of life, Data, alien or otherwise?"

"I can detect none above the bacterial level, Commander. However, the sensors are not able to penetrate to the levels at which the surges probably originated."

Data paused, seemingly consulting a readout. "Commander, the time indicated by the pattern you specified has passed. No surge has been detected."

Riker managed what he hoped was a convincing sigh of resignation as he turned to the Krantinese. "I'm sorry. Apparently the computer was wrong."

"Then can we move on to the power station?" Zalkan asked impatiently.

"Of course. Mr. Worf?"

Abruptly the circles vanished from the screen as the

shuttlecraft shot to a higher level and veered onto a new course.

At the power station, Riker and Troi accompanied Geordi, Zalkan, and Denbahr inside while Data and Worf remained in the shuttlecraft with a visibly impatient Khozak. Inside, Geordi briefly surveyed the control cubicle and stood back, monitoring his tricorder while Denbahr immediately plunged into the work, starting by calling up a series of readings to determine which of the units was the nearest to failure. Zalkan, obviously as familiar with the equipment as Denbahr, worked in concert with her, hardly a word being spoken. As soon as she selected a unit, he began temporarily disabling the associated self-repair circuitry so they would be allowed to work on the unit manually.

Finally, as Denbahr led the way into one of the cramped access corridors, Troi nodded to Riker and the two turned and left. In the airlock to the outside, Troi waited silently until the inner door had closed.

"Now that Zalkan is here, he's the calmest I've seen him," she said. "It's as if he were totally immersing himself in the work with Denbahr. Whatever his fears or motives, I'm certain he is genuinely concerned about the Plague. And he was overjoyed when the laser unit tested as well as it did."

"He didn't sound overjoyed to me," Riker said, remembering the scientist's earlier display of pessimism. "Or even very hopeful."

"It was only for a moment, Will, when Denbahr completed the final test on the unit and told us it worked perfectly. For that moment, all his fears, whatever their source, were forced into the background, but they returned the instant Geordi indicated that the vacuum in the unit was still degrading."

"What about the mines? It looked to me as if Zalkan was trying hard *not* to react when Data found the one that had been tampered with recently."

Troi nodded. "He was trying *very* hard. He also reacted very strongly, even fearfully, to the suggestion by Khozak that he was an alien infiltrator."

"You mean he could actually be one?"

"An infiltrator, yes, but obviously not an alien, if we can believe the results of Dr. Crusher's examination."

Riker shrugged. "From what the *Enterprise* sensors told us, the pilots of the disappearing ships weren't physically distinguishable from the Krantinese either."

"So if the ships are from an alternate reality, another Krantin, Zalkan could be from the same place?" She returned his shrug. "It wouldn't surprise me. It would probably surprise me more if he weren't. I'm positive he knows more about the ships than he's telling. And we discussed his illness before, and the possibility that it resulted from his having been on one of the ships. In any event, his reaction to the mine entrance was unmistakable. He was extremely tense the whole time we were over the mines, but he was almost terrified when Data located the one entrance that had apparently been collapsed by explosives."

"Which is just one more reason for us to concentrate on that one," Riker said with a smile. "Not that I wasn't intending to anyway."

Chapter Ten

RIKER EYED THE COLLAPSED ENTRANCE to the mine uneasily. Data's tricorder had pinpointed the time of the collapse—the explosion—to roughly ten years ago, but the debris was still plainly visible. On any healthy world, the plant life would have obscured it long ago, but here there were only patches of the mosslike growth they had seen elsewhere and the softening of the edges by ten years of weather.

What concerned him, though, was that the shuttlecraft's sensors, even at this close range, could not reach deep enough into the mines to tell him if whoever or whatever was responsible for the energy surges—and the collapsed entrance—still lurked in the depths, waiting.

He turned to Data. "Now that the *Enterprise* is in low orbit, would it be safe to use the transporter for a short point-to-point jump into the mine, Data? If there *is* something down there, blasting in with a phaser is more likely to warn them we're coming than a quiet beam-in."

Data considered a moment. "You are correct, Commander, and the odds are good that the transporters would be safe to use. Even so I would not recommend it. It is true that the 'background' energy would not present an obstacle at this range, but there is no way to guarantee that another energy surge would not occur. It is even possible that our entry, if it were to be detected, could trigger such a surge. And a surge anywhere in the mines beneath us could disrupt or divert the matter stream."

Riker nodded, not arguing. "Phasers, then. So be it."

Twenty minutes later, Data leading the way, they eased through the cooling, cauterized opening into the darkness. At Riker's suggestion, a constant lock on their comm units was being maintained from the *Enterprise*. If they ran into an emergency, the danger of which was more certain than that posed by an unexpected energy surge during transport, they could be instantly beamed back to either the shuttlecraft or the *Enterprise*.

Riker stood to one side, waiting for Khozak, who, though he had been fidgeting with impatience until now, trailed the others hesitantly. From the moment the shuttlecraft had left the power plant, the president had let it be known with annoying frequency that he was becoming more certain with each passing moment that the aliens responsible for the Plague were somewhere in the darkness below them. He had also been increasingly anxious to begin the search, but Riker noted that, once the final barrier had fallen to the shuttlecraft's phasers, much of Khozak's bravado had fallen with it. He had even refused Riker's offer of one of the field-effect units that generated the virtually invisible, body-hugging energy fields that all except Data used. Instead, he had insisted on the "familiar technology" of his own battered breathing mask.

Once everyone was through the phasered opening, Riker set a portable field generator directly in front of it, switched it on, and waited while the field came to life with a brief flicker. It would keep the atmosphere out while they were inside, and when they left, they would reseal the entrance with the same phasers that had just now opened it.

Satisfied, Riker turned back to the tunnel. In the glow of the handheld lights, he could see that it was less a tunnel than a two-meter-wide corridor that sloped gently downward. Floor, walls, and ceiling were all of a concrete-like substance, rough surfaced but not jagged. Every few meters, translucent hemispheres that must have once held lights protruded from the walls.

"As the shuttlecraft sensors indicated, Commander," Data said, looking up from his tricorder readouts, "the contaminant level is markedly lower here than on the surface. However, the air is still not safe to breathe for extended periods."

"And life-forms?"

"None within the tricorder's current range, Commander."

"Very well," Riker said, pulling in a breath and starting down the corridor, "let's see what we can find."

Three hundred meters in, the corridor opened abruptly into the square central shaft of the mine. There was no guardrail, only a rusty, metal-runged ladder that split the opening vertically in half and disappeared into the darkness above and below.

While Data and Worf peered into the abyss unanchored and seemingly unconcerned, Troi and President Khozak halted a good two meters short of the precipice. Riker took what he considered a prudent middle ground and stopped just short of the edge; he tested the ladder and, when it proved solid, gripped it firmly before leaning cautiously forward.

The shaft itself, he saw, was roughly five meters on a side below the level of the tunnel, a meter wider above. Over his head, the ladder continued twenty or thirty meters up the wall to the roof and the rusting metal beams that reinforced it. Because the shaft below the level of the tunnel was narrower than above, the downward extension of the ladder was recessed in a half-meter-deep groove in the wall. Similar grooves in the other three walls also contained ladders, but those only went down. Riker assumed that they had all originally been to provide an emergency escape route if the elevator ever jammed or lost power.

Below, where the elevator had once lumbered up and down, all that protruded into the shaft now were the guides the elevator must have followed. Like all the other exposed metal, they were rusting badly. The elevator itself, along with the cables and motors that had pulled it up and down the kilometer-deep shaft, had presumably been dismantled and removed, along with everything else movable, when the mine had been shut down and the shaft covered over more than a hundred years ago.

Steeling himself, Riker leaned farther out, looking down to where the ladders descended into the darkness beyond the glow from their handheld lights. Almost at the limit of the lights, roughly a hundred meters below, a shadowy rectangular opening in the far wall marked what must have been the highest level of the actual mine.

"Can you pick up any more from in here than from outside?" Riker asked as Data, standing with his toes at the very lip of the shaft, straightened and studied the tricorder.

"Only regarding the shaft and its immediate vicinity, Commander. It is at least a kilometer deep, and there are openings every fifty to seventy-five meters after the first level. There are still no life-forms within tricorder range."

"Will you be able to get down there?" Khozak asked.

"Probably only if we decide to take a chance on the transporter," Riker said. "Even if this ladder is solid enough right here, I certainly wouldn't trust it enough to try to climb down it. What we can do for a start is transport some remote-control surveyors down a few levels, possibly a tricorder as well."

"That may not be necessary, Commander," Data said. "Readings indicate that the ladder leading down this side of the shaft is sturdy enough to support at least twice the weight of any of us." He paused, adjusting some of the tricorder controls.

"You're positive about that?" Riker asked when Data remained silent over the tricorder for several seconds.

"Yes," Data said finally. "The ladder on this side of the shaft has been reinforced no more than ten years ago." He looked up where the ladder continued up toward the roof. "The mountings immediately above and below this opening have also been strengthened at approximately the same time."

"The same time this entrance was opened and resealed!" Khozak, still hovering two or three meters back, said triumphantly. "What more proof do you need, Commander? Someone—alien or not!—entered these mines and carefully covered their

127

tracks. Obviously, they're still down there! Or at least their machines are! The energy surges you detected must tell you that much!"

"What about the other ladders, Data?" Riker asked, ignoring Khozak's outburst.

Data once again leaned precariously into the shaft, holding the tricorder before him. A moment later, he straightened. "The others have not been repaired or modified at any time, Commander. In fact, the mountings of the ladder directly across from us have deteriorated to a point at which the ladder is on the verge of coming loose under its own weight."

"How far down does the reinforcement on this side go?"

"Only as far as the first opening," Data said.

"I will go down," Worf rumbled, reaching for the ladder.

"Hold it a second, Lieutenant," Riker snapped. "Data, you're absolutely positive about this? And there aren't any booby traps?"

"None that I can detect, Commander." Rather than consulting his tricorder again, he gripped the ladder and silently pressed at it in several directions, in a methodical, more strenuous version of what Riker had done a few minutes earlier. "It is mounted quite solidly, Commander," he said, stepping back. "I will follow Lieutenant Worf."

Riker frowned but finally nodded. "Very well. But neither one of you go beyond that first level until we know a little more about this setup."

"Of course, Commander," Data said, echoed grudgingly by Worf a moment later.

Data returned to his tricorder as Worf gripped the ladder, swung onto it, and started down, his broad shoulders barely fitting within the groove.

"I cannot yet be certain, Commander," Data said,

"but at least the first two levels appear to be connected internally, not just through the shaft. Once there, we may be able to descend to other levels without resorting to the ladders again."

"Not without orders, Mr. Data," Riker said firmly.

"Of course, Commander," Data said again.

Silently, they waited while Worf clambered down, Riker gripping the ladder unnecessarily, unable to completely ignore the impulse to steady it.

"I am in the first level, Commander." Worf's voice came over Riker's comm unit, each word faintly echoed a split second later as the words carried the hundred meters up the shaft.

Tricorder case and light held firmly in place by a shoulder strap, Data stepped onto the ladder and moved effortlessly downward. Incapable of vertigo, he felt no different than if he had been climbing down a short access ladder in the heart of the *Enterprise,* and in less than two minutes, he reached the opening to the first level of the mine. The ladder, instead of being in the center of the opening as it had been above, was at the left edge. A pair of rails in the floor, ending flush with the shaft, explained the placement of the ladder to him: In the center, it would have blocked the ore cars from being wheeled on and off the elevator.

Swinging off the ladder, he saw that Worf was a good thirty meters down the tunnel, a bobbing island of light. Unlike the access tunnel above, this one, except for the area immediately next to the shaft, looked more like a primitive mining tunnel from twentieth-century Earth or even earlier, not high-tech in any obvious way. Only the floor was even remotely smooth, and it was that way only in the center to provide an even bed for the rails. Dirt and rock had fallen from the roof and walls in several places between the rotting braces, often completely obscuring the rails.

Methodically, as he walked down the tunnel after Worf, Data described the scene to Riker and the others waiting above.

He caught up to Worf at a branch in the tunnel two hundred meters in. The rails curved into the left branch, which at that point began to slope downward more steeply. The right branch ended after a dozen meters, opening into the top level of a huge, irregular excavation, a jagged, underground amphitheater dozens of meters across. Its walls, like those of the tunnels, were shored up here and there with timbers that looked no sturdier than the rusting ladders in the shaft. Leaning out into the cavern, Data could see, a dozen meters down, an opening similar to the one he was in. Below that was yet another and another, the last nearly fifty meters down. The bottom of the massive excavation was beyond the range of his light.

Data stepped back, continuing to describe the scene while keeping one eye always on the tricorder. Back at the branch, he started down the left tunnel, following the rails and Worf. He paused after a few meters as certain of the tricorder readings slowly grew clear. He called to Worf, a dozen meters ahead of him, to wait.

"Commander," he said, speaking both to Riker and to Worf, "my tricorder now indicates that this level of tunnels definitely connects to the next level down, although it apparently did not originally, except through the excavation I described and others like it. It also appears now that there may be a further connection from the second level to the third."

"Not originally connected, Data? Explain."

"All the tunnels within tricorder range are essentially horizontal or, at most, sloping a few degrees. All were excavated well over a hundred years ago. At the lowest point of this top level, there is a steep, narrow opening to the next level. I cannot yet be certain, but preliminary indications are that this opening was made long after the tunnels themselves were dug."

Riker was silent a moment. "As recently as ten years ago, Data?" he asked finally.

"It is entirely possible, Commander."

Three hours later, Data was seven levels down. In all but two instances, each level had been connected to the next lower level by a short, steep passageway, some only a few degrees from vertical. Levels three and four were actually a single, complex level with two separate openings to the central shaft, and levels five and six were connected only through the central shaft, probably because, Data speculated, the two levels did not at any point come within fifty meters of each other, and whoever had created the connecting passageways hadn't been prepared to bore through quite that much solid rock. Instead, between five and six, the ladder in the central shaft had been reinforced the same as the ladder leading down to the first level. Data's tricorder indicated that all work—connecting passageways and reinforced ladders—had been done not more than ten years ago. Worf had reluctantly stopped at the sixth level when the opening to the seventh had proven barely large enough for Data.

"Time to start back, Data." Riker's voice came over Data's comm unit as he took another turn in the maze that was the seventh level. "Geordi just reported that they'll be finished at the power station in another half hour and they'll need a ride."

"Very well, Commander," Data said, continuing down the narrow side passage he found himself in. "However, I believe the connection to the next level is less than a hundred meters from my present location."

"So check it out," Riker said with a grin in his voice, "as long as you're that close."

"Thank you, Commander. I will hurry."

The tunnel he was in had obviously never been worked: no rails for ore cars, few timbers to brace the low-hanging, jagged rock ceiling. It had probably been an exploratory tunnel that had come up empty, but it was also the lowest in the seventh level. Stooping more and more, even crouching at times, Data hurried down the sloping tunnel, keeping one eye on the map displayed on the tricorder screen. In the center, around the dot that represented his own location, the nearest passageways were sharply defined, becoming blurred and uncertain only as they approached the edges of the screen. One level up and hundreds of meters in toward the central shaft, a single sharply defined symbol lay among the blurs—Worf and his comm unit.

Data rounded a final twist in the tunnel and descended a fifty-meter slope, and the opening to the next level was before him. It was, as he had already discerned from the tricorder images, almost vertical and longer than any of the previous connecting passages. He would be able to navigate it with only minor difficulty, but others would, at the least, require a safety line.

Dropping on his stomach with his face over the opening, he held the light down and peered past it. Perhaps ten meters below, he could see the shadows of the next level.

Setting the light to one side, he lowered the tricorder into the opening. He switched from the glowing map display and began cycling through the analysis modes. As expected, the passageway was recent compared to the tunnels, roughly the same age as the previous ones, possibly slightly more recent. Like them, it held traces of the explosives that had almost certainly been used in their construction. Like them, it was at almost precisely the point at which the two levels of tunnels were at their closest. Which meant, though he had yet to discuss it with Commander Riker, that whoever had made these openings had had to have either a device like the tricorder or access to detailed maps of the entire system of tunnels—the same maps that had, according to Khozak, been deleted from the city's records computer. Otherwise, how could they have known what point in each level was closest to the next lower level? Just finding the lowest point wouldn't have been enough. Here in level seven, for instance, the lowest point was three hundred meters back, but there had been no corresponding eighth-level tunnel underneath that point, only a hundred meters of solid rock all the way down to the ninth level.

For a moment he returned to the map display. The levels below him, he saw, were defined more sharply than those above. Zalkan's belief that the Plague energies had less effect the deeper you went underground appeared to be true, at least for the first kilometer below the surface.

For several seconds, he worked with the controls, juggling them for the highest sensitivity he could achieve without losing all stability. Under normal circumstances it was not difficult, but here in semi-darkness, with the varying background of the Plague energy constantly upsetting the readings, it was a tricky balancing act, even for Data. Next he narrowed the focus, which would also extend the range at the expense of a wider field. The focus, at least, did not seem to be affected by the Plague.

Finally, satisfied, he began slowly sweeping the tricorder in an expanding spiral, watching the display.

After nearly a minute, he stopped abruptly, brought the tricorder back a fraction of a degree.

And stopped again.

For several seconds more, he studied the display, alternating between analysis modes and the mapping function.

Eventually, satisfied that the readings were not an artifact of the background energy and that he had gained all the information he could, he continued the outward spiral.

And stopped again. As if unable to believe this new reading, he made several minuscule adjustments to the tricorder controls. No, he decided after nearly a minute, this too was real, no matter how unlikely it might seem.

Finally, he raised himself from the opening and stowed the tricorder. Crouching beneath the low, rocky ceiling, he brought his hand up to his comm unit but hesitated a fraction of a second as he considered the effect this double discovery would have on President Khozak.

And on their own mission here.

"I am returning now, Commander," he said, and nothing more.

Chapter Eleven

AS UNLIKELY AS THE IDEA WAS, Riker couldn't shake the feeling that Data was hiding something. During his entire trek up from the bottom of the mines, Data had remained silent except to report his and Worf's arrival at each level. Back on the shuttlecraft, the android had delivered his report with uncharacteristic brevity. Levels eight and nine, he said, were within tricorder range from his seventh-level vantage point and were connected by the same kind of recently opened passageway that connected most of the higher levels. They were also equally devoid of life-forms and machinery. When Khozak expressed angry disappointment over this negative report, the android said not a word, which raised Riker's suspicions even more. If there was one thing Data seemed to like to do, it was explain things, and Riker would have expected him to, at the very least, volunteer to clarify the limitations of his tricorder under Plague conditions.

But Data said nothing, and he seemed to avoid even looking at Khozak during the flight to the power plant. Instead, he kept his eyes glued to one of the viewscreens. Riker suppressed an urge to ask him what was going on, knowing that Data would have no choice but to answer. If Data was hiding something, it meant he hadn't thought it through yet. He would speak up when he was ready.

Besides, when Geordi and the others came aboard at the power plant, Data's uncommunicative behavior was largely forgotten in the infectiously celebratory mood that Zalkan and Denbahr brought with them. According to all tests they had been able to devise, the new laser unit worked flawlessly. Geordi had already spoken with Engineering on the *Enterprise* and asked them to start work on another dozen of the units. Those twelve would, Denbahr assured him, take care of all units in danger of imminent failure.

Further distraction came when Khozak, in a superior I-told-you-so manner, insisted on telling Zalkan about the recently formed passageways connecting the different levels. The scientist's near-euphoria turned instantly to a stiff uneasiness.

A moment later, Troi leaned close to Riker. Despite Zalkan's brittle shell of calm, she whispered into his ear, Khozak's words had pushed him to the verge of panic.

And that was the way Zalkan remained until he and Denbahr and Khozak were left at the city's airlock. Questions to him were either evaded or ignored, and an offer to take him to the *Enterprise* so that he could be "more closely involved" in the production of the laser units was flatly refused.

As the shuttlecraft lifted off and swooped up through the haze toward space, Riker turned to Data, only to find the android about to speak to him.

"You have something to tell us, Data?"

"I do, Commander. I did not wish to speak of it in front of President Khozak and the others until I informed you and the captain."

"Go ahead, Data," he said.

"You will remember, Commander, that President Khozak indicated the mine extended down just over one kilometer, which would have been approximately two hundred meters below the lowest point I reached. While I inspected the passageway between the seventh and eighth levels, I was able to adjust my tricorder to penetrate not just the two hundred meters to the eighth and ninth levels, as I perhaps implied before, but more than a hundred meters beyond the ninth level."

Riker smiled and Geordi chuckled. "Lying by omission, Data," Geordi said. "Very good. You're becoming more human all the time."

"And you found something you didn't want Khozak or the others to hear," Riker prompted.

"A number of things, Commander. First, the fact that the tricorder was able to penetrate to that depth indicates that Zalkan was correct in his theory that the background energy grows weaker as one descends below the surface."

"I suspected as much," Troi put in. "When he spoke of that belief, he seemed to be telling the truth, even though it made him uneasy to do so."

"Interesting," Riker mused, "but hardly something you would want to hide from our guests. Go on."

"You are correct, Commander. The tricorder indicated three things. First, a single, recently formed tunnel extends at least two hundred meters below the thousand meters Khozak indicated was the bottom of the mines. Second, there are humanoid life-form readings, faint but detectable, in that recent tunnel and in the lowest levels of the original tunnels, three levels below the lowest level I reached. And finally, several meters beyond the end of the extended tunnel, there are indications of a massive deposit of dilithium."

Even Worf turned from the shuttlecraft controls to stare at Data.

Picard listened intently as Troi, Data, and Riker gave their reports. Zalkan's behavior and wildly varying emotional state only confirmed what they had already known: He knew a lot more than he was telling. Data's discoveries in the mines, however, seemed to Picard to provide at least the beginnings of an explanation, if not for Zalkan's actions and fears specifically, at least for the overall picture of what was going on in the Krantin system. Whoever these interlopers were, wherever they were from, they must be after the dilithium. And, even though Krantin apparently knew of neither the existence nor the value of the dilithium, those searching for it very much wanted to keep their search a secret.

It raised more questions than it answered, of course, but it was at least a start.

But first, despite his misgivings, he would have to inform Khozak and the Council—if the Council did indeed exist—of their findings, particularly the dilithium. He looked at Data, seated across the conference table from Riker.

"How large a deposit, Mr. Data?"

"Unknown, Captain, but it would have to be substantial to register on the tricorder under those conditions. Certainly there is enough to make Krantin a wealthy world."

Picard nodded. He had assumed as much. "But unless they—or we—find a solution to the Plague, all the wealth in the sector won't help them. Mr. Data, you said these life-forms in the mines are humanoid, but are they Krantinese?"

"Also unknown, Captain, but there was nothing to indicate that they were not."

"Just as there was nothing to indicate that the pilots of the disappearing ships were or were not Krantinese," Riker said. "You may recall we've already considered the possibility that they are from this same world in an alternate reality, in which case they could be biologically indistinguishable."

Picard nodded grimly. "I'm not about to forget, Number One. The question is, how do we keep one of them here long enough to ask? Phasers and tractor beams obviously aren't sufficient."

"Engineering is working on it, Captain," Geordi said. "Logically, we should be able to generate a field that interferes with the operation of their equipment just as theirs interferes with ours. Unfortunately, computer analysis suggests that any such field would be difficult to project accurately, for reasons similar to the reasons that our own sensors and transporters are unreliable beyond relatively short distances here. We would probably have to get very close and simply blanket the entire area, ourselves included."

Picard eyed Geordi questioningly when the chief engineer fell silent. "Why do I get the impression, Mr. La Forge, that that is not as simple as you make it sound?"

"Because it's not," Geordi admitted. "There's a

good chance that any field we generate would have side effects that are just as damaging to life-forms as the field it's designed to counter."

Picard suppressed a grimace. "How soon can you be positive, one way or the other?"

"Short of trying it out on living tissue, Captain, I can't."

Picard was silent a moment. "Very well. Keep me informed of your progress."

He turned to Dr. Crusher. "Is there anything new in your search for a cure for these side effects, if that's what they are?"

"Something better than CZ-fourteen, Captain, but not a cure. Or so the computer model indicates. At best, it would slowly halt the deterioration over a period of weeks or months. It might even reverse the process to some small degree. However, it would require inducing what virtually amounts to a coma for all that time."

"And the subject would be only slightly improved when it was all over, Doctor? Is that what you're saying?"

"Essentially, yes. The chances are good that he would be stabilized at some level slightly better than the one at which treatment started. Without the treatment, he would continue to deteriorate, even without more exposure to the energy field."

Picard nodded. Beverly was right. It did not sound hopeful, at least not for Zalkan. He turned to Troi. "It would help if we knew if Zalkan's illness was indeed the result of such exposure, Counselor, and if so, how often and how long he had been exposed. Do you still feel that Zalkan knows the cause of his illness?"

"I am almost certain of it, Captain. And I am just as certain that he knows a great deal more, not only about the disappearing ships but about what is going on in the mines. As I said, the idea of our exploring those mines frightened him more than anything else we have said or done before. But once again, it was not a fear for himself."

"For the ones at the bottom of the mine, then? The ones piloting the ships? He's afraid we'll get our hands on them?"

Troi shrugged. "I don't know, Captain. Perhaps it *is* for those in the mine, but I doubt that it is for those on the ships. There was an anger, perhaps a bitterness, associated with the ships that was not present when he was forced to think about the mines. And there is still his odd reaction to Koralus. When we arrived with the laser unit, Zalkan asked about him, wondering why he hadn't come along this time."

"Did he explain his interest?"

"He said it was merely his interest in the Desertion, purely historical, but he was not being truthful. It was something more personal, but I have no way of knowing precisely what it might be."

"What of Koralus's reaction to Zalkan when they were both on the *Enterprise?* Was there any hint of recognition?"

Troi shook her head. "Not the slightest."

"Which is not surprising," Riker put in, smiling, "considering that Koralus left Krantin fifty years before Zalkan was born."

"I know that, Will," Troi said with a slight frown. "I didn't say any of this made sense. I am simply reporting what I observed. I might be able to learn more if I could observe the two of them together some more."

"In that case," Riker said with a slight shrug, "why don't we take Koralus with us the next time we go down?"

"An idea to consider, Number One," Picard intervened. "Counselor, what of President Khozak? What did his reactions tell you?"

"Little more than I already reported, Captain. He knows no more about the Plague or the mines than he has said. He still greatly mistrusts us, perhaps even more than earlier. And having Koralus accompany us will almost certainly raise that level of distrust."

The discussion continued for several minutes. In the end, Picard decided to include Koralus in the group when they went down to brief Khozak and Zalkan the next day. Troi might indeed gain some useful information from Koralus's and Zalkan's reactions to each other, and information was one thing they were desperately in need of, as they often were. Besides, Khozak's distrust of everyone from the *Enterprise* was already so great that the presence of Koralus could hardly make it worse. They would also ask Khozak to call together the entire Council, whose members might have a different perspective than either Khozak or Zalkan. In the meantime, Picard would contact Starfleet with the news of the dilithium.

It should, he thought wryly, make their day.

Data was at the ops console two hours later when another energy surge, the first in more than a day, was detected, this one relatively weak, more like the ones from the mine than the ones from space. The source was neither in space nor anywhere near either of the areas on Krantin where previous surges had been detected. Instead, it was in the vicinity of, if not actually within, the city. Data quickly noted the precise time and the necessarily imprecise location, then notified the captain in his ready room.

Summoning an ensign to take the console, Data

strode from the bridge as Picard entered. Minutes later, as he entered his quarters, he noted that Spot, while not hiding, still appeared uneasy, her eyes following him as he crossed the room to the view-screen on his desk.

"Computer, display on split screen the record of activity in these quarters and the quarters of Ensign Thompson for the period between twelve and ten minutes prior to the time of this command."

The screen sprang instantly to life, divided precisely down the middle. On the left, Spot lay curled on the heavily cushioned back of the couch, obviously one of her favorite spots, as indicated by the deep indentation she was half submerged in. On the right half of the screen, Fido, with markings similar to Spot's but with hair twice as long, was stalking one of the lifelike mouse automatons that Data had designed and distributed to all interested cat owners on the *Enterprise.*

On both screens, time displays silently counted down the minutes and seconds.

At minus eleven minutes ten seconds, Spot's eyes snapped open, followed a fraction of a second later by her tail stiffening and bristling. At eleven minutes nine seconds, Fido lurched to a halt in his pursuit of the mouse.

At eleven minutes eight seconds, both let out a brief teeth-baring hiss and darted looks in all directions. The tails remained bushed out for several seconds before beginning to subside, first on Fido, then Spot. Both remained alert, even wary, for more than three minutes. Spot, still watching Data from her perch on the couch back, had laid her ears back as her own image had hissed at her from the screen but otherwise remained comparatively undisturbed.

"Replay at one-tenth speed the period from eleven minutes twelve seconds to eleven minutes," Data said.

When he was through, Data was satisfied that the phenomenon he had suspected since the day before had been confirmed. Not only that, the computer records had pinned down some of the key parameters. Spot's first reaction to the energy surge was three-point-one seconds before the *Enterprise* sensors had first detected it. With Fido in frantic motion, it was harder to pinpoint the precise time of his reaction, but it was at least two-point-two seconds before the sensors. Not surprisingly, their reactions to the energy surge from the city were substantially less severe than Spot's earlier reaction to the much more powerful energy surge from space.

As with every piece of information he encountered, Data filed these for future reference.

Later that night, while Data observed Spot directly, she reacted minimally but unmistakably to a half-dozen energy surges even less powerful than the first. All, he discovered when he checked the computer log, were in or near the city. Space and the area around the mines remained inactive.

Chapter Twelve

IT TOOK ONLY MINIMAL LOBBYING on Picard's part to convince a nondescript Starfleet admiral that the captain should be the one to head the next day's away team despite regulations that ordinarily gave that duty to the first officer. It was not just that President Khozak, a putative head of state, was entitled to a "delegation" headed by the ranking officer, though that was the low-key argument that Picard made. It was simply that there were times—more of them than he liked to admit, even to himself—when he felt like getting off the bridge and out of the ready room. And away from the crew fitness reports, he told himself uneasily, which still were barely started.

"As always, Jean-Luc, the decision is yours," the admiral assured him in conclusion. "You're the one on the scene. However, a suggestion: Whoever goes down, leave the phasers on the *Enterprise.*"

With that not-quite-order, the distant image vanished, replaced momentarily by the Starfleet insignia. When Picard turned away, he saw Riker shaking his head disapprovingly.

"No disrespect to Starfleet, Captain," Riker said quietly, "but as the admiral said, you're the one on the scene. And he wasn't greeted at the airlock with drawn weapons the way we were."

"I understand your concern, Number One," Picard said dryly, "but carrying weapons is not conducive to trust. And we will need all the help we can get in that respect when we tell them that we have, in effect, been holding out on them about what we discovered at the bottom of the mines yesterday."

Which, he realized even as he spoke, was the real reason he had decided to take Riker's place. Another "obligation" of rank. If as captain he was responsible for withholding the information from Khozak, then he should now be responsible for so informing the president and taking whatever heat resulted.

"In any event," he went on, mentally filing the uncomfortable insight that had just come to him, "keeping the *Enterprise* in low orbit and maintaining a constant lock on our comm units strikes me as a more practical precaution than arming ourselves and hoping to shoot our way out of the middle of a sealed city with only one known exit."

Despite the field-effect suit he had activated as the shuttlecraft door opened, Picard felt like gasping for breath as he stepped out into Krantin's hazy, poisonous atmosphere. Koralus, a comm unit attached to his tunic for the duration of their visit, stepped out after Picard, followed by Data and Troi.

The Jalkor airlock was already open. Two of the same security officers who had escorted Riker's group the first day were waiting just inside. This time their weapons were at least not drawn, Picard noted, though there was little other evidence of trust. As before, the group from the *Enterprise* was hustled into a large van, apparently electrically driven, with the triangular Security Force insignia on both sides.

Picard had scanned the tricorder records and listened to Data's descriptions of the two previous trips, and he realized almost immediately they must be taking a different route. The earlier parties had been taken through what Data had described as a large industrial district, in which the buildings extended all the way up to and sometimes through the surrounding city roof. This time the van rolled through an obviously different area, this one filled with two- and three-story buildings that had probably once been individual homes. The city roof here was several meters above the tops of the buildings, supported by featureless metal or plastic columns, most of them ringed by glowing tubes. Several of the tubes, however, were dark, leaving the surrounding areas in a shadowy twilight. For one stretch of three or four kilometers, the individual buildings vanished, replaced by blocky, flat-roofed buildings hundreds of meters on a side. One of the surface hydroponics facilities they had detected from the shuttlecraft during the first trip down, Picard assumed.

At one point, while passing through a stretch of windowless blocks a hundred meters high, he heard a series of faint, popping sounds which, he realized after a moment, were very probably the signature of projectile weapons similar to the ones the security officers carried. The driver darted a glance in the direction of the sounds, but the other guard either didn't notice or ignored them. Picard couldn't help but wonder uneasily if the distant shots had anything to do with the fact that they were taking a different route today.

Except for a smaller version of the van they were in, also emblazoned with the Security Force insignia—heading in the direction of the shots? he wondered—Picard saw no direct evidence of the five million people who were supposed to still inhabit Jalkor, not even when they finally reached the canyons of what had been the heart of the city. It was as deserted as everything else.

But the empty streets were understandable, he thought. Only the security forces and their quarry would be out and around, in what passed for "the open." Most of the people still working to keep the city going were wherever the machinery was: out of sight.

And those who weren't working, those who had surrendered to despair and the computer fantasies . . .

Suppressing a sigh, Picard could think only that Jalkor was fully as bleak and depressing as any city he had ever encountered. He had seen cities nearly destroyed by wars where the survivors had at least had enough hope and determination to show themselves in the streets. But perhaps this was worse than an ordinary war. Here the enemy could not be seen or fought. As far as these people knew, it simply existed—and had existed for hundreds of years and dozens of generations. And it could not be resisted, could not be struck out at. It was everywhere, literally a part of the air they had to breathe, unstoppable.

He grimaced mentally. It was little wonder that, in the face of centuries of such seeming inevitability, the urge to retreat into computer-generated revenge fantasies was so great. Even the vandalism made a perverted kind of sense—if they couldn't strike out at a real, visible enemy, they would strike out in their blind frustration and anger at whatever came to hand. Countless riots on dozens of worlds, including Earth, had been born out of less.

Closing his eyes for a second and pulling in a breath, Picard forced such thoughts out of his mind and focused on what, in another few minutes, he must tell President Khozak.

The van swooped down from the street level and deposited them in a mostly darkened parking area, where the only lights were those triggered sporadically by the group's presence. After a brief, shuddering ride in an elevator, they were marching down a featureless corridor toward the Council Chambers.

Raised voices were audible several meters before they reached the door, which the security officer opened for them before stepping to one side and gesturing them through. Inside, Picard recognized Khozak, Zalkan, and Denbahr standing with seven others around the conference table. All of the seven looked tired and harried and impatient to be somewhere else. The two who were speaking angrily to Khozak were as smudged and disheveled as Denbahr had been when Picard had first seen her on the link from the shuttlecraft, fresh from hours of maintenance work at the power plant. The subject, apparently, was a desperate need for more technicians to care for the decaying food-processing equipment.

"Wake them up and shut off their terminals, Khozak!" the one, his back to the door, was saying loudly, his voice filling the sudden silence that fell as the others saw Picard leading the group into the room.

Scowling, the speaker turned. The scowl lightened when he saw the group from the *Enterprise,* but it didn't disappear entirely, and Khozak's angry expression when he saw Koralus more than made up for it.

Zalkan's eyes widened briefly at the sight of Koralus, but beyond that there was no reaction.

"So," the man said after a second, "these are the miracle workers from the stars."

"They've already worked a small miracle in the power plant!" Denbahr snapped, apparently angered by the man's tone. "They produced a functional laser confinement unit in a matter of hours and will have more for us in a few days. That's obviously not the answer to all our problems, but at least it will give us breathing room." She verbally lurched to a halt, glancing toward Picard and the others as she stepped back. "And they've only been here a couple of days," she added quietly.

"Technician Denbahr is correct," Khozak said into the silence that followed Denbahr's brief outburst. "They may also," he went on, looking sternly around the group, "have discovered the source of the Plague."

For a full second, there was total silence, and it was all Picard could do to suppress an angry scowl at the melodramatic announcement. But he shouldn't have been surprised by a grandstanding announcement like that from Khozak, he thought in exasperation.

Then all seven were talking at once, some directing their questions at Khozak, others at the group from the *Enterprise*. Khozak held up his hands and shouted for quiet, then pounded solidly on the table with a gavel-like object. Finally, silence returned.

Solemnly, Khozak introduced the seven, all members of the Council, all obviously impatient to get through the formalities. Then he announced the names of Picard, Data, Troi, and "the Deserter Koralus."

Picard was relieved to see that there was none of the reaction that Khozak had obviously expected to

Koralus's name. Instead, the Council members barely glanced at him while Delmak, the original speaker, didn't even do that.

"Is it true?" Delmak demanded, turning his frown from Khozak, at whom he had been directing it throughout the introductions, to Picard. *"Do* you know what caused the Plague?"

"We have discovered a *clue* to the *nature* of the Plague," Picard said slowly and deliberately, trying not to return the frown, "and we have encountered some ships that *may* have some connection with the Plague. So far—"

Another eruption of everyone speaking at once cut off Picard's words. This time it was Delmak who restored order.

"Ships?" The anger was obvious in his voice. "Are you saying that the Plague is not a natural phenomenon? That the revenge fantasies are *true* and someone is *causing* it?"

"Not at all. What we are saying is—" Picard broke off deliberately, his eyes moving from Khozak to each Council member in turn. The silence held.

"What I am saying is this," he resumed. "Let us tell you precisely what we *have* found, and you can draw your own conclusions."

Everyone nodded or muttered assent, and Picard began. With questions and other interruptions, however, it took nearly an hour to get to the point at which the mines had been entered. Khozak himself took over then with his account of the discovery of the mysterious recent activity in the mines. "I have already alerted several of my best security officers to be prepared to descend as far as necessary to determine what the intruders were—or *are*—doing there. I trust you have no objections, Captain Picard?" Khozak concluded.

Again Picard suppressed a frown. "I would not advise a course of action like that at this point, President Khozak," he said uncomfortably. "Before you make any decisions, you should be aware of a number of things. First, the most recent energy surges detected by our sensors originated neither in space nor in the vicinity of the mines but somewhere in or near Jalkor."

"Where?" Khozak demanded, his frown returning. "In what part of the city?"

Picard shook his head slightly. "It is impossible to tell. As I said, we are not even positive that they originated within the city. Neither do we know whether the surges indicated the arrival of something—or someone—or the departure."

"How many were there?" Zalkan, completely silent until now, spoke up.

"Seven, I believe." Picard glanced at Data, who nodded. "Seven. Does the number of surges mean anything to you, Zalkan?"

The scientist shook his head vigorously. "I was merely thinking that, if there were several, it is possible that someone observed at least one of them. Is it safe to assume that these surges, like the ones related to the disappearance of the ships that you showed us, would have been accompanied by flashes of light?"

"Probably," Picard said, "but these were very weak compared to the ones in space." He turned to Khozak. "It could be helpful, however, to issue an alert, asking everyone to be on the lookout and to report any unusual lights."

"Of course," Khozak said, grimacing as he turned to Zalkan. "Zalkan, is that possible? Can we still get word out to everyone in the city?"

"To everyone who still has a functioning terminal, yes. Assuming they use it for anything but continual fantasies."

"And assuming they can tell the difference between the fantasies and a message from the real world," Denbahr added.

Khozak nodded, turning back to Picard. "I believe you said there were a number of things we should know. What are the others, in addition to the energy surges within Jalkor?"

Picard pulled in another breath and held it a moment. Data had acted correctly in temporarily withholding the information from the Krantinese, but that knowledge didn't make it any easier for Picard now. "We have discovered something else in the mines, or, more accurately, below them."

"What?" Khozak's most recent expression, one of careful neutrality, vanished, replaced by the belligerent wariness he had worn during most of his stay on the *Enterprise.* It was obvious he was not going to make Picard's task any easier. "No one told me of any such discoveries when we were in the mines."

"My apologies, President Khozak," Picard said. Out of the corner of his eye, he saw Troi wince, her eyes darting to Zalkan. The scientist's face was frozen, his chest motionless, as if even his breathing had stopped. Something must have upset him, and badly, for Troi to allow her own reaction to his emotions to show through that much.

"However," Picard resumed, focusing again on Khozak, "it seemed advisable to inform the entire Council at one time."

"So," Khozak said stiffly, "this is as much of the Council as still exists. What are these discoveries?"

"First," Picard said, plunging ahead, "assuming the

maps you provided of the mines are complete, a tunnel has been extended downward approximately two hundred meters from the lowest level."

Some of the stiffness went out of Khozak's bearing. He almost smiled. "Extended by the same ones who entered the mines ten years ago and tried to conceal their existence."

"In all probability, yes, Mr. President. And, as you suspected, they are apparently still there. Mr. Data's tricorder indicated several humanoid life-forms in or near the extended tunnel, life-forms that may or may not be Krantinese. That, however, is not the most important thing we have found."

"Not to you, perhaps," Khozak said, glancing triumphantly at the Council members, "but I can imagine nothing more important to us than finding the very people responsible for destroying our world!"

"President Khozak," Picard said, an edge of exasperation creeping into his voice even though he could understand, even sympathize with, Khozak's reaction, "I repeat, there is nothing to indicate that these people—or *any* people—are responsible for the Plague!"

"There is enough!" Khozak snapped. "You have yourself told us of the evidence!"

"Suggestions of an association, nothing more! Whoever they are, they could be victims, the same as the Krantinese."

Khozak was silent a moment. Finally he shrugged. "Very well, I admit there is something in what you say. However, I intend to speak with these people, whoever they are, and on my terms!"

"I can ask for nothing more."

"Now, Captain Picard, you said there was something even more important than the presence of these beings?"

Picard took another breath. "Not far from the tunnel extending down from the mines is a deposit of an extremely valuable mineral called dilithium."

"Dilithium?" Khozak frowned. "I have never heard of it. What is it? Why is it valuable?"

"To Krantin, with its present level of technology, it isn't valuable. However, to the Federation—to anyone with matter-antimatter technology, particularly warp-drive starships—it is one of the most valuable substances in the galaxy." Picard looked around at the Council members. He was at least slightly relieved to see that their faces, unlike Khozak's, reflected more curiosity than anger.

"And this dilithium is what these . . . invaders are after?" Khozak asked.

"It almost certainly is," Picard admitted, "whoever or whatever they are."

"And you, a servant of this Federation, to whom this substance has great value," Khozak said, his voice suddenly filled with disbelief, "you only discovered the presence of this dilithium—when? Yesterday?"

"Yesterday, yes. When Mr. Data descended to the lower levels of the mines, he was able to adjust his tricorder to obtain readings hundreds of meters farther down. Zalkan," Picard went on, glancing toward the scientist, who twitched nervously at the sudden attention, "your belief that the effects of the Plague become weaker as you descend underground appears to be valid."

Khozak waved off any reply by Zalkan, though the scientist did not seem inclined to speak in any event. "And you had no suspicion," Khozak persisted, "that this dilithium existed until your Mr. Data discovered it?"

"Of course not," Picard said, forcing himself to

ignore the sarcastic tone of Khozak's words. "How could we? We have explained how our sensors are hampered by the Plague."

"And yet you offered to help us," Khozak continued, his tone even more sarcastic. "You even provided a superior laser unit for our power plant and promised several more—all before you even *suspected* the existence of this valuable substance."

"Khozak, don't be a complete paranoid fool!" Denbahr exploded, somewhat to Picard's relief. "You've seen their ship! Don't you realize, if all they were interested in was this dilithium, whatever it is, they could have taken it anytime they wanted? Why would they even *tell* us about it?"

She shook her head in renewed exasperation. "Why would they even tell us they were *here*? They could've set one of their shuttlecraft down at the mines and dug for years, like those others apparently *have* done—they could've set off skyrockets to signal shift changes, and we'd never have had a clue they were even there! We didn't have a clue these others, whoever they are, were out there, doing whatever they've been doing for the last ten years! Except for the power plant, we don't have a clue about *anything* that's happening outside Jalkor, am I right? So tell me, President Khozak, if they want to steal this dilithium or anything else, why have they gone to all the trouble they've gone to to let us know about it? And about themselves and everything else they've told us, even about the Plague?"

When Denbahr had first started to speak, Khozak had glared at her furiously, but by the time she finished, he had gotten control of himself and forced his features into a smile.

"You misunderstand," he said. "I merely wish to understand the situation. This could, after all, be the most important event in a hundred years. It must be dealt with thoroughly, not with a casual word or two." He turned to Picard. "You understand my motives, I trust, and are not offended by my questions."

"Of course not, Mr. President," Picard said, noting Troi's continuing presence out of the corner of his eye. "In matters of this import, full and mutual understanding is imperative. I'm sure, for example, that the Federation will want a similar depth of understanding when it comes time to make formal arrangements regarding the dilithium."

"Of course, of course. But first we must dispose of the invaders."

"Dispose of?" A frown flickered across Picard's brow at Khozak's choice of words.

Khozak nodded. "Clear them out somehow. Now that we know they are there, we can take them by surprise and—"

"In the first place, Mr. President," Picard interrupted, "the layout of the mines being what it is, your men would have to descend one at a time, slowly and probably noisily. Second, if whoever is in the mines has the same ability to appear and disappear that the ships have—and the fact that we have detected energy surges in the vicinity of the mines indicates they do— then whoever you send down there will probably be helpless against them. As helpless as the *Enterprise* was to keep the ships from vanishing from under our very noses. And finally and most importantly for Krantin, even if these people *are* responsible for the Plague, there is no reason to believe that simply killing them or driving them out would end the Plague. If we are to have a chance to understand and end the Plague, we need to talk to them, not drive them away."

"But if they are responsible for the Plague—"

"All the more reason to be cautious, I would think," Picard interrupted again. "There's nothing to say that they are responsible, but if they *are,* they are likely to be capable of much more. Nor are they likely to be reluctant to make use of those capabilities, whatever they may be."

Khozak paled at the thought, slumping in his chair. He nodded weakly. "You are right, of course. I obviously hadn't thought the matter through thoroughly enough. I could only think—these could be the creatures who destroyed our world."

"The feeling is understandable, Mr. President," Picard said blandly.

"But what *can* we do?" one of the seven asked abruptly. "Whether they are responsible for the Plague or not, we could be at their mercy." He shivered, looking around. "You said they were already in the city!"

"I said we had detected energy surges in the vicinity of the city," Picard corrected him. "We have no idea what those surges meant. They could have meant things—or people—were arriving; they could have meant things were leaving. Or both. All we know is that the surges were smaller than those we detected in the area of the mines. But since we don't know what happened in the mines either, that doesn't help much."

"This dilithium—" Khozak seemed to have recovered from his momentary despair. "You say it is valuable but not to us directly. Your Federation would— What would you give us for it? What kind of help? What kind of help is *possible* for a world like Krantin?"

Picard was silent a moment, relieved that Khozak finally appeared to be ready to deal rationally with the situation. "At this point," he admitted, "I don't know. At the very least, if your present population is as low as you say—five million, I believe you said—a mass evacuation is conceivable, provided a suitable world, or worlds, can be found. And provided your people wish it. What the Federation can *try* to do is find the cause of the Plague and stop it. If that is successful, then it might be possible to eventually restore Krantin to something approaching its original state. But in even the most optimistic case, any meaningful restoration would be decades away."

"And your Federation would do this—would attempt these things? In return for the dilithium?"

Picard suppressed a sigh, wondering what Troi was picking up from the president. He supposed the man's cynicism and distrust was justified, considering Krantin's history, but that didn't make it any easier to deal with. Denbahr looked as if she was on the verge of reading him the riot act again.

"I cannot yet speak officially for the Federation," Picard said carefully, "but I assure you they will do whatever is feasible to help your world, regardless of what you decide to do regarding the dilithium."

"Need I again point out, President Khozak," Denbahr said, intensely but quietly, "that they have already given us essential help for the power plant? And that it was given before they even knew of the existence of this dilithium?"

Khozak ignored her, turning to Zalkan. "You said it would be possible to contact everyone in Jalkor."

"We can send messages to every functioning terminal," Zalkan said. "As you well know, however, ninety percent of the populace is largely beyond reach."

"As I well know, yes," Khozak sighed. "But now we can give that ninety percent a reason to rejoin us. It may take some time, but—"

"A reason, Khozak?"

"Yes, a reason! If we announce the discovery of this dilithium, and if we can explain what it means, what the help of the Federation means—"

"No!" Zalkan snapped, and Picard was surprised both at the scientist's reaction and at its vehemence. "You must not make any such announcement!"

"Don't be ridiculous!" Denbahr shot back angrily. "If Jalkor is going to survive long enough for any of this to come true, we need at least *some* of these people to keep the machines running, to keep our air breathable. You of all people know how much needs to be done and how few there are to do it."

"I know, but—but it is dangerous! You just heard how these—these 'invaders' may be in Jalkor itself. Seven energy surges, Commander Data said, *within the city!* And you would make this announcement, letting the invaders know that we know about them! What might they do then?"

"Zalkan is right," another of the Council members said. "You don't know who these invaders are or what they are capable of. If, as you yourself believe, they are indeed responsible for the Plague—" She shook her head. "And we all know how vulnerable we are. A break in the roof is all it would take. Or in a wall. We have quite enough trouble keeping our own people from destroying what's left of the city. No, until we know who these invaders are, we can't let them know that we know they're here."

"If they don't already know," Delmak said. "If they were able to tamper with the records computer, who knows what else they may have done? They could be monitoring us this very minute!"

For a long moment there was total silence. Finally Khozak turned to Picard. "We must do *something!* You are the ones who told us of these invaders, of the material they are doubtless trying to steal. You have told us it would be suicidal to send our security forces down to confront them. What *do* you suggest we do? Simply wait for them to take the dilithium?"

"Of course not," Picard said, glancing toward Data. "We suggest that we return to the mines and that Mr. Data descend as he did yesterday and continue down to the levels where the life-forms were indicated. Once at that level, his tricorder should be able to pinpoint the individual life-forms and may enable him to observe them without being seen. We will try to keep a transporter lock on him so that he can be pulled out if he feels the danger has become too great."

Khozak frowned. "But I was given to understand that your 'transporters' could not be safely used within the Plague."

"They aren't as safe as we'd like, but with the *Enterprise* in low orbit, it should be safe enough, provided one of the energy surges doesn't occur during the few seconds required for a transport. In any event, depending on what Mr. Data finds, he will either try to establish contact or return undetected to a higher level of the mines, at which time his observations could be evaluated and further plans made."

Khozak didn't like it. At the very least, he said, he wanted a number of his security officers to accompany Data. At one point he even proposed flooding the lower levels of the mines with a deadly, fast-acting gas, until it was pointed out that even the fastest-acting gas couldn't possibly reach all points of the tunnels rapidly enough.

"You might kill one or two," Picard pointed out patiently, "or even a dozen, but all you'd do to the rest is make them angry—assuming they're not angry already."

Finally, reluctantly, Khozak abandoned his opposition to Picard's cautious, nonlethal plan. Data would descend into the mine the next day. In the meantime, one shuttlecraft would be stationed near the mines, another near the city, watching for energy surges, hoping a pattern of some kind would emerge in either location or that the location of the surges within the city could be pinpointed.

As they were preparing to leave, with Picard and Data still answering the Council members' questions about the uses and value of dilithium, Troi took Zalkan aside and motioned for Koralus to follow. Except for a few moments immediately after the captain had first disclosed what they had found at the bottom of the mines, the scientist had somehow maintained a stiff, emotionless exterior. His inner agitation, however, had been a shrill and painful assault on Troi's empathic sense ever since. The only times it had lessened even slightly had been the rare moments when his eyes had settled briefly on Koralus.

"What is it?" he asked, his voice as neutral as his appearance as he stood facing her, carefully avoiding looking at Koralus, who stood a meter to her right.

"Zalkan," she said softly, her voice not carrying the few meters to the nearest of the Council members, "perhaps we can help you."

"Your doctor?" He shook his head. "She has already—"

"Perhaps medically also, but that is not what I meant."

"Then what? Help Krantin, you mean?"

"That, too, but I meant you, personally, in dealing with whatever it is that has you so frightened."

He shook his head, frowning, and she felt his terror ratchet even higher. "You do not make sense. I am no

162

more frightened than Khozak or any of the others. This news of the ships and the Plague has unnerved us all."

"I know that, Zalkan. But I also know that there are things that frighten you and you alone."

"Nonsense! Are you saying I am a coward? Well, perhaps I am. I am a scientist, not a warrior."

"That is not what I meant." She paused, realizing that by trying to ease up to what she had to say, she was making him more terrified, not less. She put a hand lightly on his arm. "I am an empath," she said. "I can sense emotions, and those emotions very often allow me to tell whether a person is being truthful or not."

With her words, she winced, feeling his terror abruptly escalate to new heights. Shaking his head, he tried to jerk free of her grip. "I don't know what you're talking about!" he hissed. "Now let me go!"

Grimacing at the flood of fear that poured out of him, stabbing into her mind like a hundred daggers, she found that it was all she could do to retain her grip on his arm despite his physical weakness. Abruptly, she began to fear he would collapse on the spot.

"I know you are sincere in your concern for Krantin," she said quickly, forcing her voice to remain soft and reassuring despite her pain, "but I also know that you are in far more trouble than you have let anyone know. That is what I meant when I said we might be able to help you."

For another second, the fear continued to batter at Troi's mind and Zalkan continued to struggle feebly against her grip.

But then his eyes flickered toward Koralus and, like a punctured balloon, he went limp, no longer struggling. The bulk of the fear that had filled his mind to the bursting shriveled as well, replaced by a painful mixture of resignation and relief. All this with barely a sound, certainly none that reached the ears of the Council members, though Picard had been carefully watching the two of them out of the corner of his eye.

"You wanted to tell us the truth," Troi said even more softly, "but you were afraid to trust us."

Weakly, he nodded, saying nothing. Troi looked toward Picard, and for a moment their eyes met.

Chapter Thirteen

"AT LEAST YOU MUST PROMISE to hear me out," Zalkan said weakly, "before you make any judgments."

"Of course," Picard agreed, his eyes again going worriedly to Troi, who nodded her reassurance. The emotional battering that Zalkan's terror had subjected her to had left her shaken, but she had insisted on staying close and monitoring the scientist while he told his story. Data and Koralus stood to one side, listening.

The five of them were in Zalkan's private lab, a small, locked room several floors away from the one in which the tests on the laser unit had been run. It was cluttered with jury-rigged circuits and machines of all kinds. The only "standard" items, on a bench at the rear of the room, were a massive vacuum pump, one of the laser units for the power plant, and several vacuum chambers, each studded with a mass of sensors capable of detecting and analyzing virtually any form of matter inside the jars.

Picard had offered to take the scientist to the *Enterprise* to talk, but Zalkan had insisted on returning to this lab. He had given no reasons, but Troi had indicated that it was not a trap of any kind and that Zalkan still seemed intent on telling them the truth. He wanted them to promise not to tell Khozak or any of the others, but in the end he had had to settle for Picard's promise to listen to the entire story before making any judgments.

As if still delaying what he must say, the scientist gestured at the jumble of equipment. "Can you tell me," he asked, "if any of this—if *anything* has a chance of blocking the Plague? I've been trying for ten years to develop an energy field that would at least keep it from infecting the vacuums in the laser units."

Picard turned to Data, who seemed to consider for a moment. "If they were in operation," Data said, "it is possible I could compare the field characteristics with those of a device Commander La Forge is building for a similar purpose on the *Enterprise,* but I would not suggest activating it while anyone other than myself is in close proximity to it. If the field characteristics are similar, it could be just as harmful to living organisms as the fields it is intended to block."

Zalkan was silent a moment, then nodded. "You know about those effects, then?"

"We have only speculated," Picard said quietly, "based on similar fields we have encountered in the past. And on your own failing health."

Zalkan smiled faintly. "Your doctor's examination of me, yes."

"That and more. Counselor Troi saw that you knew more about your illness than you admitted," Picard said. "She also saw that you recognized the ships when we showed you the holograms. Based on those insights and previous experiences of our own, we suspected that your illness could be the result of having been aboard similar ships when they made their jumps—to wherever they go."

"And you thought I was one of them . . ."

"We didn't know what to think. You recognized them and you were afraid of—of something, she could not tell what."

Zalkan nodded and then shivered. "There is little I am not afraid of." He was silent a moment, then smiled, almost chuckled. "Except death. I'm sure your doctor knows how close I am to that."

"She has an idea," Picard admitted. "But she also has been searching for something that could help you."

"And has she found anything?" A resigned smile.

"No miracle cures, but she tells me there is a treatment that could stabilize your condition, perhaps even reverse it to a modest degree."

"But that would require, I would guess, that I no longer expose myself to the energy fields that seem to have caused my problem in the first place."

Picard nodded. "And it would, essentially, put you in a coma for several weeks, if not months."

This time Zalkan did laugh. "At this point, a coma sounds very attractive, if only I could afford the time. Has she found nothing else?"

"Nothing that offers any long-term hope."

"But short-term?"

"Only very short-term—a powerful metabolic enhancer called CZ-fourteen. In all likelihood it would briefly restore your strength, but it would also very probably kill you in a matter of hours."

When the scientist did not respond for several

seconds, Picard prompted, "The quicker you tell us what the situation is here, the more time we will have to address it."

"Obviously. But it is difficult to admit this kind of truth, even when I have no choice." Again he fell silent for a long moment, shaking his head. When he looked up again, his eyes fell on Koralus, who had been standing silently in the background throughout the exchange.

"Koralus," Zalkan said, "I must ask. Before you left on the *Hope,* did you know a woman named Endros?"

Koralus's eyes widened, as did Picard's. "How did you know?" Koralus asked softly.

Zalkan let out a sigh, not of relief but of something else, something even Troi could not completely identify. "She was my grandmother," he said softly.

"Impossible!" Koralus snapped, scowling at the scientist. "Endros left *with* me on the *Hope.* Nearly half a century ago, she died while I slept."

Zalkan closed his eyes a moment. "In this world, yes," he said, his words barely audible. "In my world, you and she—"

He broke off, shaking his head again. When he spoke again, his voice was firmer. "It is so complex, it is difficult to even know where to start in order for it to make any sense."

Picard nodded sympathetically, gesturing to an agitated Koralus for patience. "The world that you come from?" Picard asked. "Is that the world the ships and the people in the mines are from?"

Zalkan nodded. "Krantin. My Krantin. But where it is in relation to this Krantin, I have no idea. No one knows. Wherever it is, the two worlds were once virtually twins." He glanced again at Koralus. "Even now, despite the massive differences caused to both worlds by the Plague, people who exist here also exist there."

"An alternate reality," Picard said, remembering. "We don't fully understand it ourselves, but we have encountered enough examples to accept the existence of such things."

"'Alternate reality,' yes, as good a way to describe it as any. Some of our scientists—including our Koralus—have advanced the concept."

Picard glanced at Troi before speaking again. "Zalkan, *are* you or these others somehow responsible for what the Krantinese call the Plague?"

Zalkan was silent for several seconds, then shuddered. "God help us, yes, we are all responsible." Abruptly his voice was trembling with emotion, as if he were finally letting go not only of the secrets he had been hiding but of the iron control he had had to exert for so long. "For five hundred years— But we had no idea what we were doing! I swear, all we knew—"

He broke off, almost sobbing, his sudden surrender to anguish reflected momentarily in Troi's face as she reached out to touch his arm again.

After a minute, he straightened, his breathing returning to normal. "Thank you, Counselor Troi."

He turned to face Picard and Koralus, his face once again an emotionless mask. "The ones in the ships, they—or their leaders, the Directorate, what passes for a government on our Krantin—know now what they are doing. The Directorate has known for decades, but they have kept it a secret from all but those directly involved. And they simply do not care what they have done—are still doing to Krantin. I am part of a small underground network of scientists, but we are powerless to help in any meaningful way—unless we are able to obtain at least a small portion of the dilithium we are searching for in the mines. Then we will at least have a chance to save ourselves and perhaps even Krantin. If the Directorate obtains it, both our worlds are doomed. That is why the dilithium must be kept as secret as possible here. Those energy surges you detected in the city, they are almost certainly the work of the Directorate."

"This Directorate has people here?" Picard was not surprised. "In Jalkor?"

"None live here, as I have done for more than a decade. They come and they go, we believe." The scientist seemed to have regained complete control, now speaking calmly, almost formally, the only indication of any distraction an occasional sideways glance toward Koralus. "We also believe they have monitors attached to the computer system. Normally they rarely check them. The Directorate sends someone through once a year at most, primarily to confirm that Krantin still presents no real threat to them. But now that they have seen your ship and you have told them you intend to help Krantin—they will at the very least check their monitors, perhaps even activate new ones. The surges you detected in the city almost certainly were theirs. Anything that is in the city computers, they will soon know, if they don't already." Zalkan shivered and fell silent.

Picard looked questioningly at Troi, though he was already convinced that what he was hearing was true. It would explain much, particularly Zalkan's terror when Khozak had wanted to make the dilithium general knowledge throughout Jalkor.

"He is telling the truth as he knows it," Troi confirmed.

Picard turned back to the scientist, still silent, looking frailer than ever, his thin shoulders hunched forward.

"What *is* the Plague?" Picard asked when Zalkan did not resume speaking.

The scientist pulled in another breath. "It is the waste material of our world," he said softly, "reduced to its component atoms and molecules by the process that sends it here. Five hundred years ago, our scientists were experimenting with matter transmission, what you call transporter technology. They were never successful, but purely by accident they discovered something else—an energy field that made material objects disappear. Forever."

To his own surprise, Picard found himself having to suppress an impulse to laugh. *The Plague was the result of a planetwide high-tech garbage-disposal system!* But then he wondered: What would Earth have done if its scientists had stumbled onto such a device when the water and air were thick with pollution and the landfills were overflowing? Would they have been able to resist the temptation?

"Did they know where the waste was going?" Picard asked, sobering. "Did they try to find out?"

Zalkan shook his head. "Many probably did try, at first. But not knowing where the material went didn't stop them from sending it. It was just too easy, too convenient. Anything subjected to the energy field simply disappeared and was never seen again. As far as anyone knew, it was being snuffed out of existence. Within a few years, the process was being used everywhere by virtually everyone, and the ones who controlled it controlled our world, and they were no longer interested in where the waste was going. They eventually became the Directorate, and no one objected. After all, because of them, our industries became pollution-free virtually overnight. Within fifty years, our world—our Krantin—was cleaner than it had ever been. Not that it wasn't disfigured. The Directorate used the process for mining as well, stripping great chunks of soil and rock away in order to get at the material they—we—wanted. The same happened in space—that cloud of interplanetary dust that is smothering this Krantin is simply the ninety percent and more of tens of thousands of asteroids that the Directorate 'mined' over the last four hundred years."

"What of the ships out there among the asteroids in *this* reality?" Picard asked. "What are they doing there? Are they the Directorate's as well?"

"They are. They are looking for the dilithium." Zalkan grimaced. "It is a complicated story. Our world once had the same dilithium deposit as this Krantin, but before anyone knew of its value, it had gone the way of all the rest of our 'waste products' and could not be reclaimed."

Picard nodded when Zalkan paused. "Our sensors detected a molecular form of dilithium in the Plague cloud," he said.

Zalkan almost laughed. "A thoroughly useless form, at least to us."

"And to us," Picard agreed.

"But then a small group of scientists and engineers—one of them my father, the son of our Koralus and Endros—discovered how to use the crystalline form. The Directorate of course confiscated the tiny amount that still existed. They apparently assumed they could find more, or that it could be duplicated, but they soon found it could not. So for the first time, the Directorate began a serious effort to learn *where* over four hundred years' worth of our world's trash had gone. It took nearly twenty years to learn to 'look' through to this world and another ten to develop a way to physically come through—and to learn that the dilithium, like everything else we sent through, was unrecoverable. But they had also discovered that the two worlds—the two realities—were virtually identical physically. So they assumed—hoped—that this world would still have its dilithium."

"But if the dilithium is here on Krantin," Picard asked puzzledly, "why are they searching for it out among the asteroids?"

"Because we were incredibly lucky," Zalkan said. "The only ones who knew precisely where the dilithium originated in our world were not of the Directorate, and they were able to tamper with the computer records and fool Directorate scientists into thinking it had come from the asteroids. That gave us the chance to—"

Without warning, the single door to the lab burst open, slamming back as if it had been hit by a battering ram, and a flood of Khozak's security officers, their projectile weapons drawn, stormed in. Before anyone could react, the comm units were torn from the tunics of the three *Enterprise* officers and, more violently, from Koralus's. Only Zalkan reacted, his right hand, released by Troi, darting into a pocket of the coveralls he wore. Then, like the others, his every muscle seemed to freeze.

Behind the officers came Khozak, a weapon in his hand as well. His face was flushed as he pushed Troi roughly to one side and stood facing Zalkan.

"Who *are* you?" he grated, bringing the weapon up until it was leveled at the scientist's sunken chest. *"What* are you, that you would destroy our world?"

Zalkan flinched at the rage in the president's face and voice.

An instant later, a brilliant flash of light blinded everyone in the room.

And the roar of Khozak's weapon slammed at their ears.

When vision returned, Zalkan was gone.

And, Picard noted with hope, if not quite relief, the door of one of the vacuum chambers that had been on the bench directly behind Zalkan had been shattered by the projectile.

174

Chapter Fourteen

"Captain!" Riker's voice erupted from one of the comm units, still clutched by one of the guards. "There has been another energy surge, apparently very near to your present location."

Picard couldn't help but smile slightly despite the situation. *I noticed, Number One.* "President Khozak," he said quietly, "I would suggest you allow me to reply."

Khozak, still scowling furiously at the spot where Zalkan had stood moments before, spun toward Picard.

"And let you be snatched from under our noses, like your murderous friend Zalkan? Remember, I heard your Commander Riker in the mine yesterday—and you, just minutes ago—speaking about keeping a 'lock' on those devices with your transporters. That is why they were taken from you!"

"Precisely," Picard said mildly. "And the lock is still functioning. Additionally, if there is no reply, the transporter will be activated, and anyone holding a unit will find himself on the *Enterprise*. Unless there is another energy surge during transport, in which case he could find himself anywhere—or nowhere."

The three guards holding the comm units darted quick looks at Khozak, who seemed to be thinking furiously but reaching no conclusions.

"Just tap one lightly on the front, gentlemen," Picard advised. "That will activate it. It will pick up anything said in the room."

"On the bench," Khozak ordered, emerging from his momentary paralysis. "Put them on the bench and tap one and stand back." Before he had finished speaking, the four comm units had clicked onto the bench near the door and all six guards were edging hastily backward. Their weapons were still pointed in the general direction of Koralus and the three from the *Enterprise,* however.

Picard smiled faintly, thinking that they might survive the situation after all. "That will be acceptable, under the circumstances."

When none of the guards returned to touch the abandoned comm units, Khozak stepped up. Darting angry looks between Picard and the comm units, he extended his hand slowly.

"Captain, this is Commander Riker. Respond."

Khozak's hand jerked back from the offending comm unit as if he'd been burned.

"Tap it, Mr. President," Picard repeated. "Lightly with one finger will suffice. And I should warn you that Commander Riker's instructions, in the event he cannot obtain a response, are to set the transporter to scan a wide area and then activate it. I don't know the exact parameters, but I suspect everything in this room would be taken."

"Data! Deanna! Koralus! Respond!" Riker's words erupted from all four units, sending another twitch through Khozak.

"Mr. President?" Picard prompted.

Like a man attempting to pet a scorpion, Khozak sent one hand darting downward, pulled it back too quickly, hesitated a moment, and brought it down again.

Cautiously, Picard moved a step closer to the comm units. "Number One," he said, raising his voice only slightly, "we have a situation here. Stand by."

He turned to Deanna. "Counselor, what is your reading of our circumstances?"

"Now that Zalkan has left," she said after a moment, "there is no specific hostility except toward Koralus, only fear and uncertainty. It is similar to what President Khozak has felt all along, only it is now much more intense."

Picard nodded, relieved that he had not miscalculated. "None of them wants to kill us," he said quietly, "but it could happen anyway, either accidentally or intentionally. Is that fair to say?"

"Something like that, Captain."

"Kill you, Captain?" Riker's quadrupled voice rattled off the walls. "What *is* the situation down there?"

Picard looked inquiringly toward Khozak. "May I explain?"

Khozak once again gave the impression of furious but fruitless thought. Finally he nodded.

Picard turned back to face the comm units, marshaling his thoughts. "Number One, it's a long story. The essentials are these. Both the ships and the humanoids in the mine are, as we suspected, from an alternate reality, containing a world once much like Krantin. Zalkan is from that world as well. He told us that the Plague is, essentially, the waste from that world, unknowingly transmitted here by the people of that world using a method they accidentally discovered five hundred years ago."

Picard paused, observing Khozak, then resumed. "I assume that this constant transmission results in the low-level energy field that blankets the system. Sometime in the last few decades, they have found a way to come through themselves. The most recent energy surge you detected was Zalkan vanishing from this very room in a flash equally as blinding as those in which the ships vanished. If we can believe him—and Counselor Troi has said that we can—he is part of an underground network of scientists working against what he calls the Directorate, the people in control of that world. The Directorate, he says, has no interest in stopping the Plague. Zalkan's is the group in the mines, and he hopes that, if they can get a small portion of the dilithium, they would be able to . . . set things right and perhaps stop the Plague, although he did not have time to elaborate before President Khozak and his men burst in, precipitating his abrupt departure.

"He has been experimenting here," Picard added, looking again toward Khozak, "in this lab, trying to develop a means of blocking the transmitted material from small areas, possibly an energy field similar to what Commander La Forge is working on. I suspect Zalkan's exposure to the energy fields generated by his own experiments is more responsible for his current state of health than his travels between realities."

"You left out a couple of small details, Captain,"

Riker said when Picard fell silent. "For example, since there was some mention of your possibly being killed, can I assume the four of you are being held against your will? If so, by whom? And why?"

"I can answer only the first two of those questions, Number One. President Khozak will have to answer the last."

"He's the one who's holding you?"

"He and a group similar to the one that first met you at the airlock."

"I see. Can I speak to President Khozak?"

"You have been speaking to him, Number One. The question is, will he speak to you? Mr. President?"

Khozak blinked, his grip on his weapon faltering for a moment but recovering. "What do you wish to speak about, Commander Riker?"

"I should think that was obvious, Mr. President," Riker snapped. "Why are you holding three Starfleet officers and one of your own people against their will?"

"I'm curious about that myself, Mr. President," Picard added when Khozak didn't respond for several seconds.

"I *heard* Zalkan and you," Khozak said finally, with the angry sound of a man who was beginning to have second thoughts—or, worse, perhaps his *first* real thoughts—about an overly hasty action. "I heard the two of you calmly discussing the fact that he had destroyed Krantin!"

"Zalkan's world, perhaps," Picard said, "as represented by the Directorate, not Zalkan personally. He personally, along with his friends, appears to be risking his life opposing the Directorate." Picard gestured at the benches of jury-rigged equipment. "He has even been trying to develop a means of blocking the Plague."

"And am I supposed to take his word for that? He, whose people have destroyed our entire world?"

"You can take our word for it that he was telling the truth, Mr. President. Counselor Troi is an empath. She knows if a person is lying, and she is convinced Zalkan was telling the truth."

Khozak swallowed audibly. "But *I* can *not* tell if a person is telling the truth. I do not know if you and your—your so-called empath are telling the truth or lying." He shook his head angrily. "You come here with your ships and your Federation and you tell us things that no sane person would believe, that you can travel between the stars not in centuries but in hours, that you can 'transport' yourselves magically from place to place, that you have brought Koralus back from the dead, and now you tell us to take the word of someone who just admitted—"

Khozak broke off. His voice had been rising with each phrase. With an obvious effort, he lowered his voice. "How am I to know your so-called Federation is not just another 'Directorate'?"

"Your reaction is quite understandable under the circumstances," Picard said calmly. "However, if you will consider the situation rationally, you can surely see that we have no reason to—"

He was cut off by a half-gasp, half-scream from the doorway. All eyes darted in that direction, most of the weapons, including Khozak's, following suit. Ahl Denbahr stood there, mouth agape.

"Technician Denbahr—" Khozak began.

"What are you *doing?*" she almost shouted.

"It's all right," Picard said hastily, but Denbahr wasn't listening. She seemed oblivious to the weapons, as well, as she stalked forward and stood confronting Khozak.

"I went to the lab, and Zalkan wasn't there. I'd seen

him talking to Counselor Troi, and he looked really bad, and I wanted to know—" She broke off, looking around. "Where *is* he?" Her scowl refocused on Khozak. "What have you done with him? I know you've never trusted him, but—"

She broke off again, shaking her head violently, as if trying to jar her thoughts into coherence. Her eyes went again to the weapons. "Are you completely insane? These people are the only chance Krantin has to survive! Without them, the power plant will shut down or destroy itself in five years at the most! Can't you *understand* that?"

"I understand more than you imagine!" Khozak snapped. "Zalkan's people are responsible for the Plague! I heard him admit it! And these people—I just can't take a chance on—"

"The rest of you!" she said, her voice still almost a shout as she abandoned Khozak and jerked around to glare at the guards. "This is crazy! I swear, these people are our only chance! You're going to ruin everything if you keep listening to Khozak! Put down those—"

As her eyes cast about from guard to guard, she suddenly spotted the comm units. She darted a quick look at Picard's unadorned tunic, and without hesitation lunged forward, grasping the comm units and turning to throw them to him.

Khozak, taken unaware by Denbahr's sudden action, recovered and lunged after her and caught her arm, his weapon forgotten as it clattered to the floor. An instant later, the comm units were jarred from her hand and hit the floor and bounced noisily. Picard winced, knowing that it must have sounded like a series of explosions to the listeners on the *Enterprise*.

"Captain!" Riker's voice erupted from the comm units again. "What happened? Are you all right?"

"Affirmative, Number One," Picard said quickly. "Continue to stand by."

"Data? Deanna? Someone respond! Koralus!"

His comm unit's transmit function must have been deactivated by the fall, Picard realized abruptly. "Activate one of them, now!" Picard snapped. "The fall—"

"If no one responds in five seconds, I'm engaging the transporter, wide scan!" Riker's voice announced from all four comm units. "If any of you can hear me, I still have a lock on your comm units. Stand by to beam up!" Immediately he began a countdown.

Suddenly, Khozak released Denbahr's arm and both lurched toward the comm units, but Khozak roughly shoved her aside as she leaned down to pick them up.

Khozak didn't lean down. Instead, he raised his foot and, as Riker's voice reached "Two" in the countdown, brought the heel of his boot down solidly on two of the comm units and, at "One," on the other two.

The silence was total. Picard's stomach knotted as he wondered if perhaps Riker had been right after all when he had recommended carrying phasers.

Khozak looked around, shivering. His eyes met Picard's, and what Picard saw there began to loosen the knot in his stomach.

"I'm sorry," Khozak said, his voice shaking, "but I couldn't take the chance."

Picard grimaced. Not that they were out of the woods yet.

Chapter Fifteen

"ENERGIZE!" RIKER COMMANDED.

"Something's happened," the transporter chief's voice came seconds later. "We've lost the lock."

"Get it back!"

"Trying, Commander, but there's nothing there. The comm units have shut down."

"All four?"

"All four."

What the hell is going on down there? "Can you scan the last known location?"

"Negative, Commander, not under these conditions. Without the fluctuating energy field, we might be able—"

"Understood, Chief. Keep trying for the comm units. Mr. Worf, anything more on that energy surge? Could it have been so close it knocked out the comm units? And can the sensors locate our people?"

"It's unlikely that the energy surge had anything to do with the comm units' failure, Commander," the Klingon said. "The captain's was operating normally for minutes after the surge. And even from low orbit, the sensors can neither distinguish individual life-forms nor distinguish between Krantinese and human."

"Chief," Riker said, returning his attention to the transporters, "can we transport down to approximately the last known location of the comm units?"

"Not safely, Commander. You could be placed within a few hundred meters of the location, but that's a few hundred meters in any direction, including up and down."

"You're saying we could end up, say, a hundred meters above the city's roof?"

"Entirely possible, Commander."

"Would point to point from a shuttlecraft on the ground be more accurate?"

"Yes, but not accurate enough to be safe, not if you're trying for the captain's location."

"But accurate enough to get someone inside the city, close to ground level, as opposed to in midair a hundred meters up?"

"Affirmative, Commander. It would get you well within the range of the surface proximity detectors, even under these conditions."

Riker was silent a moment, grimacing, then stood abruptly. "Stores, bring five comm units to the shuttlebay. I'll be taking them down. Mr. Worf, assemble a security detail and meet me in the shuttlebay. Chief—"

"Commander," Worf interrupted, "there have been . . . several more energy surges, all from the vicinity of the mines."

Riker's stomach lurched. If he *had* been able to

reestablish the lock and had been in the process of beaming them up—

"Shuttlebay, Mr. Worf," he said, striding toward the turbolift, tapping his comm unit as he went. Behind him, Worf surrendered the tactical station to Ensign Thompson. "Commander La Forge, to the bridge. You have the conn."

"On my way, Commander," Geordi's voice came back an instant later.

Riker was emerging into the shuttlebay when Ensign Thompson's voice came through his comm unit. "Commander Riker! An EM signal from the planet."

"Patch it through, Ensign." Frowning, Riker waited. What did these people think they were doing? Was this going to be a ransom demand of some kind? And it should be *him* down there, not the captain, he thought angrily. That was his job as first officer, and it was also his job to tell the captain when—

A crackling of static snapped him instantly out of his litany of self-recriminations. A moment later, an out-of-breath female voice was shouting over the static and the distortion: *"Starship Enterprise,* please respond! *Starship Enterprise,* it is urgent that you respond immediately! *Starship Enterprise—"*

"This is the *Enterprise,* Commander William Riker. Go ahead."

"Commander! Thank God! This is Ahl Denbahr—"

"What happened to our people, to their comm units?"

"They're all right, Commander!" Her voice came down from the level of a shout to being just loud enough to be heard over the continuing static. "Captain Picard and the others, I mean, and Koralus, not the comm units. The comm units are smashed."

"Smashed? What happened?"

185

"Khozak smashed them, don't ask me why! He'll be here in a minute, they all will be, if they ever quit arguing, and you can ask *them*. Him. He'll say it was my fault, but—You heard me yelling at Khozak, right? Your gadgets were still working then?"

"We heard you, yes."

"Khozak wouldn't listen, so I grabbed the comm units and tried to toss them back to your people, but Khozak grabbed me and they fell on the floor, and then you started acting like you couldn't hear us but you could still grab everyone in the room as long as the comm units were working, so Khozak panicked and smashed them, or at least stepped on them as hard as he could, and then your captain started warning him he'd better get in touch with you *some* way, there was no telling what you might do, but Khozak was still arguing, so I ran back here to the radio we use when I go out to the power plant and I remembered you were able to pick it up on your shuttlecraft and I just hoped— Anyway, here we are. Or here I am, anyway."

Riker almost laughed, partly at the breakneck speed of her account, partly in relief at the news that Deanna and the others were all right. "You're saying our people are definitely in no immediate danger, is that right?" he asked, turning as he heard the turbolift doors hiss open. Worf and four phaser-armed ensigns emerged.

"Definitely. I don't think even Khozak is *that* insane. Although some of the stuff he was ranting about— I mean, he was trying to tell me that Zalkan was responsible for the Plague!"

"Not Zalkan himself," Riker said, gesturing for Worf and the others to wait, "but the world that he's from apparently *is* responsible."

For a long moment there was silence except for the continuing static.

"The world that he's *from?*"

"An alternate world, much like Krantin," Riker said. "I gather it's a complicated story, but true. They can explain it better down there than I can. As I understand it, however, they got the information directly from Zalkan himself before he . . . left."

"Left? Where *is* he? That's why I came barging in there in the first place. I couldn't find him, and he'd been looking even worse than usual after that meeting with your captain and the Council. But *Zalkan* isn't from any other world! He's the one who pulled me back out of the computer fantasies ten years ago, and he's been trying to find a way to *block* the Plague, not make it worse!"

"That's quite probably true, but as I said—" Riker broke off as he caught the sound of faint voices from Denbahr's end of the hookup. "Captain? Are you there?"

The thin sound of footsteps, and then: "We're right here, Number One. I assume Technician Denbahr explained about the comm units."

"She said President Khozak smashed them. Correct?"

"Correct."

"I was about to come down with Lieutenant Worf and a security detail. Is that advisable?"

"Not at the moment, Number One. The situation is calm but not yet resolved, and I suspect a security detail would be counterproductive at best."

"You're still being detained, then?"

"Affirmative, Number One, but Counselor Troi assures me we are not in any immediate danger."

"So has Technician Denbahr. But I heard what you

said earlier, Captain, about intentional harm versus accidental. Does that still apply?"

"I do not believe so, Number One. Their weapons have been put away. Our problem now is to convince President Khozak of our good intentions, not an easy task under the circumstances."

"Zalkan and the Plague and the rest?"

"Precisely, Number One. Mistrust and suspicion are understandable reactions," Picard said, his diplomatic tone obvious even over the static that still plagued the connection. "Were I in President Khozak's position, without the aid of Counselor Troi, I don't know that I wouldn't have the same suspicions as he."

"Understood, Captain. But about the comm units—"

"He has apologized, Number One, but he would prefer they not be replaced, at least not immediately. President Khozak has agreed to keep this link open, however. He assures me it will be monitored at all times."

"As you wish, Captain. You should know, however, there was another series of energy surges just minutes ago, all from the vicinity of the mines. I assume they were related somehow to Zalkan's disappearance."

"I would assume the same, Number One. My own speculation would be that the mines were being evacuated."

Or extra people and machines were being brought in to get at the dilithium quickly, now that Zalkan's people know they've been discovered, Riker thought, *but if the captain isn't saying it out loud, neither will I.* "Mine, too, Captain," he said. "Would President Khozak object if we sent another shuttlecraft down to verify it?"

"I would!" Khozak's voice came over the link. "Until we—"

"And how would you even *know* if they went down in the mine?" Denbahr asked angrily. "President Khozak, if you—"

"I'm well aware of your views," Khozak snapped, sounding rattled. "And of your friendship with the traitor Zalkan!"

"Zalkan is no traitor! He's done more for this city than—"

"I believe," Picard's voice overrode Denbahr's, "that a few minutes of rational discussion are in order."

"I am being rational!" Denbahr shot back. "It's this—this *president* who's being totally irrational."

"Calm discussion, then," Picard said. "President Khozak?"

"It would be a great relief, Captain," Khozak said, "but with Technician Denbahr present—"

Picard cut off another outburst by Denbahr. "We can start the discussion," he said, "by bringing her up to date on the matter of Zalkan."

With questions and loud expressions of disbelief, the updating took nearly half an hour, by which time Riker and Worf were back on the bridge. In the meantime, some inventive work on the EM link had reduced the static to a more tolerable level. Picard, with occasional assists from Troi, had kept the discussion, if not calm, at least not explosive.

The only exception was when, reluctantly, Khozak admitted there were secret "listening devices" in offices, labs, and apartments all over the city, and that it was through one of those that he had overheard Zalkan's revelations.

"I didn't put the devices in," Khozak protested when Denbahr finally calmed down. "Most, I was told, were installed at least fifty years ago. Some were in use before the cities were sealed. This was almost the first time I've ever used them, any of them. Most don't even work anymore. But when I saw Zalkan talking to these people in the Council Chambers and looking as if he were about to go into shock, and then when I saw they were going into that 'private' lab of his, the purpose of which he has *never* satisfactorily explained to me . . ."

He shook his head. "I tried the system, and it worked. All I can say is, it was extremely fortunate that I did, considering what I learned."

Obviously not everyone agreed, but in the end an interim "agreement" on most other matters was reached. The next day, a second shuttlecraft would bring someone down to check the mines, to try to determine what the dozen or more energy surges had signified. The same shuttlecraft would then pick up Khozak and return him to the *Enterprise* while Picard, Data, Troi, and Koralus remained in the city. Meanwhile, Riker would contact Starfleet and arrange for one or more someones "in authority" to speak directly with Khozak. Riker had expected Denbahr at some point to wonder angrily—and rightly—why Khozak would believe someone "in authority" hundreds of parsecs away when he wouldn't believe Captain Picard or anyone else when they were standing directly in front of him, but to Riker's surprise she remained silent, as she had for much of the later discussion. Perhaps, he thought, she was simply trying to digest the news she had finally been forced to accept about Zalkan.

Finally, after a last-minute request by Data that Ensign Thompson check on Spot occasionally, particularly in the event that more energy surges were detected, the static-laced EM link was broken. Riker passed the request on, even tried to feign interest as Thompson explained the discussions he and Data had been having about their increasingly nervous cats. Finally, he settled back in the captain's chair, grimaced inwardly, and began to prepare a series of subspace messages to Starfleet.

Somehow, Zalkan managed to hang on to consciousness as the blinding light faded from around him and he collapsed to the cold, concrete floor. Then the once-familiar face of one of his fellow conspirators was looming over him in the near darkness.

"Zalkan? Is it you?" The muted voice was filled with easily as much disbelief and shock as Zalkan had expected. No one left behind on this Krantin had seen him since he had jumped to that other Krantin nearly fifteen years ago, so they would be prepared for his having aged. What they would not be prepared for, he knew, was his weakness, his deterioration. He had jumped only twice, once to Krantin and now back, and yet he knew that, because of his attempts to develop a blocking field, he looked far worse than even those Directorate pilots who had jumped fifty and sixty times and were due to be "lost" in another flight or two, before their deterioration became too obvious.

"Everyone must be pulled back from the mines," he managed to whisper before utter exhaustion pulled his eyelids down like lead weights and the rasping sound of his own breathing faded from his ears.

When Zalkan awakened, it was to the painful pricking of a needle being withdrawn from his left arm. Forcing his eyes to open, he saw an empty, red-stained bottle being disconnected from the other end of the tube that ended in the needle.

Blood.

They had given him new blood, he wondered how much. However much, it would revive him only temporarily. It would give him the strength to tell them what needed to be told. After that, he might last an hour or a day, certainly little more.

But that was enough. He would almost welcome the end. There was nothing left for him but the anguish and guilt that racked him for having failed. He would have to tell them that his gamble—a gamble he had been trapped into but one which, hindsight told him, he could still have avoided—he would have to tell them that his gamble with the strangers from the stars had not only failed but backfired.

And, in all probability, his people's decades-long struggle would then be ended. Barring a miracle, the Directorate spies would learn of the true location of the dilithium and would take it. With their massive machines and virtually unlimited power, with no need for the secrecy and caution his own tiny group had been shackled by, they could jump the dilithium and the surrounding rock from that Krantin to this with little more effort than it took to jump their massive ore carriers in the asteroid belt. The likelihood that the entire tunnel system would collapse when tens of thousands of cubic meters of rock and soil and dilithium vanished in what amounted to a massive underground implosion was of no concern to them, any more than what the Directorate had done to the rest of that Krantin over the centuries.

Struggling to sit up, Zalkan began to talk.

When he finished speaking and the others began, he learned that the situation was even worse than he had known, worse even than he could have imagined.

Chapter Sixteen

As ALWAYS when he was snatched from a sound sleep, Commander William Riker lurched toward consciousness with shreds of dreams still clinging to him. This time, not surprisingly, they involved Deanna. And Lwaxana, who was seated imperiously in her luxurious home on Betazed in a transplanted captain's chair while all around her swirled the polluted, acrid-scented atmosphere of Krantin. Riker himself, transmuted into the clean-shaven ensign he had once been, stood defiantly before her while Deanna's body appeared and disappeared in the noxious mists that billowed around his feet and he struggled to formulate a satisfactory response to the question Lwaxana seemed to have been asking since the beginning of time: "Will Riker, what have you let happen to my daughter?"

"Commander Riker!" Not Lwaxana's imperious tones, but the anxious voice of Ensign Thompson exploding out of nowhere, sending the distorted images of Betazed swirling into chaos.

"Commander Riker!" the voice repeated, yanking him the rest of the way into full wakefulness.

Blinking away the last remnants of the images, Riker responded even as he threw his legs over the side of the bed and sat up. "Riker here. What is it, Ensign?"

"A massive energy surge, Commander, probably nearby in space. Sensors indicate a ship proceeding toward us on impulse power from the direction of the surge."

"On my way. Notify Lieutenant Worf."

"In the process."

"Is the EM link to Krantin still open?"

"Yes, sir. Shall I—"

"Not yet. Just be sure it stays open."

Signing off, Riker quickly finished dressing and raced for the bridge. When he arrived, a small ship not unlike the one that had approached and fired on the *Enterprise* earlier was visible at the center of the screen. A faint halo of light only partially obscured it.

"This is what came through?"

"Apparently, Commander." Ensign Thompson was still at the tactical station. "It is approaching at the equivalent of minimum impulse from the direction of the surge."

"Response to our hails?"

"None yet, sir."

"Weapons?"

"Laser devices similar to the earlier ship, sir, but none appear to be activated."

"A pleasant change. Pilot?"

"Presumably, and three passengers."

Worf, making a last-minute adjustment to the ceremonial sash that always adorned his uniform, emerged from the turbolift and strode to the tactical station, where Ensign Thompson quickly filled him in.

"Keep hailing it, Lieutenant," Riker said. "Ensign, take Science One and see what more you can get from that ship."

"Another surge, sir," Worf announced as the ensign hurried to the back of the bridge, "from the same general direction as the first. It was roughly twice as powerful as the first."

"Another ship?" Riker wondered.

"Apparently, Commander," Thompson said from the science station. "There is *something* there, at least."

"EM response from first ship, Commander," Worf said.

"Let's hear it."

A male voice, speaking rapidly and loudly, filled the bridge. "You must protect us, take us aboard. The Directorate will send someone after us the second it realizes we have jumped."

"There is a ship behind you already," Riker said. "It appeared in approximately the same area that you did. Now—identify yourself."

There was a gasp through the EM link. "They have found us already! I was certain we had at least a few minutes! Please, you must protect us!"

"I repeat, identify yourselves."

"They will kill us! Is that not reason enough?"

"Not until you identify yourself. And your pursuers."

"They are the Directorate! They are responsible for virtually destroying this world below you!"

Riker's mind flashed back to what Picard had told him only hours ago. "This 'Directorate' is responsible for the Plague?" he asked.

"If 'Plague' is what you call what has fouled the world's atmosphere—and the space around it—for hundreds of years, yes!"

"You still have not identified your*selves*. Who are you and why is the—Directorate, you said?—pursuing you?"

"Commander," Worf said, "the second ship is overtaking the first. If its weapons are comparable to those on earlier ships, they will be in firing range within three minutes."

"We are part of a group working against the Directorate," the voice from the approaching ship said, speaking rapidly, "but we have been helpless until now. The Directorate controls everything!"

Zalkan's group? Riker wondered but said nothing.

"When we learned of your presence here," the voice continued, "we thought—"

"How did you learn of us?" Riker interrupted. On the screen, the second ship had become visible as a ball of light many times brighter than the faint halo around the first. It must be traveling at least at quarter impulse, Riker thought.

"The ships you encountered when you arrived were the Directorate's," the voice said. "Word of your existence is everywhere in the Directorate now."

"And how did your opposing group learn—"

"We do not openly oppose them!" the voice almost screamed. "No one can! We are—"

"An underground group?" Riker interrupted. He held back from mentioning Zalkan's name. If this was a trick—

"Yes! We were part of the Directorate, and we heard—"

"If you were part of the Directorate, if your organization was secret, what happened? How did they find out you were working against them?"

"I don't know! When we heard about your ship and what it was capable of, we began to make plans to contact you, but we must have been careless—or the Directorate has spies in our midst or maybe they've known about us all along but it never mattered until now, when we decided to contact you!"

"The second ship will be within laser range of the first in less than a minute, Commander," Worf said.

But the pursuing ship wasn't waiting. On the screen, a series of laser bursts emerged from the ball of light that was the pursuer. One struck the nearer ship squarely but seemed to have little effect except to increase the halo that still surrounded it. The others swept past harmlessly, though one produced a faint glow as it grazed the *Enterprise* shields.

"You see?" the voice from the nearer ship shouted. "They will kill us all!" The nearer ship was in direct visual range now, its impulse engines reversing, bringing it to a halt only kilometers distant. The halo faded and vanished.

"Damage, Lieutenant?" Riker snapped.

"Minimal. They are still out of effective laser range, but—"

A second series of laser bursts flared across the screen, two of them buffeting the nearer ship, two others flaring more brightly against the *Enterprise* screens.

"Minor damage to their impulse drive, Commander," Worf said. "The range is decreasing rapidly. Another direct hit would almost certainly disable the drive."

"Very well," Riker said, grimacing, knowing the decision had to be made, and made now. "Lieutenant, extend our shields to enclose the nearer ship. And keep close watch on *its* lasers. Any indication they're preparing to fire, bring the shields in, fast!"

"Shields extended, Commander. Lasers remain inactive on the first ship. The pursuing vessel still does not respond to our hail."

"Warn them about the shield, whether they respond or not."

As expected, there was no response. Riker briefly debated contacting Krantin and the captain but decided against it. Unless Zalkan had returned—and there had been no surges to indicate that he had—no one there would know any more about this other Krantin or the Directorate than Riker himself.

On the screen, the nearer ship now hovered almost in the shadow of the *Enterprise*. The second ship emerged from the ball of energy as its impulse engines reversed and brought it to a halt barely a kilometer short of the *Enterprise* shields.

"Its lasers are primed to fire again, Commander," Worf said.

"Only one life-form on board," Thompson added from Science One. "Humanoid, possibly Krantinese."

"Transmit on all EM frequencies, Lieutenant," Riker said, pausing while Worf tapped at the comm panel.

"Ready, Commander."

"Identify yourself," Riker said. "And in case you don't already know it, your lasers are ineffective against our shields."

For a full minute, there was only a tense silence. Then: "Lasers returning to standby," Worf said.

Moments later, a new voice, even deeper than Worf's, rumbled through the bridge. "Alien starship," it said stiffly, "we demand that you allow us access to the ship you are shielding."

So, you do know how to speak. "Identify yourself and state the reasons for your demands," Riker said.

"And I might remind you that threats against a Federation starship are not taken lightly." *Not that similar reminders regarding the kidnapping of Federation officers did much good with Khozak,* he thought irritably.

"I don't know what or where this 'Federation' of yours is," the voice shot back, "but this star system is surely outside its jurisdiction."

At least it's in the same universe. "We are assisting the people of Krantin," Riker said. "I repeat: Identify yourself."

Another silence, and then: "I represent the Directorate. The people aboard the ship you are misguidedly protecting are wanted criminals."

"They say that you are the criminals, not they. They say that you are responsible for the near-destruction of Krantin."

"They are lying! They are traitors, no more, no less. I demand you surrender them to me."

"Not until I know more. If you would care to come aboard and discuss the matter face-to-face, together with those from the other ship, I can send a shuttlecraft for you."

For several seconds there was only silence. Then: "We do not 'discuss' those or any other matters with wanted criminals and traitors, nor with their so-called protectors."

"Energy surge—" Worf began, but before the words were out, the viewscreen and the sensors were blinded. When vision returned to the screen and the sensors recovered from their brief overload, the Directorate ship was gone.

"So," Riker said, eying the remaining ship, "I suppose we had best invite this lot aboard for a chat. And see if you can raise the captain."

* * *

Each breath of the toxic air burned Ahl Denbahr's unprotected lungs. Desperately, she scrabbled on the floor of the lab, searching for the breathing mask she knew must be there. But there was something more important than the breathing mask, she realized abruptly, and she looked up and found herself no longer in the lab but on a barren hilltop that was rising higher with each aching breath. Overhead another world appeared through the poisonous haze, rushing at her from the depths of space, but as it grew larger and larger she saw that it wasn't another planet, wasn't another Krantin as she had thought, but a gigantic face with mountains and valleys for features, a face that she knew she should recognize but could not, a face which, if she could only recall the name that went with it, she could call to and it would stop its crushing descent before it smashed her and her world into—

Gasping, she came awake, her muscles achingly tense, her body bathed in an icy sweat. For a disoriented moment, the terror-laden thought shot through her mind that she had once again surrendered to the fantasies of the computer, but it was gone as quickly as it had come. No one would willingly submit to such surreal horrors as these, let alone seek them out.

Then it all came rushing back: Zalkan. The Plague. The people from the stars. Her impotent rage at Khozak and his unconscionable wasting of valuable—vital, irreplaceable!—time, his stubborn refusal to look beyond his own blind paranoia.

But there was nothing she could do about it, she thought, grimacing at the memory of her last confrontation with him, when she had tried to return the comm units to the one called Picard. It had only made the situation even worse. Khozak had destroyed the comm units, leaving them dependent on the radio in the lab, which, like everything else, could die at any moment.

What they *should* be doing was begging this Federation for all the help it could give. What Zalkan was or was not responsible for didn't matter. Whose side he was really on was of no importance. All that mattered was, something called the Federation existed, and it had ships like the *Enterprise,* ships and people capable of—of she didn't know what. This Federation was Krantin's only hope.

And even if Khozak's worst paranoid fears were true, if the *Enterprise* was out to "steal" the dilithium or do other terrible things, what difference did it make? How could matters be worse than they already were? When your entire world will be dead in little more than a decade, there's not a lot to lose by taking a chance and trusting in the goodwill and kindness of strangers.

Grimacing, she threw back the covers and sat up. No more sleep tonight, not the way her mind and stomach were churning, and even if she were able to sleep, she would be faced with dreams even more terrifying and bizarre than reality.

Not turning any lights on, she crossed to her terminal and voiced it on as she sat down. Only a microphone and speaker and screen. After Zalkan had pulled her loose from two years of fantasies, she had ripped out the helmet and all the tactile connectors.

"Plague revenge fantasies," she said, and titles began scrolling up the screen.

"Description. Forty-eight," she said, spotting a likely title.

The screen froze, number forty-eight highlighted. "An expedition to the fifth planet discovers an abandoned alien base, suspected of triggering the Plague," the computer's neutral voice began. "Artifacts found on the base are returned to Krantin, where they are analyzed and improved upon, thereby enabling a second expedition to track the aliens to what is thought to be their homeworld and to turn the Plague back on them when evidence is found proving they were indeed responsible for the Plague. The surviving aliens, however, are able to send a distress signal to their true homeworld, and—"

"Terminate description. Terminate session."

She sank back in the chair as the screen faded to black. She remembered the fantasy she herself had been submerged in when Zalkan had pulled her free that morning ten years ago. In that one, as in countless others, aliens had come to Krantin to check on the results of an experiment they had casually started a thousand years before, but they were found out. In the end, as always, their homeworld—or had it been an Empire that time?—had been destroyed by an avenging fleet from Krantin.

Could she blame Khozak for his paranoia? Like everyone, he had been raised on the revenge fantasies, a thousand variations on a single theme: Aliens found to be responsible for the Plague are destroyed. They were second in popularity only to pastoral fantasies about the world Krantin had been a thousand years ago, its air clean and breathable, its lands fertile, its pretechnological cities open to blue-green skies.

And her own sharp reaction to Khozak's paranoia had only reinforced it. She should have held her tongue. She realized now that the one called Picard had been following the sensible course—diplomatic discussion, not angry confrontation.

But Khozak was so infuriating, and these people from the stars were so obviously a—

A rasping buzz shattered the silent darkness, sending her bolt upright in the chair, her skin tingling, heart pounding. It had been ten years since she had last heard that sound. Zalkan had been at her door, and she had been lying on the cot, working up the energy to detach herself from the computer long enough for her daily meal.

She stood at the door, her room still dark. "Who is it?" she asked loudly, pressing her ear against the door. Even ten years ago, the buzzer had been all that worked. The voice system had died sometime in the two years she had been prisoner of the fantasies.

"Zalkan has sent me," a muffled voice said. "He desperately needs your help."

Her heart leaped. Ten years ago, he had saved her from the fantasies, and now—

Without hesitation, without thinking or wondering about the accusations she had heard leveled at him, without wondering how she could possibly help him, without even wondering if the person on the other side of the door had really been sent by Zalkan, she snatched open the door.

Chapter Seventeen

AHL DENBAHR SWALLOWED AWAY her jittery nerves and seated herself before her computer screen. Zalkan's messenger, Ormgren, stood to the side, well out of reach of the video pickup, frowning skeptically. He was not happy with her "plan," but he had been unable to suggest anything better after nearly half an hour of discussion.

"Here goes," she said, and spoke Khozak's access code into the audio pickup. To her surprise, the president's face appeared on her computer screen within seconds. From his image, she couldn't tell if he had simply not even gone to bed and tried to sleep or if, like her, he had been awakened and been unable to go back to sleep. Whatever the situation, he didn't look happy, and he looked even less happy when he saw it was Denbahr who was calling him.

"What do you want *now?*" he snapped. His voice

sounded as frayed and exhausted as he looked. "Haven't you caused enough trouble?"

A sharp retort formed instantly in her mind, but she forced herself to pause and swallow the words. Without his cooperation, she couldn't get near the people from the stars, and if she failed in this, Krantin's last chance for survival would be gone.

"I'm sorry," she said, forcing herself to sound penitent rather than defiant.

"I'm sure you are, for a great many things. Or you should be. But what's so important it can't wait till morning?"

"I have an idea how to find out if the people from the stars are telling the truth or lying."

His eyes widened skeptically. "How?"

"I have to talk to them."

"Why?"

"I told you, to find out if they're telling the truth or not."

"You're talking in circles, Technician! Now tell me precisely how you can determine if they're telling the truth."

"It's not something I can explain easily."

"Try, Technician. If you don't, this conversation is over."

Stifling an almost irresistible surge of anger, she managed to limit herself to a frown while she thought furiously. Wherever they were, Khozak had doubtless posted guards, so even if she managed to find out where they were, she didn't have a chance of getting to them without Khozak's cooperation.

"You see these?" she said abruptly, holding up a half-dozen tiny gray disks less than a centimeter across. From the other side of her dimly lit room, out of reach of the video pickup, a startled gasp was abruptly cut short. She kept her eyes straight ahead, focused on Khozak's image on the screen, and hoped he hadn't heard Ormgren.

"I see them," he said, still frowning but giving no indication he'd heard anything other than her words. "What are they?"

"I don't know. They were given to Zalkan the first day by the one called Riker—rather secretively, now that I think back to it," she improvised. "But so much was happening, I didn't think any more about it, and I'd completely forgotten about them until tonight."

"And?" Khozak prompted irritably when she paused, trying to think what to say next.

"And," she went on, "whatever they are, they must be important to Zalkan. I *think* he sent someone back for them."

Khozak's frown turned to an angry scowl. "What happened?"

"I couldn't sleep, so I went back to the lab. I don't know what I was hoping to find, maybe just look through my records and see if they'd help me remember more about the last ten years with Zalkan, see if I could remember anything he'd said or done that would mean something, now that we know what he is, where he's from." That much was almost true; she'd *thought* about doing just that and probably would have eventually—if Ormgren hadn't shown up.

"But when I was in the hall outside the lab," she went on, "I saw a flash of light inside, just like the one when he disappeared. I thought maybe he'd come back, so I rushed in as soon as I could get the door unlocked, only it wasn't Zalkan. It was a young man I'd never seen before, dark like most of the ones from the stars. And he was digging through Zalkan's desk."

Denbahr shrugged. "I yelled at him, and he ran. Practically knocked me over getting by me. So I started looking through the desk, too, and that's when I found these things. And then I remembered what they were—or where Zalkan had gotten them, anyway."

"And how will these objects, whatever they are, prove whether the people from the stars are lying or not?"

"I'll show these things to them," she said, suddenly proud of herself for coming up with such a story on the spur of the moment, under this kind of pressure. "I'll make up some story about how I found them and how I think maybe they might be from Zalkan's world, and I'll ask them if they can analyze them and tell us what they are. If they say they don't know what they are, then we'll know they're lying, that they're involved with Zalkan and probably whoever's responsible for the Plague."

"And suppose they see through your simple little trick?" Khozak asked, scowling. "Suppose they admit they gave them to Zalkan and make up an explanation? If you don't know what the objects are, how will you know if their explanation is true or not?"

Denbahr sighed, though she wanted to explode. "I admit, I probably wouldn't. But at least there's a chance we'll prove they're lying, which is more than you've been able to do so far. And if we do, you'll be in a much better position when you speak to those higher-ups tomorrow. You'll know *they're* probably lying, too."

Khozak was silent for several seconds, his scowl deepening at first, then distorting into a look of anguish.

"But I don't *want* them to be lying!" he burst out. "I really don't!" His image shuddered.

"Then just assume they're telling the truth," she said, forcing herself to speak calmly, "as I have. And let me do this test, which they will almost certainly pass."

Still he hesitated.

"What do you have to lose?" she asked, unable anymore to totally bottle up the anger and frustration at his resistance. "Are you afraid I'll try to pull something? Is that it? Look, you and your guards can stay with me the whole time. You can have me hauled out and arrested whenever you want to." She paused, shaking her head in angry disbelief. "What is it you're afraid of, Khozak? That I'm going to help them escape? If I were able to do *that,* I'd've done it already, before you locked them up and hid them away!"

For a long moment he was silent. Finally he sighed resignedly, very much like a man who's decided he does indeed have nothing left to lose. "Very well, Technician. But don't blame me if waking them up at this time of night irritates them."

Twenty minutes later, Denbahr and Khozak and half a dozen of his security officers were at the door to the suite Picard and the others had been confined to. Denbahr was carrying Data's tricorder. The disks— the markers—were in her pocket.

Data, who must have heard them approaching, was waiting for them just inside the main room of the suite when Khozak opened the door. Picard and Troi, still in their uniforms, were emerging from two of the bedrooms. Koralus came through a third door a moment later. All eyes but those of Koralus fell on the tricorder, but none of the three spoke.

"I'm sorry to disturb you," Khozak began, but was cut off by Picard.

"If you truly do not wish to disturb us," he said dryly, "you might consider returning us to our shuttlecraft."

Khozak swallowed nervously. "Technician Denbahr has found something that could be important," he said.

"I found some things in Zalkan's lab," she said, stepping past Khozak. "I've never seen anything like them before. They certainly aren't anything either he or I had ever worked on, and I wasn't able to analyze them. I was hoping you might be able to tell us what they are."

"Is that why you brought Lieutenant Data's tricorder?" Picard asked when Denbahr paused and reached into her pocket.

She nodded and pulled four of the gray disks from her pocket and quickly handed one to each of the three from the *Enterprise*.

"They could be computer chips of some kind," Troi said, turning hers over in her hand.

"You don't recognize them, then?" Khozak said a moment later.

"Recognize?" Picard looked at Khozak, who in turn looked toward Denbahr.

Denbahr turned to Koralus and handed him the fourth rectangle. "What about you?" she asked as he took it in his hand and frowned puzzledly. "Is this something you might've seen a hundred years ago?"

"What nonsense is this?" Khozak asked. "You said you had a plan—"

Denbahr's hand had returned to her pocket as Khozak started to speak. She took one of the remaining disks and, as Zalkan's messenger had instructed her, squeezed it as hard as she could between thumb and forefinger.

She felt a tingle over every square centimeter of her body, then a numbness, a dizziness. If she had been able to move, she would have fallen.

In the distance, she heard Khozak—or someone;

she couldn't be sure, the sound was so muffled—
shouting at her. She caught none of the words.
Koralus and the three from the stars were turning
toward her.

Suddenly, she was enveloped in a blinding glare. A
moment later, her ears popped painfully, as if she'd
just undergone an atmospheric pressure change.
When her sight finally returned, the room and
Khozak and the guards were gone.

Riker scowled as he turned from the tactical station, once again under Ensign Thompson's ministrations. Despite Khozak's promise, a dozen attempts
had failed to get a response on the EM link to Jalkor.
There had also been an unexplained energy surge
from somewhere in the city.

At least the team he had sent down to check on
Picard's shuttlecraft had found it apparently un-
touched. It sat deserted outside Jalkor's only functioning airlock, its security system armed and operational, set to send a subspace message to the *Enterprise* at the first sign of attempted tampering and to
lift off if the tampering persisted and grew forceful
enough to threaten damage. As instructed, the team
left an activated comm unit attached to the
shuttlecraft entrance, another in plain sight on the
ground immediately outside the city's outer airlock
door, and two more hidden in the rubble at the side of
the decaying road.

But there were more immediate concerns than
Khozak's broken promise and the unchanged condition of the captain's shuttlecraft.

Riker returned his full attention to the double
image on the main viewscreen. On the left, the ship of
the alien "defectors" floated in space, still inside the
extended shields. On the right, the shuttlecraft return-

ing from the alien ship was settling to the deck of the main shuttlebay.

Lieutenant Worf emerged within seconds and turned to wait for the other occupants. The four aliens appeared then, moving hesitantly, wearing gray-green tunics, trousers, and boots, all of which had the look of uniforms, particularly the rectangular and triangular insignia that were distributed in varying numbers and arrangements on all the tunics. Unlike the Krantinese with their Data-white faces and hands, these were darker, almost coppery, although the eyes of two of them appeared haggard and lifeless even as they looked around, gawking at the comparative immensity of the shuttlebay. One flinched and stumbled, half falling, when he saw the massive doors still open to space, the atmosphere contained only by the invisible annular forcefield. One of the three security officers immediately behind the aliens caught his arm and helped him back to his feet.

Worf glanced in the direction of the monitor that was transmitting the image to the bridge, then stepped back out of earshot of the four. "Commander," he said quietly into his comm unit, "none of them are carrying anything my tricorder can identify as a weapon. However, it does show that each has a microchip-sized device implanted near the base of the skull."

Riker grimaced. Yet another problem. "Could it be a communication device?" he asked.

"Perhaps, but if so, it is currently inactive."

"Very well, take them directly to sickbay. Dr. Crusher's instruments can probably tell us more, maybe even how to remove the devices, if that's possible."

"On our way, Commander," Worf said, turning and signaling to the security detail.

"Dr. Crusher," Riker said, "you heard?" Crusher, as a senior officer, had been roused shortly after Riker and had been observing events on a small monitor in her office in sickbay.

"I heard and saw, Will. Implants aside, none of them look to be in particularly good health. However, if nothing else, examining them may give me more of a database to work with, and the medical computer and I need all the help we can get."

On the screen, the alien ship continued to hang silently in space while Worf and the aliens and the rest of the security detail crowded into the nearest turbolift.

Khozak stood frozen in Zalkan's lab, his stomach seeming to drop through the floor as he waited for his vision to return. Finally, after several tortured seconds, individual figures and objects emerged from the curtain of constantly shifting shadows, and he almost cried out as his fears were confirmed.

They were gone! All four prisoners—and Denbahr, of course.

He should have known it was a trick! The warning signs had all been there for him to see. The woman's naive belief in the miracles these people from the stars—*supposedly* from the stars—had promised. Her blind loyalty to Zalkan. Even after learning who the scientist really was, what his world was responsible for, she had continued to defend him. She might even have known all along, might have been a part of what had been destroying Krantin for more than five centuries. And in his desperation, he had fallen for her outlandish story of a "test"—which had been nothing more than a ruse to gain her access to the prisoners, to allow her to—to do whatever she had done that had enabled them to go wherever Zalkan had gone.

He shook his head violently, as if to shake the thoughts free, and turned to the six guards, who seemed even more stunned than he. Fighting to keep his voice steady, he issued his orders—send guards immediately to the airlock and don't let anyone through without his personal approval. And take as many men as could be found and do what should have been done hours ago—take charge of the ship, the so-called shuttlecraft, if, as he hoped, it still sat waiting for the escaped prisoners.

If it was already gone—

He shuddered. Whether it was gone or not, whether Denbahr was simply a dupe or an active agent of the Plague, no matter what the nature and motives of these people from the stars, he had bungled the situation badly. If this Federation was indeed a potential benefactor, he had alienated it by taking its representatives prisoner and now had let them be kidnapped from under his nose. And if the Federation was an agent of the Plague, in collusion with Zalkan's world, he had let his hostages escape and had lost what little influence they might have given him.

And, one way or another, sooner or later, he was going to have to respond to their ship hovering in orbit above Jalkor and try to find out which kind of disaster he had precipitated.

Chapter Eighteen

COMMANDER WILLIAM RIKER turned abruptly from the main viewscreen as he heard the turbolift hiss open. It was, he was glad to see, Dr. Crusher.

"Conclusions, Doctor?" he asked as she strode down the ramp toward him.

The four defectors, after she had thoroughly examined them, had been deposited temporarily behind a detention screen in the security area, and Riker had been waiting impatiently for her report.

"For one thing," she said, dropping into Counselor Troi's seat next to Riker in the captain's, "they said they already knew all about the implants—which did have a number of microchips in them, by the way, along with some other items I wasn't able to identify. I gave Geordi the results of the scans; maybe he'll be able to make sense out of them."

"They knew about them?" Riker echoed after a moment.

214

"They're disciplinary devices, apparently—and one of the chief reasons the four of them defected. Or escaped. Everyone who works for the Directorate, even if it's just sweeping the floors, has to have an implant like that. They didn't know precisely what the implants could do to them, or so they said. But they didn't know of anyone who'd ever been able to successfully defy or escape the Directorate, either."

"Did they want you to try to remove them?"

She shook her head. "They're not in a hurry for it. For one thing, the Directorate lets it be known that any attempt to remove an implant results in a slow and painful death. And from what the exams told me, that might just be true. The implants could be booby-trapped. Those items I couldn't identify might do anything. Some of them looked as if they were wired directly into the nervous system."

Riker grimaced. "Nice bunch, this Directorate. Did you tell them all this?"

"I did, but they didn't seem worried. The only way the implants can be activated, they say, is by the Directorate's main computer network, and there's no way it can reach through and get at them here."

"How did they react to the idea that jumping from one world to the other had already been slowly killing them?"

She shook her head. "They didn't believe it, at least not at first. But when I 'guessed right' about which ones of them had made the most jumps, and explained the results of a few of their metabolic tests, they looked a little less confident."

"And when you compared their metabolic functions with those of Zalkan?"

"None were as low as Zalkan's. However, all four of them had a problem that Zalkan didn't: a decided deficiency in what I assume are vital trace elements."

215

"Did you—"

"Commander," Worf rumbled from the tactical station, "an energy surge, roughly the same heading as the previous ones."

"Stand by to raise shields. Any indication of a ship?"

"None yet, Commander."

"Open all EM channels. If there's something there and it transmits anything at all—"

"Low-level EM pulse on the same heading as the energy surge, Commander. It was apparently directional, centered on the *Enterprise.*"

Riker frowned. *What now?* "Any information content?"

"Unknown, Commander. The computer has found none other than frequency and duration. Unless—"

Worf broke off, his eyes darting across the displays. "A second energy surge has just been detected, on the same heading as the previous one."

"Lieutenant Worf!" The voice of one of the ensigns from the security detail came over Worf's comm unit. "The prisoners—something's happening to them!" The distant sound of screams could be heard in the background.

Dr. Crusher was on her feet, racing for the turbolift, a split second after the ensign's words.

"Looks as if they were wrong, Commander," she said over her shoulder. "Apparently the Directorate *can* reach them here."

Riker hesitated only a moment, then raced after her.

All four prisoners were dead by the time Dr. Crusher and he arrived at the detention area.

Picard was gripped by a feeling of paralysis, and for just an instant, he thought that Riker had somehow located them and was beaming them up despite the loss of the comm units. But then the similarity to being transported ended in a wave of knee-bending weakness and a brilliant, all-enveloping flash, and he realized that whatever had happened to Zalkan a few hours before must now be happening to him.

When his vision returned, he was standing on a bare, concrete floor, his legs wobbling from the feeling of weakness that still gripped him. Data, Troi, Koralus, and Zalkan's assistant were almost on top of him, not nearly as far away as they had been a second before. Data was steadying Troi, his android body obviously not as affected by the process as the flesh-and-blood bodies of Troi and himself and, from the look of them, the Krantinese.

Khozak and the guards were nowhere to be seen. Not surprising, Picard thought abruptly as he realized what must have happened. It had been the mysterious devices Denbahr had "found" in Zalkan's lab. Like Starfleet comm units, they must enable people and things to be located by whatever machine it was that snatched them between worlds. And Khozak and the guards had not been given any.

All around him in the dim light was what looked like a random collection of dilapidated consoles of all sizes and shapes, with all manner of controls and screens. A bearded man with none of the sunless pallor of the Krantinese stood at one of the consoles, the only one in sight that had a lighted screen and controls. From somewhere, not from the console but seemingly from beneath the floor he stood on, came a deep-throated humming. The man stood with his left hand raised beside his face, as if still shielding his eyes from the bright flash that had undoubtedly marked the group's arrival. He wore what struck Picard immediately as a uniform—gray-green tunic, trousers, and boots with geometric insignia on the front of the tunic. The room itself had the look of an abandoned warehouse—concrete block walls barely visible beyond the stacks of crates and cartons that took up most of the space not occupied by the paint-chipped consoles. No doors or windows were visible anywhere.

The man at the controls frowned as he lowered the shielding hand and looked around from the screen and saw Picard and the other three standing there. The fingers of his right hand remained poised over the controls, as if he were about to enter another set of commands.

"Who are you?" he asked warily. "Where is Ormgren?"

"I am Ahl Denbahr," the technician said quickly, setting Data's tricorder on the floor. "These are the people from the stars that Ormgren was sent to warn. He came to me for help in finding them, but they were being held captive by Khozak. Bringing them here was the only way we could think of to set them free so they could get word to their ship."

"But Ormgren—"

"He had to stay behind to place a marker near the city's airlock. As soon as we know it's in place, we can return there and I can take them through the airlock to the smaller ship they came down in."

"Then no one on their main ship yet knows what we suspect?"

Denbahr shook her head, bringing a grimace to the man's face.

"Perhaps it is just as well," he said. "Our informant has had more to say since Ormgren was sent. And Zalkan now has an idea that the situation could be turned to our advantage, might even bring an end to the Directorate."

He stepped away from the console. "I will have to take a chance and let this run unattended. You must talk to Zalkan, all of you."

Then he was striding toward them. "Come," he said, "follow me, quickly. It may already be too late."

"Too late for what?" Picard asked, balking as his strength returned. "Where are we? And why have you—"

"Too late to save your ship," the man snapped, starting toward a narrow corridor between a ragged line of consoles and stacks of cartons. "And Krantin. Your entire crew may be about to be killed, your ship stolen by the Directorate. Then, with that out of the way, what's left of Krantin will probably be next."

Picard's stomach tightened at the words, but he merely looked questioningly toward Troi, who, except for still breathing heavily, seemed to have recovered her strength and composure.

She looked at the man, her dark brown eyes meeting his as he paused and turned back to frown at them impatiently. After a moment, she nodded. "He is telling the truth, Captain."

Ensign Thompson, his round, bearded face bordering on haggard as he emerged from Data's room and headed for the nearest turbolift, wanted nothing more than a good night's sleep. Volunteering for the late-night shift on the tactical station had seemed like a good idea at the time—he could get the experience working the station and its myriad readouts and controls without the added pressure of Captain Picard being on the bridge to look over his shoulder. And even at the Academy, he had always been a night person, though in space the distinction was more academic than real. Despite the twenty-four-hour "days" that were generally observed on the *Enter-*

prise, he had no way of knowing if they bore any relationship to the days and nights he had grown up with. His biological clock had been reset so many times, he often wondered if it hadn't long ago cracked a mainspring—or a microchip—in confusion.

His inner clock, however, wasn't the main problem. The main problem these days was that he was a light sleeper, and ever since they had entered the Krantin system with its so-called Plague cloud and its energy surges, Fido had not been his usual placid self. Normally the cat would curl up on one corner of the bed and rouse himself only when the covers were tossed back on top of him and he caught the odor of a feline breakfast coming from the replicator terminal. Now, however, if Thompson so much as turned over in his sleep, the motion would wake Fido, who would complain just loudly enough to make sure he wasn't the only being in the room that was awake. If one of the energy surges occurred—and Data's computer records of both Fido and Spot seemed to confirm the connection—the complaint seemed loud and violent enough to wake people in adjoining quarters. Several minutes of patient reassurance was the least that was required before further sleep could even be considered.

And now that Data was being detained—temporarily, he assumed—on Krantin and Spot needed similar ministrations, as well as someone to get her food down from the replicator terminal, his moments of sleep were even sparser. This time, Spot had been fairly easy to calm, as if she were becoming accustomed to the energy surges, or perhaps it was just her feline ability to ignore unpleasant aspects of her existence once she determined they were merely unpleasant rather than dangerous.

Yawning, he entered the turbolift, which waited

patiently for the yawn to be completed and a deck number to be requested, then closed its doors and silently flowed away.

The doors were just opening on Thompson's deck and he was stifling yet another yawn when a brilliant light erupted behind him in the lift. His immediate thought that, despite the *Enterprise*'s almost foolproof systems, something had exploded shocked him into full alertness and sent him leaping into the corridor even as the light vanished.

Spinning around, he was confronted with a figure all in black, including gloves and tight-fitting hood with openings only for the eyes. The figure had a weapon of some kind in one hand, the other hand clenched tightly into a fist. For a moment, the figure staggered and seemed about to fall, as if it had dropped from a great distance and was having trouble regaining its balance.

"Intruder, Deck Seven," Thompson snapped, slapping his comm unit on in the same moment he leaped back into the turbolift and made a grab for the weapon. For an instant he thought he had it, almost ripping it from the black-gloved hand, but then, as if triggered by the attempt, the grip tightened and a deafening explosion smashed at his ears. A moment later he realized he was falling, his left leg giving way under him, and the weapon was being jerked away. A sudden pain erupted in his collapsing leg, and he thudded to the floor of the turbolift, convinced that in another moment the weapon, now gripped tightly in the other's hand, would be turned on him again.

Pushing against the side wall with his good leg, he grabbed for the figure's feet, hoping against hope he could upend him and get a second chance at the weapon or even jar it from his grip in the fall.

But his fingers closed on air. The figure, instead of

standing and turning the weapon toward him, had leaped out of the turbolift. Without even a glance at Thompson, the figure spun around and raced away down the corridor of Deck 7.

"Intruder on Deck Seven," he reported, avoiding looking at his leg, "armed with handheld projectile weapon. He's already used it on me." He slumped back as the doors hissed shut. "Sickbay," he said to the waiting elevator, "and when we get there, don't close the door until someone comes and gets me."

By the time Dr. Crusher was working on his leg in sickbay, a red alert had been issued.

Chapter Nineteen

DENBAHR AND KORALUS and the three star people silently followed the bearded man—whose name, he had finally told them, was Albrect—through the maze of consoles and cartons. Finally they came to a large metal sliding door, which he quickly unlocked and relocked behind them. Then they were in a corridor with similar doors on both sides, labeled only with letters and numbers. After a good fifty meters, they passed a freight elevator and continued on to a small passenger elevator around a corner in an alcove. Albrect's right thumbprint opened it, and the six crowded inside.

Denbahr's ears popped twice as the cramped elevator shot upward. When it came to a relatively smooth if sudden stop, Albrect placed a thumb—his left one this time—over a scanner and waited as the hidden circuits did their work and released the door.

Denbahr squinted as the door opened into brightness, then gasped as she realized what she was seeing. Sunlight as brilliant as any computer fantasy flooded into a large room through a floor-to-ceiling window that filled most of the facing wall. Centered in front of the window between two large but wilting indoor plants was a massive desk with what looked to be a computer screen angling up out of its surface, but she barely noticed the furnishings as, almost reflexively, she ran to the window. Only dimly was she aware that Koralus had come to stand beside her, as wide-eyed in wonder as she.

She hadn't seen anything so beautiful since she had been extricated from the computer fantasies. She had *never* seen anything so beautiful—no one now living on Krantin, even Koralus, had ever seen anything even remotely so beautiful in the real world. A brilliant sun just shedding the redness of dawn was a few degrees above the horizon, shining through a sky as pure and clear as Krantin's was dark and polluted. Looking down, she gasped again. Two hundred meters below the window was a wooded area with half a dozen trails meandering through acres and acres of trees. A score or more of people, seemingly unaware of the miracle they were walking through, were visible on the trails. The only blemishes were a dozen or so trees that were dead or dying, their branches bare, but they were as nothing to the hundreds and hundreds of others still vibrant in their blue-green splendor.

Beyond the other three sides of the forested area were what looked like dozens of massive power plants, some with the cooling towers that proclaimed them prefusion nuclear, others with the smokestacks that once on early Krantin had indicated the burning of fossil fuels. But here the stacks were short, protruding only a dozen meters or so above the broad roofs, each one ending in a rectangular cap of some kind. The air above all but one was as gloriously clear as the air everywhere else, but above the one, clouds of black smoke billowed.

Albrect cursed as he saw the smoke and rushed across the room, brushing past Denbahr and Koralus as he rounded the desk. A voice responded within a second of his tapping a code into the computer screen. "Number seventeen has shut down again," he snapped to whoever was on the screen. "Get the burner shut down *now* before someone less forgiving than myself discovers it! And have it back on-line before the day is out, is that understood?"

There was a pause as the screen made an unintelligible reply.

"If you're short of parts, requisition whatever you need! I'll authorize it in advance. Just get it done!"

Picard and Data had crossed to the window while Albrect had been talking. Picard gazed out through the glass next to Denbahr while Data, after a brief but comprehensive glance, turned to one of the wilting plants and pulled his tricorder from its case. After a quick check of a series of readouts, he glanced out through the window a moment, then detached a half-dozen of the drooping leaves from the plant and stowed them in a compartment of the tricorder case.

Picard's attention, meanwhile, had remained on the outer world. "Those are some of the devices Zalkan told us about?" he asked, pointing at the rectangular caps on the tops of the stacks as Albrect stepped away from the desk. "The devices that keep your air clean and Krantin's unbreathable?"

The man nodded as he headed toward a door in the wall on the right. "Those are the grids," he said, "the visible parts the public sees. The drivers—the controls and generators—are somewhere in this building, behind so many locked doors and Directorate guards that even I have trouble getting in."

"You're Directorate, then?" Picard asked.

Albrect glanced down at the insignia on his tunic as he pressed his right thumb against a sensor and waited for the door to be released. "The ones who count think I am, at least for now," he said glancing back toward Denbahr and Koralus, who still seemed to be in the grip of what they saw beyond the window. "Or until they catch me at something like this," he added as the door finally opened.

"Come," he snapped. "We have no time for gawking."

Denbahr straightened with a start. With an obvious effort, she tore her eyes from that outer world and turned her back on it. For a fleeting moment, her eyes met Picard's, and he saw the longing in them, the plea for the help he only hoped he could give. A moment later Koralus turned from the window, his face revealing nothing. Then they were all following Albrect as he hurried down the lushly carpeted hallway beyond the door he had opened.

"Not that anything will matter much longer if you can't keep your ship out of their hands," Albrect said grimly, glancing at Picard. "What few hopes we still have would all be finished then, along with what's left of both Krantins."

At a door at the far end of hall, he repeated the identification process, this time with his right index finger. This door slid open more ponderously than the other, revealing what appeared to be a meeting room with table and chairs that had been pushed to one side to make room for a bed.

And on the bed—

Picard's eyes widened as he realized that the emaciated figure on the bed was Zalkan. The scientist looked as if he had aged a decade or more in the hours since he had been snatched from his lab. He was still fully dressed, his eyes closed. A man, as dark as Albrect and with Directorate insignia on the front of his tunic, sat stiffly in a chair at the table, the upper half of his face covered by a heavy blindfold. A woman, slightly darker than the blindfolded man, sat across the table from him, holding a projectile weapon loosely on the tabletop as she faced him.

"You are all familiar with Zalkan, I gather," Albrect said quickly. "As for the others, the blindfolded one is called Strankor. He claims to have defected from the Directorate for reasons of conscience. The one guarding him is one of our agents within the Directorate. She brought him to us when she heard what he had to say." Albrect grimaced. "I sincerely hope he is a spy and has not told us a word of truth. That would be immeasurably better than believing his story."

On the bed, Zalkan roused enough to open his eyes. He smiled weakly as he saw Denbahr, but his face fell when he recognized the others standing just behind her.

"Why are they here?" he asked, his voice barely audible.

Quickly, Albrect recounted Denbahr's brief explanation of how Ormgren's mission to warn the *Enterprise* had gotten twisted out of shape by Khozak's paranoia.

On the bed, Zalkan struggled to raise himself, and Denbahr hurried to help him and then support him once he was sitting up. "Picard," he said, his voice seeming to gain strength now that he had forced himself to sit up, "I must return with you to your ship. It is the only way to save Krantin."

Then it is surely lost, Picard thought bleakly. The

scientist could probably not survive being taken from the room, let alone the jump back to that other Krantin.

"Before we make any rash decisions," he said, nodding at Troi, "I would like to hear just what it is we're up against." He turned to the blindfolded man. "Whatever you told them, tell us now—quickly!"

The man stiffened, his head coming up as if to look at Picard despite the blindfold. "You are the captain of the ship from the stars?"

"I am. Now tell me your story."

And he did, quickly and succinctly, painting a picture of a Directorate leadership as self-centered and callous as any group Picard had ever encountered. The moment the leaders had learned of the existence of the *Enterprise* and that it was proposing to help Krantin, they panicked and withdrew all the ships the Directorate had operating in the asteroid belt. They also immediately ordered that all the secret recording devices linked to Jalkor's computers be monitored continuously in hopes of finding out what the Krantinese knew about the "star people" and what sort of "help" the *Enterprise* and its "Federation" were offering. The only worthwhile piece of information they found, however, came when they stumbled across Khozak's search of the records computer and learned that the records involving the onetime mining area had been virtually wiped out. This led them to have their own Directorate computers checked more closely, where they found similar smaller alterations in the hundred-year-old records of a massive strip-mining project in the corresponding area—now a pit nearly two kilometers deep—on their own world. And in what appeared to be overlooked remnants of even older records, they found that it was this mine, not the asteroids, that was the actual source of the scraps of dilithium that still existed in their world.

Their immediate reaction was to want to call in one of their biggest machines, even more powerful than those used to jump the massive ore carriers in the asteroid belt. They would use it to scoop out the ground above the dilithium in great chunks, then retrieve the dilithium itself.

But they were too afraid of the *Enterprise* to actually put that plan into action. Instead, they decided they would first have to either destroy or take over the *Enterprise,* which, with their jump machines, they felt confident they could do. With the *Enterprise* out of the way, they would take the dilithium and then breach the walls of Jalkor, killing its five million inhabitants—not because they posed a direct threat but because the Directorate feared that, if they were allowed to live and if another Federation ship ever came to that other Krantin, the story of what happened would come out and the Federation might someday be able to pursue the Directorate to their own Krantin.

When Strankor was finished, all questions answered, the guard, at a word from Albrect, prodded the man to his feet and took him into the hall, closing the massive door behind them.

Troi looked up at Picard and nodded grimly. "He is frightened and far from certain that he has done the right thing," she said, "and there is more to his reason for defecting than his professed horror at the Directorate's planned destruction of Jalkor. There is a fear that he might be in danger himself. But I am virtually certain that he is otherwise telling the truth."

* * *

"Engineering, Deck Thirty-six," the computer announced, following up with a set of precise coordinates.

On Deck 36, the security ensign nearest the coordinates, phaser set on heavy stun, had already seen the flash around the nearest curve in the corridor and was racing toward it, eyes peeled for yet another of the black-clad invaders. All other lookouts, on 36 and all other decks, maintained their positions, backs against the corridor walls, eyes scanning both directions, phasers ready. On Decks 35 and 37, at least one pair of eyes darted to each door that opened on the emergency stairs that gave access to every deck on the *Enterprise* in the event of a catastrophic power failure that put even the turbolift system out of commission.

This time it had actually been two almost simultaneous flashes. One of the black-clad figures was lurching in one direction, firing a projectile weapon seemingly at nothing, when the security ensign came in view. The other, momentarily unnoticed as the ensign's eyes focused on the first, seemed to have overcome the initial unsteadiness that had plagued all the others and raced full speed toward Main Engineering.

The first was brought down within seconds and vanished like all the others in a second flash as his unconscious body skidded along the corridor floor. The second, both hands seemingly empty, came within a few meters of Main Engineering before he went the way of the first, brought down by one of Geordi's people, on loan to security for the duration of the alert.

On the bridge, Lieutenant Worf continued to monitor the tactical station readouts, wondering if the current lull—the twin surges in Engineering had been the only ones for more than a minute—was just that, a lull, or if whoever was sending them was finally running out of volunteers. With the phasers set at their current level, just short of lethal—Worf had recommended an even higher setting—the intruders would not be available for a second run for some time yet.

Worf had long ago lost count of the number of energy surges. The first intruder, the one who had wounded Ensign Thompson, had gone uncaught for nearly five minutes, racing around the decks of the crew quarters like someone lost and frantically looking for a way out, finally somehow finding the emergency stairs and darting up to Deck 5.

Three others had appeared within seconds of the first, two in the shuttlebay and one in the corridor outside sickbay, and a minute later another four. For nearly an hour it had continued—so far. Setting up security fields had helped, but not enough, and they often were a hindrance to getting a wounded security officer to sickbay. Several times intruders had slammed into fields full-tilt, but the effect was the same as that of a phaser. Within seconds, they vanished, and sooner or later another would show up on the other side of the field.

At one time, there were at least thirty scattered about the *Enterprise* like a cloud of biting gnats, firing their projectile weapons at any crew members they saw, then racing off in seemingly random directions, sometimes firing blindly down an empty corridor. One had even emerged from the turbolift onto the bridge but had been phasered by Riker before he could fire his own weapon. Like all the others, he had vanished in a burst of light almost the moment he hit the floor.

Geordi had experimented briefly with the blocking field but found it essentially useless under these conditions. As he had feared from the start, its effects had proven at least as damaging to living tissue as the fields it blocked, so it could not simply be turned on and left running. To be effective at all, it would have to be timed to come on only for the second or two during which an intruder was attempting to come through, and there was no way that that could ever be predicted. Even if he were able to hook directly into the sensors and set them to trigger the blocking field at the first indication of a surge the sensors picked up, it would not be soon enough. The time to build up the blocking field seemed to match within a few milliseconds the time it took the field they were trying to block to build up. And even if he *could* have cut the buildup time of the blocking field, even if he could have blocked every intruder, he wouldn't have dared do it. By the hundredth one, if his computer models were correct, the cumulative effects of even those brief bursts of the blocking field would have been verging on lethal for everyone within range, which was essentially every living being on the *Enterprise*.

What finally seemed to have stemmed the tide was nothing technological, unless you counted turning the task of announcing surge locations over to the computer, just an application of common sense. Riker had blanketed the ship with security people and regular crew members, every one with a ready phaser set on heavy stun. In the last twenty minutes, no crew member had been wounded and no intruder had remained active more than twenty or thirty seconds. Most were dispatched almost before the flash announcing their arrival had faded.

If this was an attempt to take over the *Enterprise,* Riker thought as he waited for the next energy surge and the virtually simultaneous announcement of its location by the computer, it was an extremely clumsy one. If they had sent the intruders all through simultaneously, it might have worked. At the very least, the casualties would have been much worse, the damage to the ship from their projectile weapons much greater. Whatever it had been—

"Commander!" Worf announced abruptly. "Someone is attempting unauthorized entry into the shuttlecraft on the surface. It is lifting off on automatic, no occupants."

The captain's shuttlecraft? "You're certain no one is inside? Not even one of our shoot-'em-up friends from up here?"

"No life-forms are indicated, Commander. The shuttle sensors, however, indicate a half-dozen life-forms on the ground directly beneath the shuttlecraft."

"The ones who tried to break in," Riker said with a grimace. "Did those communicators we left outside the airlock pick up anything?"

Quickly, Worf called up the records, but there was little in them. The grating sound of the airlock opening, which at least indicated that the would-be shuttlecraft hijackers had come from the city. Footsteps, several sets, as they approached the shuttlecraft. Noises, subdued at first, then louder, as they poked and prodded at the shuttlecraft. And finally, unintelligible shouts and the sound of the shuttlecraft lifting off.

"Khozak again," Riker said with a scowl. "First he takes the captain prisoner and now he tries this!" He turned to Ensign Curtis at the Ops station. With the tactical station fully occupied with the seemingly omnipresent intruders, the comm function—and the continuing attempt to establish an EM link with

233

someone on the surface—had been transferred to Ops. "Any response at all, Ensign? Any indication anyone is even *listening* to us?"

"I believe someone is, Commander," Curtis reported. "An unmodulated EM carrier is present, indicating at least that the equipment down there hasn't been turned off. Whether anyone is listening, however, is another matter."

"Very well, Ensign. Keep at it." He shook his head. "Tell them that until they respond and give us proof that our people are still safe, President Khozak can forget about talking to anyone higher up in the Federation."

"Yes, sir."

"You might also mention that we do not appreciate attempts to tamper with the captain's shuttlecraft and—"

"Energy surge, Commander," Worf broke in, "on the planet." He darted looks at other readouts. "The shuttlecraft sensors picked it up as well. The surge was inside the city, within a few hundred meters of the shuttlecraft's original position outside the city's airlock."

Riker thought for a second. "Lieutenant, access the shuttlecraft's computer log for the last hour. See if it picked up any surges down there while we were being swamped up here."

"Only one, sir," Worf announced a moment later, "somewhere near the center of the city. Its magnitude was similar to the more recent one—and to those on the *Enterprise.*"

Riker turned back to Ensign Curtis at Ops. "Is their equipment still turned on down there?"

She glanced at a readout. "It appears to be, Commander."

"All right. Patch me through and set it up to repeat

until we get a response. I'll take a shot at them. Figuratively speaking—at least for now."

Her fingers darted across the face of the console. "Ready, Commander."

Riker pulled in a breath. "President Khozak or whoever is listening down there: This is Commander William Riker of the Federation *Starship Enterprise*. First, unless you respond and provide proof that Captain Picard and the others are still safe, the discussions you requested with Federation authorities will not take place. Nor will any such discussions ever occur unless and until you satisfactorily explain the attempted assault on the captain's shuttlecraft. Second, there have been two energy surges in your city in the last hour, one near the center, the second only moments ago in the vicinity of your airlock. Finally, the *Enterprise* has been under attack for more than an hour. Black-clad intruders with projectile weapons not unlike the ones with which your guards greeted my away team have been appearing on all decks, and I would very much appreciate any information you might have. If you do not respond, we will have no choice but to assume you are in some way responsible and act accordingly."

Signaling he was finished, Riker grimaced as he turned back to the tactical station and wondered just what "accordingly" meant. With any luck—not that they'd had much so far—Khozak would come to his senses and he wouldn't have to figure it out.

Chapter Twenty

KHOZAK LISTENED to Riker's message for the third time, his stomach knotting more tightly each time. Virtually everything he had done had turned out wrong, and now—*now* they suspected him of having something to do with an attack on their ship! And the energy surge near the airlock—Denbahr and the star people returning, hoping to reach their shuttlecraft? He hoped it was as benign as that, and not someone from the Directorate coming through.

Blinking, he came out of his self-induced paralysis and stabbed at the button that put him in communication with his people at the airlock. Tersely, he ordered them to recall the ones who had attempted to enter the shuttlecraft and then to leave, to disregard his earlier orders to allow no one through. The last thing he wanted now was for them or anyone to try to recapture the onetime prisoners.

He turned to the radio, the same one Denbahr had

used to contact the ship a seeming lifetime ago. There was nothing for it but to throw himself on these people's mercy and hope against hope that Denbahr's naive belief in their goodwill and patience was closer to the truth than his own far darker suspicions. And that whatever Denbahr had done to or for the four, it had not resulted in death or capture by the Directorate, even though he could not keep from his mind the thought that the Deserter Koralus and the Directorate deserved each other.

He touched the switch that would send his voice on its way. Pulling in a shuddering breath, he said, "This is President Khozak, Commander Riker."

Picard was grim-faced as they descended in Albrect's private elevator, made even more crowded by the presence of Zalkan, his frail body cradled in Data's arms. He knew the scientist was right, that his plan was the only chance to save both the *Enterprise* and what remained of Krantin, but that knowledge didn't make it any easier to watch a man purposely hasten his own death. He would unhesitatingly offer himself up for lesser gains, had in fact done it more than once and had found it far easier than this. His creed, one of the reasons he had joined Starfleet, was to protect others, not to stand by when others sacrificed themselves, no matter how high the stakes or how narrow the options.

"Picard," the scientist had said when Troi had vouched again for the reality of the threat and the truthfulness of his own analysis, "you spoke earlier of a short-term treatment your doctor could administer to me, a metabolic enhancer. Would it give me the time I need?"

"I don't know," Picard said. "There are too many

variables. The only certainty is that you would be dead within hours."

The scientist had smiled faintly. "That is already a certainty, Captain, no matter what I do, if not within hours then within days. Only a substantial infusion of new blood has given me what little strength I have, and even that would not help after the transfer back to Krantin. And I do not propose to lie here, clinging to a few more useless days, while there is even the slightest chance that the Directorate can be defeated and Krantin saved."

And Picard had nodded grimly, conceding the truth in Zalkan's words.

The elevator door slid open at Albrect's command and the group hurried down the still-deserted sub-basement corridor. As Albrect approached the massive sliding door they had emerged from earlier, the faint humming coming from beyond the door suddenly increased in volume. Albrect stiffened and lunged the remaining meters to the door and jammed his key into the lock. Through the tiny crack at the bottom of the door, a sliver of light flashed. Then the door was open and Albrect was racing back through the twisted corridors of consoles and packing cartons. The others followed, Picard pausing to slide the door shut.

A young man in dark coveralls sat on the floor near the active consoles, apparently recovering from the transfer. He lurched to his feet when he saw Denbahr.

"It won't work," he said, still short of breath. "I left the markers in an abandoned house near the airlock, but the area is crawling with guards. Several of them were sent outside, either to guard the ship or to try to take it over."

"They won't get in," Picard said, frowning, "but if

they try too vigorously, it would lift off, out of their reach. And out of ours, too, unfortunately. Either way, I don't see how we could reach it if Khozak is determined to stop us from getting through the airlock." He turned to Albrect. "Is there any way you can transfer one of us to the area outside the airlock and bring him back? If the shuttlecraft is still there—"

Albrect shook his head. "With one of the new Directorate machines, perhaps, but not with this one. All it can do is home in on a marker. Or make a random transfer to the general vicinity of this same area on that Krantin, and that would be more than a hundred kilometers from the city."

"Are there other markers in the city?" Picard asked. "If one of us could get to a radio, we at least could warn the *Enterprise* even if we couldn't get back on board ourselves."

Albrect shook his head. "Very few."

"And the only radios I know of that I could guide you to," Denbahr said, "are the ones I used before, in the lab, and the ones in the machines we use to drive to the power plant. But those are all in the storage and repair area that the airlock opens into, so they'd be almost as hard to get to as your shuttlecraft."

"If I were to transfer alone," Data, still cradling a weakening Zalkan in his arms, said, "I believe the odds are good that I could either evade or overpower the guards long enough to reach one of the machines you speak of and make use of the radio."

"If the radio in the first one you try works," Denbahr said. "Or in the first half-dozen. We might have a better chance going after the one in the lab." She glanced at Ormgren. "You did say there was a marker somewhere in the building?"

The young man nodded. "In the subbasement. It might not be functional, however. It is one that Zalkan placed there several years ago."

"At least I'd be in familiar territory," Denbahr said. She shook her head. "It's too bad there isn't a way to come out around the power plant. That's where I left my machine when you people picked me up that first day, and its radio is working, or at least it was when I left it there a couple of days ago."

"The power plant?" Albrect brightened. "There may be a way," he said. "For a time, we used an area only a kilometer or so from it for a dump site." When Denbahr looked at him questioningly, he went on. "The material from the mine. The only way to get it out is to transfer it here, and we obviously can't leave it lying around. It's tricky enough to keep a functioning jump machine down here without someone from the Directorate stumbling onto it. Storing the dirt and rock from the mines here would be impossible, so we have to jump it back to Krantin, somewhere far away from the mines. One of those somewheres was not far from the power plant. We stopped using it when we realized what it was and that you technicians were visiting it every few months. Now, if the marker there is still functional . . ."

As he had been speaking, Albrect had turned back to the console and tapped in a series of commands. After several seconds studying the screen, he nodded. "I can lock on to it," he said. "That's a good sign."

Picard nodded, beginning to have hope. "If it works, this could be better for us than reaching a radio inside the city. Mr. Data, you can go through and proceed to the power plant and the radio and contact the *Enterprise*. Have them send a shuttlecraft down immediately. Return for us the moment it arrives. If you do not return—" He turned to Albrect. "He *can* return, can he not?"

Albrect nodded. "As long as the Directorate doesn't find us here. And the more often we use the jumper, the more likely it is that someone will stumble onto us. That's one reason progress in the mines has been so slow. But yes, he can return."

"Very well. Data, if you do not return within half an hour, we will utilize the marker that Ormgren left near the airlock in Jalkor."

"Yes, Captain," Data said.

As the android lowered Zalkan gently toward the floor, the scientist stirred in his arms. "Tell them also to bring their magical potion," he whispered. "I begin to suspect I overestimated my ability to survive another transfer."

Riker scowled as he broke the connection with President Khozak. The man was a raving paranoid lunatic. Despite Khozak's mea-culpa confession and professed conversion, it didn't take a Deanna Troi to realize that he still didn't "trust" Riker or anyone connected with the Federation. If anything, he mistrusted them now more than ever. It was just that, finally, he must have decided he had dug himself into a hole so deep that no other choice remained.

But at least now Riker had some idea what had happened, and it wasn't good. Denbahr, presumably with help from Zalkan, had "rescued" Deanna, the captain, Data, and Koralus from under Khozak's nose, though he had trouble imagining why. Despite Khozak's rampant paranoia, the president hadn't been about to harm them. Unless, Riker thought uneasily, Denbahr had learned something about Khozak that might contradict that assumption. Or unless there was some connection between the rescue and the seemingly short-lived "invasion" of the *Enterprise,* which appeared to have drifted to an end with the twin surges in Engineering.

And the timing *was* suspicious, Riker had to acknowledge. The rescue had come at almost the peak of the Directorate assault—*assumed* Directorate assault—on the *Enterprise.* As a result, the energy surge associated with it hadn't been noticed for another half hour, when the review of the shuttlecraft records was conducted.

And the second surge, the one near the airlock, had coincided roughly with the end of the assault. Possibly sheer coincidence in both cases, but Riker mistrusted coincidence almost as much as President Khozak mistrusted the *Enterprise* and the Federation.

The only questions of any real import, however, were: Where had the four been taken, and why? And, *most* important, where were they now? From the evidence of the energy surge and Khozak's description of the "rescue," Riker assumed they had been taken to that other Krantin, the Krantin of the Directorate.

But why? Denbahr knew the ill effects of the transfers; she had seen Zalkan and now knew the reason for his condition. Admittedly, it would take several transfers to cause irreversible damage, but still, for her to subject not only them but herself to even one transfer, she must have thought it important.

But it wouldn't be just one transfer, not if it was indeed a rescue. They would have to be returned to this Krantin, or they would be prisoners forever in the Directorate Krantin, never able to return to the *Enterprise* or the Federation.

Or had they *already* returned? Was that what the

second surge had been, the one near the airlock? Had they returned there, hoping to get through the airlock to the shuttlecraft? If so, what had happened to them? Khozak swore that none of the dozen or more guards at the airlock had seen anyone other than each other since the time of the surge.

Was it even remotely possible that one of Khozak's paranoid fantasies was actually true, that Denbahr and/or Zalkan were in league with the Directorate and they had not rescued the *Enterprise* officers but kidnapped them? From his own impressions of the woman, not to mention Deanna's more informed opinion, he found that extremely hard to credit.

But the "rescue" made no sense either. Unless he was missing a major piece of information, which unfortunately was entirely possible, even likely.

For what seemed like hours but was in reality less than a minute, Riker remained in the captain's seat, his mind continuing to circle in frustration. If there was one thing he couldn't abide, had never been able to abide, it was sitting on the sidelines, simply waiting for developments when something inside him kept shouting at him to do something, if only to stir the pot and see what, if anything, floated to the top. That was one reason he preferred an away team to bridge duty. And when Deanna was the one who might be in danger—

Abruptly, he stood and turned to the tactical station. Speaking quickly, formulating his thoughts as he spoke, he issued a series of orders, then strode to the turbolift. "You have the conn, Mr. Worf," he concluded as the doors hissed shut behind him.

Chapter Twenty-one

LUCKILY DATA WAS NOT SUBJECT to the weakness and disorientation that humans experienced immediately after a transfer. It was even luckier that he had made the jump alone, carrying only a tricorder and a half-dozen markers, rather than with Denbahr, who had given him complete instructions for locating and operating the radio. As it was, he was able to recover his balance and catch himself before he had slid and lurched more than two or three meters down the steep slope of rocks and dirt he found himself on. His uniform was torn in several places, but his body suffered only the android equivalent of minor scratches.

And the tricorder, in its field case suspended from his shoulder, was unharmed despite several impacts.

Carefully, dislodging as little of the rubble as possible, he made his way to the bottom and level ground. Visibility was even worse than it had been the other times he had been exposed to this Krantin's atmosphere. Low clouds hid even the reddish glow that was all that reached the planet from its sun. Even the power plant, little more than a kilometer distant according to Denbahr, was lost in fog and Plague.

But it was there, he saw a moment later as the tricorder zeroed in on the powerful and easily identifiable fusion processes. Depositing one of the markers on a flat area a few meters from the mound of rubble, he broke into a run, unhindered by the unbreathable atmosphere.

Once the plant came in sight, Data altered his course to head directly for the spot on the road where he remembered Denbahr parking her vehicle, and he was at its door only minutes after he had emerged on the rubble slope.

As Denbahr had said, the outer and inner doors were unlocked and the magnetic card that turned on the electrical system was protruding from its slot beneath the button that started the engine.

Quickly, he pushed it all the way into the slot and waited as the screen came to life, a series of icons indicating what was operating and what was not. Almost immediately, he saw that the radio was not among the indicated functions. Just as quickly, he located the radio itself and checked the associated switches. All were set as Denbahr had indicated they should be.

He pulled the card out and replaced it. Like everything else on Krantin, Denbahr had said, the radio often showed its age and needed coaxing.

This time, it came on, but when Data set it to transmit, it crackled briefly and fell silent, and a moment later its "active" icon vanished from the screen.

Data considered the situation for all of half a

second. Time was of the essence, if Zalkan was to be believed, and Counselor Troi had said he was. Given time, he might be able to repair the radio. It might even come back to life on its own. But it might not. And there were other radios, Denbahr had said, in the area near the city's airlock. The chances of his eluding or quickly overpowering the guards there, if they opposed him, were better, he decided, than continuing to try this radio.

Placing one of the markers on the other seat so he or Denbahr could return and try again if the captain desired, he took the marker that would return him to Albrect's basement station in his hand.

Restlessly, Riker circled low over the mounds and sinkholes that marked the mines. There was no progress anywhere. Examination of the captain's shuttlecraft, returned by remote control to the *Enterprise,* had yielded nothing. The security detail he had sent in another shuttlecraft to the airlock had reported no activity and, except for one ensign remaining on board, was in the process of being let inside the city. Khozak himself had come on the radio and assured both Riker and the leader of the security detail that neither Denbahr nor any of the *Enterprise* personnel had been seen in the vicinity of the airlock or anywhere else in Jalkor. However, he had no objection to the detail's coming in with tricorders and conducting their own search.

Riker grimaced as he took the shuttlecraft to a higher altitude and continued to watch the sensor displays. What had he been expecting? For Deanna or the captain or Data to conveniently materialize at the entrance to the mines? The only even semilogical reason for his patrolling the area was that it was the primary area on Krantin in which energy surges had been detected and the *only* place outside of Jalkor where humanoid life-forms had been detected. The real reason, though, was that he couldn't bring himself to stay on the *Enterprise* bridge, simply waiting. In that respect, he was no Captain Picard. The captain seemed to have infinite patience, a characteristic Riker had sometimes envied but never shared with him. His impatience had served him well sometimes, ill others, but if he didn't give in to it now and then he would—

Suddenly, a change in the readouts leaped out at him.

An energy surge! But not here! In the city?

No, the indicated heading was at least ninety degrees from Jalkor. What—

The power plant! That was at least approximately on this heading, but more than a hundred kilometers distant. And the first time they had encountered Denbahr, she had been just leaving the power plant!

His heart was pounding as he took the shuttlecraft up sharply, locked the sensors on to the prominent signature of the fusion units, and accelerated along the new heading.

Within minutes, the power plant, blocky and sprawling, emerged from the rusty haze.

And there was a life-form somewhere down there!

But only one, not four. Who—

Abruptly, the readings solidified: an artificial life-form, humanoid and—

Data! But where was Deanna? The captain?

Locking the sensors on to this new target, he brought the shuttlecraft swooping down to ground level—and found himself only meters in front of the vehicle he had first seen Denbahr in.

* * *

Zalkan, his head still cradled in Denbahr's lap, opened his eyes again. This time Koralus stood over him, and the scientist smiled. It had been right, that first instinctive reaction to Koralus's name and face, the face he had seen a thousand times in his mind, though never before in reality. *His* Koralus, one of the first of the so-called underground, had been killed by the Directorate long before Zalkan had been born. But Zalkan had known him, if not in the flesh, in the words of his grandmother, and seeing and listening to this Koralus was like having her words come to life. The lives of the two men had been as different as the two Krantins they had inhabited, but their characters had been the same, just as the characters of the other "twins" had proved essentially the same in both worlds despite lives different in every detail. In one, rebelling against the Directorate had cost that Koralus his life. In the other, championing the Migration had cost this one even more dearly.

But now, if this desperate plan worked . . .

Albrect, once Zalkan had explained who Koralus was, had agreed immediately that Koralus's presence greatly strengthened the chances for stability if the Directorate was—*when* the Directorate was brought down.

But for that to happen, for the Directorate to be destroyed, he himself had to survive for another few minutes, until the one called Data returned with the magic potion.

But until then . . .

His eyes closed and again he drifted into exhausted sleep, his almost-grandfather's face still floating before him.

Data froze, his thumb millimeters from pressing down on the marker that would return him to that other Krantin. He very nearly decided to run a diagnostic on his own perceptual circuits, so unlikely did he consider what had suddenly appeared only meters in front of the vehicle: an *Enterprise* shuttlecraft. But the urgency of the situation and the tremendous amount of time the shuttlecraft, if real, would save him overcame the positronic logic circuits that, otherwise, would have demanded a diagnostic.

Opening the vehicle's outer door, he climbed out and dropped to the ground. An instant later, the door to the shuttlecraft opened and Commander Riker's voice boomed from the little ship's PA system. "Data! Get in here! What happened?"

Data was inside almost before Riker's words were out. "I will explain in a moment, Commander. Has a group claiming to be Directorate defectors been allowed on board the *Enterprise?*"

"Four of them came on board two or three hours ago," Riker said, frowning. "But how the devil did you know?"

"After the four were killed, has the *Enterprise* been invaded by several individuals, each——"

Scowling, Riker cut Data off. "How did you know— Never mind. Yes, we were almost overrun. There were hundreds of them, popping up everywhere, firing their weapons at anyone they saw, racing around with no rhyme or reason. But that's over now. No one was killed, at least not permanently, and the damage to the *Enterprise* was minor. And if they try it again, we're ready for them."

Data held out a marker for Riker to see: neutral gray, less than a centimeter in diameter. "Their purpose was not to invade or attack, Commander. Their sole purpose was to distribute objects similar to this as widely as possible."

"This? What is it? We found something similar implanted in the skulls of the defectors. They said they were for disciplinary purposes."

"Those may have been, but they were also assassination devices. They were almost certainly the cause of death of the so-called defectors, whom the Directorate killed in order to confirm their story and divert attention from their real purpose. Those devices, however, were not the same as these. The only similarity, I suspect, is that both types contain, for want of a better term, markers. They are similar to our comm units in that they allow the Directorate to lock on to them and transfer objects or personnel from their world to this and vice versa, to wherever the markers are located. The purported defectors planted the first ones, and the 'invaders' then used those first ones to come and plant more."

"So that's—" Riker grimaced. "There could be thousands of them. Those 'invaders' were everywhere. But what are they planning? Another even bigger 'invasion'? Bombs?"

"No," Data said, "an invasion could be easily countered, and explosives would damage the *Enterprise,* which they would prefer not to do. The Directorate plans to transfer great quantities of a deadly, fast-acting gas into all parts of the *Enterprise* simultaneously, killing everyone on board but leaving the ship intact."

"Field-effect suits—" Riker began, but Data cut him off.

"Neither field-effect suits nor breathing masks would be effective. Like the Plague on Krantin, the gas will materialize everywhere at once, including inside any protective devices, even within the lungs."

Abruptly, Riker turned to the shuttle's comm system and opened a channel to the *Enterprise*. Worf responded immediately.

"Lieutenant," Riker said, launching into a quick reprise of the essentials of what Data had told him, ending with instructions to institute an all-out search for the markers. "The objects in question are roughly circular, approximately—"

"There is no need to describe them, Commander," Worf broke in. "I have one here. The invader who reached the bridge apparently dropped several before you brought him down. I will assign all personnel to the search."

"Get to it," Riker said. "We'll be there as soon as we can." As he had been speaking, the shuttlecraft had reoriented itself, and now it zoomed upward. "Now," he said, turning again to Data, "where are Deanna and the captain? And Koralus?"

"They are safe in the other Krantin for the moment, waiting to be brought through. But first I must speak with Dr. Crusher."

Suppressing the impulse to ask if they were ill or injured, Riker instead got the shuttlecraft patched through to sickbay and nodded to Data.

"Dr. Crusher, this is Lieutenant Commander Data. Do you have a supply of CZ-fourteen available?"

"A small amount," she said, a puzzled frown evident in her voice, "but why do you—"

"Please, Doctor," Data broke in uncharacteristically, "I will explain in a moment. I need a hypospray with at least enough CZ-fourteen to administer to Zalkan, who will almost certainly not survive the transfer from his world to this without it."

"I don't understand either, Doctor," Riker said when Crusher hesitated, "but you know Data well enough to know that he wouldn't ask for something unless it was essential. Just have it ready by the time we arrive, which will be in approximately three minutes."

In those three minutes, Data raced through his explanation of the plan Picard and Zalkan had arrived at, concluding, as he exited the turbolift on Deck 12, "The captain feels the risk is justified in light of the almost certain consequences to both worlds if we attempt to flee instead of accepting that risk."

"Particularly since this Plague soup we're embedded in might not let us get out of range in time anyway," Riker said as the doors closed, cutting off any further words.

When Data reached sickbay, Beverly Crusher was on her hands and knees searching the floor of her office for markers. All nurses and medical technicians were doing the same in other areas, particularly the area around the biobeds the defectors had occupied during their examinations. When Data entered, she looked up with an uncharacteristic scowl, took a hypospray from her pocket, and handed it to him.

"You understand that this could kill even a healthy person in a matter of hours, Data," she said severely. "And even if Zalkan survives, the long-term treatment will be useless."

"I understand, Doctor. Zalkan understands as well. He feels it is the only rational course open to him, and the captain has come to agree with him."

"I see," she said in a tone indicating that she didn't see at all. "Very well. It's out of my hands."

"Thank you, Doctor. Now please, stand back. I must return."

"To that other world?"

He nodded, taking one of the markers and placing it on the floor of her office. "Do not allow that one to be disturbed, Doctor. I will need it to return with Zalkan and the others. And stand well clear of it until then."

With that, he took the return marker in his hand and, as soon as Dr. Crusher had turned away and started for the door to resume her search, squeezed it solidly between thumb and forefinger.

Chapter Twenty-two

PICARD WINCED in spite of himself as Data, even before the flash of his return had faded from the retinas of the watchers, knelt on the cold concrete floor and pressed the hypospray to Zalkan's arm. The scientist opened his eyes at the touch, managed a weak smile to Data, then an even weaker nod.

Data triggered the hypospray.

For a moment, there was no reaction, and Picard found himself leaning forward, searching the man's face for he knew not what. A hint that, now that it was too late, the scientist regretted his decision? Picard grimaced, wondering if he would allow himself any regrets if his own decision turned out to be wrong and in the last moment of his life he realized that the *Enterprise* would not saved but lost with all hands.

Zalkan stiffened, a slight moan escaping his lips. Then he shivered, not quite writhing, and Denbahr, her hand trembling, softly stroked his forehead. Troi knelt down opposite Data and laid her own hand lightly on Denbahr's.

Abruptly, the scientist went rigid, his teeth gritting, his head pressing harshly backward against Denbahr's legs, and Koralus, standing tensely next to Picard, seemed to wince in sympathy with his almost-grandson.

Just as abruptly, Zalkan went limp, and Denbahr gasped his name, as if afraid that he had died.

But his eyes opened then, and he smiled, a fleeting but normal smile despite the emaciated face.

And he sat up, stayed that way for a moment, as if to let his head clear, or perhaps just to savor the simple fact of the movement, then got to his feet with only a slight lurch.

"Come," he said, his face now grim as he moved toward the clear area in front of the active console, "we may already be too late."

Data caught Zalkan's arms and steadied him as the flash of the transfer faded and the scientist lurched and almost fell to the floor of Dr. Crusher's office. Fending off Crusher's efforts to subject Zalkan to a quick scan with her medical tricorder, Data guided him into the corridor.

"Knowing I have two minutes more or two minutes less is unimportant," Zalkan said over his shoulder as he seemed to regain his strength, "and taking the time to gain that knowledge would only deprive me of yet another minute of useful life."

In the corridor, two of Dr. Crusher's medical assistants were on their knees, looking for the tiny markers. A dozen meters down the corridor past the turbolift, near where an engineering ensign was doing the same, a transporter field shimmered into existence. Data's enhanced vision could distinguish a pile of a half-dozen markers surrounding a comm unit for an instant before the entire pile vanished. A second later, he knew, the pile would materialize with dozens of others on one of the cargo transporter pads where, as rapidly as the comm units could be pulled from the pile, they would be dispatched into space.

In the turbolift with Zalkan, Data silently and repeatedly reviewed the plans that had been developed literally a world away. Repeatedly, he came to the same conclusion: Under the circumstances, there was no way he could think to improve them. All reasonable eventualities were covered, and the probable result in all cases was the capture or destruction of the Directorate leadership and the survival of Jalkor. Unfortunately, the *Enterprise* and her crew fared less well in some scenarios.

But everything was being done that could be done. Every available crew member was involved in the search for the markers. The *Enterprise* had already moved into a higher orbit, high enough to put the planet below out of danger. Six crew members were in a shuttlecraft, standing off a thousand kilometers, maintaining a constant link with Starfleet.

In the most optimistic scenario, in which Zalkan had the time to give the computer a complete picture of all the possible ships the Directorate leadership might arrive in, the *Enterprise* crew would begin evacuating to the surface of Krantin the instant his work was completed. Every available shuttlecraft, including those normally used only for cargo, would be used, taking them to a spot safely away from Jalkor, where there would have been a small but unacceptable risk that their arrival would be noted and somehow passed on to the Directorate, thereby accelerating its schedule. Those still on board awaiting evacuation would continue the search-and-transport operation until transportation became available. With a great deal of luck, either all the markers would be found and disposed of or everyone but Data would be evacuated before the gas came.

In either case, Data, unaffected by the gas, would remain on the bridge. He would be there, waiting, when the Directorate leaders came through an hour later, by which time the reverse binary gas would have developed into its harmless component parts, allowing them to board safely. Then he would see if Strankor had been right. The man had assured him that the entire Directorate leadership would come through, and Troi had indicated that he was telling the truth. They would all come through because not a single one of them would trust any of the others to board such a valuable prize as the *Enterprise* without him. Their fear of treachery—a thoroughly justified fear, apparently—was too great for them to do anything but board it together. Then, when the number of ships matched the number of Directorate leaders that Strankor had indicated, Data would direct the computer to target the precise locations that Zalkan had specified in each ship. Finally, when they were within range, dozens of pinpoint, millisecond bursts of highest-intensity phaser fire would, theoretically, disable the jump circuits of every Directorate ship. Unlike the much longer bursts that would be required to destroy the ships, the millisecond disabling pulses could all be fired before any of the ships had a chance to react. And keeping them all from returning to that other Krantin was essential. If even one escaped, the Directorate would continue, and nothing the *Enterprise* could do could stop them from snatching the dilithium and destroying Jalkor.

The second scenario was less optimistic. If Zalkan was able to finish his work but evacuation was not completed in time, Data would still be waiting for the Directorate ships when they came through, but an indeterminate number of his fellow crew members would have been killed by the gas.

In the third scenario, the gas came before Zalkan was finished, and everyone but the six in the shuttlecraft would die. Without Zalkan's information, Data would not be able to simply disable the Directorate ships. He would have to destroy them. And the only sure way to do that was to wait until they drew close and the leaders began to board the *Enterprise*. Data would then override all the safety devices and programs and breach the containment field of an antimatter storage pod. The *Enterprise* and any ship within twenty kilometers would be vaporized. The six in the shuttlecraft standing off a thousand kilometers would report the demise of the *Enterprise* to Starfleet and wait for the arrival of another ship.

The turbolift door hissed open on the bridge, bringing Data's mind instantly back to the immediate present. At the science stations stood a pair of specialists in the design, construction, and history of impulse-drive ships; the station screens were blank and waiting for Zalkan's input. Seemingly fully recovered despite a flush that had begun to suffuse his features, the scientist strode rapidly to the stations at the rear of the bridge. Speaking rapidly even before he reached them, he began, essentially, to re-create on the screens and in the computer memory the half-dozen ships that he had helped design more than twenty years before, the ships which, according to Strankor, the Directorate leadership still used.

Barely a minute into his task, the turbolift doors opened again and Picard emerged alone.

"Counselor Troi, Technician Denbahr, and Koralus," Picard answered Riker's unspoken question, "have joined the search for the markers."

Riker nodded as he surrendered the captain's chair and quickly brought Picard up to date. "I'll join the search as well," he concluded, hurrying toward the turbolift. By the time he reached it, an area assignment by the computer was issuing from his comm unit. As the turbolift door opened, he almost tripped over an ensign on the floor on his hands and knees searching for the chip's faint signature.

For another few seconds Data continued to watch the first ship growing in detail and complexity on the science station screen. Abruptly he turned away. There was no need for him to watch the ships take shape. The computer was absorbing it all, and when the time came—*if* the time came—that he needed the information, it would be there for him. He could be more useful now in the search.

He was halfway to the turbolift when he heard Geordi's voice: "Commander, I'm getting nowhere on this. I can probably accomplish more if I join the search."

"Commander Riker has joined the search himself, Geordi," Picard said. "You're referring to the blocking field? Will said you had proven it to be at least as dangerous as you originally feared."

"Captain? Yes, the blocking field. And unless my computer models are way off, ten minutes' continuous use would almost certainly be fatal even to someone in perfect health. Even one or two minutes would produce noticeable and permanent effects. The only way this thing would be of any use is if you had a damned good idea of when the gas was coming. Then I could switch it on at the last second, but as it is, we can't use it without killing everyone on board, but if we don't use it—"

"Geordi," Data broke in. Listening to Geordi had somehow prompted an unexpected idea to emerge from the positronic storehouse that was the android's mind. To a human, it would have seemed like a sudden inspiration. To Data, it was only logic, a matter of making an association between two separate bits of information. "How much advance warning do you need?" he asked.

"Data? Approximately a second more than the sensors will give us."

"An additional three seconds, then, would be sufficient?"

"You mean five seconds total? That would do it easily, Data. But when we were being invaded, I tried everything I could think of to boost the sensors or speed them up, but nothing helped. The first inkling the sensors have of an upcoming jump is just under two seconds. I've even consolidated all the functions into the master systems-display panels down here in Engineering in order to cut out the lag time between the controls and the generator and between both of those and the deflector array. But no matter what I do, the generator takes almost half a second too long to reach full strength and get the energy into the deflector array. By the time the deflector array projects the field in and around the *Enterprise,* it's too late. Whatever was being sent is already here."

"Thank you, Geordi," Data said as he turned to Picard. "Captain, I suggest we locate Counselor Troi and tell her to meet me in my quarters immediately. And send someone to Ensign Thompson's quarters as well."

Picard, despite having no idea what Data was up to, agreed to the plan before the turbolift doors closed behind the android.

Chapter Twenty-three

"DATA, I CAN'T BELIEVE we're actually going to do this." Commander Geordi La Forge stood on one side of the reconfigured master systems display in the middle of Engineering, his VISOR focused on the sensor readouts that would indicate the beginnings of an energy surge. With some internal rerouting of signals, he had tweaked another millisecond or two off the blocking field buildup time, but it was still essentially half a second too slow. "Talk about your low-tech solutions . . ."

"It will work, Geordi," Data said, his eyes on the dual image on the display screen that angled up out of the tabletop station. In the left image, Ensign Curtis was shaking her head despairingly.

"It's not happening, Data," she said.

"Do not concern yourself, Ensign. Yours is a back-up function, in the event that Counselor Troi fails, which is not likely."

On the other half of the screen, Troi's eyes were closed as she concentrated. Uncharacteristic beads of sweat had appeared on her brow in the last minute.

Finally, she looked up. "Ready, Data," she said, though her subdued voice lacked some of its usual conviction.

"Geordi, make the transfer," Data said, positioning his fingers barely a millimeter above the control surface of the panel before him.

Geordi, shaking his head, tapped in the commands that disconnected the sensor-activated trigger and substituted the control a millimeter below Data's fingers.

For nearly a minute there was only silence. Then Geordi, his VISOR still focused on the display screens, said, "If this *doesn't* work, Data, don't blame yourself. It at least has a chance, which is more than I can say for anything I've managed to come up with."

"The only reason it has a chance, Geordi," Data said, his yellow eyes remaining unblinkingly on the image of his own room on the screen before him, "is that you first developed the blocking field."

"You know what I mean, Data. No matter what happens, it's not your fault. Hell, it's not my fault either. I just—" He paused, swallowing audibly. "I just wanted you to know that *I* wouldn't blame you, no matter how this turns out. And it's been good working with you." He risked a split-second glance at the image on the screen. "You, too, Counselor."

"It has been good for me, too, Geordi," Data said. "I have always considered you—"

His fingers dropped onto the control. Sensor readings streaked across both panels. Geordi's heart lunged for his throat. Seconds later, seeing no indication of an energy surge other than that created by the blocking field, he slumped in a queasy mixture of disappointment and relief. Quickly, he deactivated the field.

"False alarm, Data," he said.

"I see that now, Geordi," he said, observing the activity on the screen. His fingers had already returned to hovering above the control.

"At least we proved your reaction time," Geordi said. "And I guess we can stand a few false alarms. Better that than missing one and—"

Again Data's fingers dropped suddenly onto the control and the sensor readings once again filled the displays, but this time—

This time they indicated the buildup of an energy surge of unprecedented proportions.

But a surge that plateaued and stalled as the blocking field built to full strength at least a second before the surge would have reached its peak.

Then it faded and was gone.

Geordi let out a wordless shout and barely resisted the impulse to race around to Data's side of the display station and pound him on the back or hug him.

"That was it!" he said when he had control of his voice again. *"That was for real, Data! You did it!"*

Somehow, Geordi continued to watch the readouts. When the last traces of the energy surges faded, he waited another five seconds. Then, his body almost limp from relief, he deactivated the blocking field.

In Data's quarters, Troi also breathed a sigh of relief. Then, on the off chance that a second attempt would be made, she lowered herself to the floor and began to try to reset the detector, which had already stopped growling but still had a tail fuzzed out to twice its normal size.

* * *

There was no second attempt, although the detector was set off three more times as groups of Directorate ships flashed into existence a hundred kilometers out. The total exposure to the blocking field as a result of those false alarms, however, was less than thirty seconds, and Dr. Crusher was able to detect only the slightest effect in the few crew members she checked before she returned to the bridge.

Zalkan, his face seeming to grow more flushed with each minute, finished his computer reconstructions only moments after the last of the ships themselves appeared on the viewscreen. Leaning on Denbahr, he watched as Worf targeted the phasers, locking them on to a series of specific points inside each Directorate ship so that those points would be hit regardless of the positions of the ships.

Despite Crusher's insistence that he be taken to sickbay, Zalkan remained on the bridge, Picard helping him into the captain's chair, where he slumped, seemingly staying conscious by sheer effort of will. Troi was in her own chair on one side of the scientist, Denbahr in Riker's on the other. Each rested a hand gently on his. Tears streaked Denbahr's cheeks.

Finally, the Directorate ships began their approach. The sensors were still crippled by the Plague field, but what they did reveal confirmed at least the broad strokes of what Zalkan had given them.

And listening to the EM exchanges between the ships confirmed what Strankor had said: Neither the leader nor any of his lieutenants would trust any of the others out of their sight for a second when booty of any kind was involved, let alone something like the *Enterprise,* control of which was potentially even more valuable than the control the Directorate had for centuries exercised over the dimensional-transfer technology.

An hour and ten minutes after the gas had been sent—and blocked—the ships came within what Worf at the tactical station considered a safe range, the lead ship almost in the shadow of the *Enterprise.* Glancing at Zalkan, he initiated the firing program he and the scientist had so carefully constructed. In less than a second, the precisely targeted and timed phaser bursts struck every programmed target. A second later, tractor beams flashed out, freezing the ships in place.

"Energy buildup!" Worf said sharply, and for a moment everyone's stomach lurched as their eyes fastened on the screen, waiting helplessly for the flashes that would mean they had failed after all.

But there were no flashes. And Zalkan roused himself and smiled, a final moment of strength coming from somewhere deep within him. "They can try to pull the ships back," he said in a whisper, "but they cannot succeed, not without power provided by the ships themselves, which they no longer have."

He grimaced, much as he had when Data had first administered the CZ-14, and his eyes met Picard's. "We have won the battle, Captain," he said, the whisper even fainter. "Now you must not lose the peace."

His eyes closed and, a moment later, his breathing stopped.

When Picard turned away, he saw that Koralus had been standing quietly behind him, a tear trickling down one cheek.

Chapter Twenty-four

KHOZAK'S EYES BLAZED as he faced Picard and the other *Enterprise* officers across the table in the ship's main conference room. "You have these monsters in your hands? And still they live? And now you want me to *meet* them?" He turned to glare at Albrect, who sat at the far end of the table beyond Koralus and Denbahr and the rest of the Jalkor Council. "Is it not enough that you have tricked us into the same room with the *new* leader of the Directorate?"

"There is one in particular I would like you to meet, President Khozak," Picard said, ignoring the president's jab at Albrect. "We felt it might be instructive, particularly in light of your desire at one point to inject poison gas into the mines, not to mention your recent treatment of myself and my fellow officers."

"I have explained my reasons for those actions," Khozak said, his anger seeming to fade beneath a momentary facade of apologetic defiance. "In my situation, you might well have done the same."

"Perhaps, perhaps not," Picard said, "but it is good that you feel that way. It is good that you can acknowledge that the situation a person finds himself in can cause that person to take actions he would not take under other circumstances. In any event, Mr. President, because you have requested that the Federation aid you in the destruction of an entire world in retaliation for the Plague that that world has unknowingly inflicted on Krantin, we thought it only fair that you meet the one who was leader of that world until a few hours ago."

"Unknowingly? These creatures have known precisely what they were doing to Krantin for decades, particularly this so-called leader you want to force me to meet! Zalkan himself said it—they knew and they did not care!"

"The leader, yes, and all members of the Directorate," Picard acknowledged, "as well as a very select number of their underlings. They were, however, the only ones who even knew of the existence of your Krantin, let alone what was being done to it. And it was one of those few, by the way, who came to Zalkan's group and told them of the plan to capture the *Enterprise* and breach the walls of Jalkor. Without his action, we would almost certainly all be dead today." Picard did not add that self-preservation had also played a role. When the informer had learned that the Directorate planned to kill the four "defectors," simply as a precaution, he had realized that, like them, he was expendable and would never be safe as long as the Directorate remained in power.

"Even those involved with the search for the dilithium in the asteroid belt were not aware that an inhabited planet existed here," Riker added. "Only the leaders and the very few they needed to install and monitor the recording devices in your computers were fully aware of the existence of your Krantin and what had been done to it."

"And they, like the pilots, were as much victims of the Directorate as you," Dr. Crusher said. "They weren't told, for example, that they were killing themselves. They knew nothing of the ill effects of repeated transfers. Only the leaders knew that."

Khozak snorted skeptically. "Surely the pilots themselves noticed they were becoming ill and dying after certain numbers of trips."

Crusher shook her head. "Before they reached that stage, the Directorate made sure they simply 'disappeared.' The Directorate never denied that being a transfer pilot was dangerous; they just substituted a more acceptable form of danger. One in every hundred transfers went wrong, they said, and ship and pilot were lost, possibly in yet another alternate reality. This was a lot different than saying, 'Each trip makes you sicker until finally you die.'"

"But Zalkan and his group obviously knew the truth!" Khozak protested. "Why didn't they simply expose the Directorate's lies?"

"They tried at least once," Picard said, "but the Directorate's control was so complete, no one paid them any attention. And the ones who made the effort 'disappeared' more quickly than the pilots."

Khozak shook his head angrily. "Why are you telling me this? What is the point in trying to prove that virtually everyone in that Krantin is innocent and that only the members of the Directorate deserve our hatred?" he asked with a sideward glance at Albrect. "You have already made it abundantly clear that my desire to protect Krantin from their continuing depredations will not even be considered."

Picard suppressed a sigh. "Protecting your Krantin is not synonymous with destroying theirs."

"Is it not? How many years will it take before they are willing to shut down their world in order to stop exporting the Plague to ours? And from what you have said, those infernal devices are so universally used that shutting them all down would amount to just that—shutting down their world!" He turned to glare at Albrect. "Is my understanding not correct?"

"A slight exaggeration," Albrect said, "but essentially correct. However, we have little choice in the matter. I thought you understood that."

"Understood what?"

Albrect looked questioningly toward the *Enterprise* officers but particularly toward Data. "Have you not verified our fears?"

Data nodded. "The samples I took, and the ones you brought with you, do bear them out," Data said.

"How long would we have if we did not shut down our 'infernal devices'?" Albrect turned to look at Khozak with a grim smile. "And they are that, in more ways than you could imagine."

"My computer models," Data said, "indicate that, at the current rate, you have no more than five years."

Albrect grimaced. "Even worse than our own figures showed." He turned back to Khozak. "That is why we will shut the machines down. If we continue to use them, if we continue to spew out the Plague onto *your* Krantin, *our* Krantin will be dead before yours. I believe you were given perhaps ten years before it was irreversible."

"Dead? Your world?" Khozak shifted his glare from Albrect to Data. "What nonsense is this?"

"The collapse of their entire ecosystem," Data said, and even Khozak greeted the statement with a stunned silence.

"For five hundred years," Picard picked up the explanation, "they have been transferring matter from their world to yours, but it has not all been 'waste,' not nearly all. The dilithium is but one example. While transferring the smoke from their industries, for example, they also transferred great quantities of their atmosphere. Their atmospheric pressure is at least five percent lower than yours. In transferring organic waste in a thousand ways, they have transferred elements essential to plant and animal life. Dr. Crusher noted a deficiency of certain trace elements in the bodies of the so-called defectors who brought the first markers aboard the *Enterprise*. Zalkan, on the other hand, who has lived on this Krantin for more than a decade, did not suffer from such deficiencies. Similar deficiencies were found in the plant samples Mr. Data brought back, and in Albrect himself. Those deficiencies are only the tip of the organic iceberg, so to speak, the first signs of what is rapidly approaching. The dead trees that we saw in the park area beneath Albrect's window are another. At this point, the process can be reversed, but sometime between three and five years from now, it will reach a point at which it cannot. If Data's models are correct, all life, even microorganisms, will be gone within two years of that point unless certain key elements begin to be replaced. Or returned."

A gleam of satisfaction radiated from Khozak's eyes, but only for a moment. Then the scowl returned as he turned back to Picard. "No!" he almost shouted. "For you to even suggest that we *help* them, that we *give* them even an ounce of Krantin's lifeblood— No! It is too monstrous even to—"

"Captain Picard did not suggest it," Denbahr broke in angrily. "Nor did Albrect or anyone from that Krantin. *I* suggested it."

"And I agreed," Koralus said. "The Ten Thousand on the *Hope* will return—Captain Picard has agreed to transport us all—and we will help in whatever ways we can."

Khozak snorted. "Ten thousand Deserters will help a billion murderers to survive! Why am I not surprised!"

"Only seventy-five Deserters at the most," Koralus said mildly, "myself and those of the One Hundred I did not awaken to die. None of the others have ever seen Krantin except in images. And there may well be another sixty thousand, if the other ships can be located."

Khozak shook his head violently. "It makes no difference. I will not be a party to an obscenity like this! I will not allow that world to save itself by stealing back the very stuff with which it destroyed Krantin!"

"Even if the 'stealing' is a part of the process by which Krantin is itself restored?" Picard asked. "The Federation will assist in whatever way it can— terraforming technology and equipment, if that is what is required."

Khozak shook his head again, even more violently. "Never!"

Picard let his breath out in a controlled sigh and stood up. "Come, Mr. President. It is time for you to meet the former leader of the Directorate." He motioned to Albrect, who stood as well. "You can return them all to your Krantin when the president is finished."

"You can return them now, then!" Khozak snapped.

"Not until you have met their leader," Picard said. He turned to Worf. "Lieutenant, if you would assist President Khozak?"

Khozak continued to scowl, but he was on his feet before Worf had taken a second step. "Why am I singled out for this unique honor?" he asked sourly as they descended in the turbolift. "Why not the entire Council?"

Picard suppressed a smile. "If, after the meeting, you wish the Council to meet him as well," he said, "you can bring them down yourself. Albrect will delay their return."

The turbolift door hissed open. Picard led the way to the same detention area the four defectors had died in. The Security lieutenant on guard silently acknowledged Picard as they walked by his station.

"There," Picard said, indicating the compartment with a single prisoner standing with his back to the forcefield.

They came to a stop less than a meter from the forcefield, but the prisoner did not acknowledge their presence.

"Khozak," Picard said, "there is someone I'd like you to meet."

"You've already established that!" Khozak snapped, but a second later he gasped.

The prisoner had turned at Picard's words.

"So," the prisoner said as he eyed the president, "this is my twin from this misbegotten world."

When President Khozak returned to the conference room an hour later, he offered no reason for changing his mind, nor did he suggest that the rest of the Council be taken to speak with the prisoner. He merely nodded to Denbahr and Koralus and said, "I will not stand in your way. Do as you wish, you and your ten thousand."

Picard breathed a sigh of relief. Zalkan's peace, if not won, had at least not been lost.

"Of course, Data," Geordi said, laughing as he reached down to scratch a purring Spot behind the ears, "I'll be glad to come to your thank-you party for Spot and Fido. However, maybe you should include the counselor in there, too. After all, if she hadn't been able to calm Spot down after all those invaders were popping in and out, it never would've worked."

Data considered a moment. "You are right, Geordi. I will of course include Counselor Troi. Or should hers be a separate affair? I would not wish to offend her."

"Don't worry, Data, it'll be fine. For that matter, if you want to include me, too—didn't you tell me that Spot's reflexes wouldn't have done us much good without the blocking field? And yourself, come to think of it. You're the one who realized what was setting both of them off and put a stopwatch on the phenomenon."

"But then perhaps we should include Commander Riker as well," Data said thoughtfully, "since it was he who returned me to the *Enterprise* so expeditiously."

Geordi laughed again. "Maybe you better just stick to Spot and Fido after all, before we find a reason to include everyone on the *Enterprise*. You don't want to spread the Spotlight too thin. There is just one thing, though."

"What is that, Geordi?"

"I hope you don't want me to 'watch' either one of them. After all, it is a party."

"I had not thought of that, but you are correct again. However, if you could spare some time later, it could be of help in my ongoing study."

"Come on, Data, don't you think they've earned the right not to be stared at for a while, particularly Spot?"

"Of course, Geordi, but I do not think it disturbs them. Besides, now that we have proven that Spot and Fido are both sensitive to at least one phenomenon that is beyond the capabilities of the sensors, do you not think it would be worthwhile to attempt to discover what other phenomena they may respond to?"

"You mean their 'I-gotta-be-someplace-else-fast' act?" Geordi sighed. "As a famous psychoanalyst is reported to have once said, Data, there are times when a cigar is just a cigar.

"And there are times," he added, grinning and pulling back abruptly as Spot suddenly decided she needed to play with his comm unit, "when a cat is just being a cat."